99 LIES

LIES

RACHEL VINCENT

99

KATHERINE TEGEN BOOKS
An Imprint of HarperCollins Publishers

Katherine Tegen Books is an imprint of HarperCollins Publishers.

99 Lies

Library of Congress Control Number: 2018936240
ISBN 978-0-06-241159-4

Typography by Carla Weise
18 19 20 21 22   PC/LSCH   10 9 8 7 6 5 4 3 2 1
❖
First Edition

For my husband and children, who were there
with me every step of the way.

NOW

I push my way into the kitchen, expecting to be stopped. I'm wearing a twenty-thousand-dollar custom gown and four-inch heels. I obviously do not belong in here, but no one even looks up from the plates they're preparing or the trays they're loading. They don't have time to notice me.

Thank goodness.

Determined, I lift my skirt to keep from dragging it or tripping over it and follow the fleeing woman down an aisle on the right side of the kitchen, careful not to bump into anything or anyone in the bustling, steam-filled room. She takes a left at the end of the aisle, and I see her in profile.

Then she opens a door and disappears.

My skirt forgotten, I race after her and throw open the door. The hall is dark after the brightly lit kitchen, and I can't see much beyond the threshold.

My pulse races as I step into the hallway. It's time to finish this.

From the darkness, I hear a pistol cock.

"Good evening, *princesa*."

10 DAYS, 16 HOURS EARLIER

I have no choice.

MADDIE

Lights flash in my eyes. Ambulances. Helicopters. Rescue boats. They paint the night in bursts of red, blue, and bright white. The cacophony is so overwhelming that it's lost focus. I hear it all as if there's cotton stuffed in my ears. As if it's all very far away. As if I'm not really here at all.

There's sand in my boots. In spite of the sensory over-load, that one sensation remains clear and focused.

I stare out at the water, trembling, though the night is warm.

Someone wraps a blanket around my shoulders. It's a metallic Mylar panel crinkling every time I move as it reflects my own body heat back at me.

Something brushes my shoulder, and I turn to find Luke standing next to me in the sand, staring out at the water as helicopters and boats pull people from the remains of my uncle Hernán's cruise ship, the *Splendor*.

There are bodies in the water. I can't distinguish them from the rest of the wreckage, but knowing they're there feels like having a terrible secret.

Knowing how they got there feels like telling a terrible lie.

Rescue boats keep bringing people to shore. The ones who are breathing go into a waiting ambulance or into the triage area set up in a tent. The ones who aren't breathing go into the long line of still figures on the beach. Each one is covered, and I wonder where all the blankets came from.

There are *so* many bodies.

"What happened?"

I turn to find Penelope Goh on my left. She stares out at the water, clutching a Mylar blanket around her shoulders, and she sounds stunned. Lost.

She, Domenica, and Rog fled the terrorist base camp in the first boat. They were gone before the *Splendor* exploded. That was an hour ago.

That was a lifetime ago.

"Maddie." Pen nudges me. "What happened?"

I look around for Domenica and Rog, but I don't see them. Maybe they went to the hospital.

"Sebastián blew up the cruise ship," Luke says, and for a second, I feel a bright, terrible wash of relief, because he's told the lie for me. But he doesn't know it's a lie—that Genesis had the detonator. That makes him innocent. "Or maybe it was Silvana," he says. "I don't know who pulled the trigger."

Every second I spend not correcting him is a lie of omission. Which makes me guilty. But I have no choice.

Family first.

3

"Why were there bombs on a cruise ship?" Pen frowns at the water, her voice hazy with shock. "I thought they were on submarines."

"So did we." Luke's hand finds mine, and it's shockingly warm. Or maybe I'm just cold. We thought they were going to transfer the bombs to a cargo ship. Not a cruise ship full of passengers.

My eyes water, and the line of blanket-draped bodies blurs in front of me.

"Ms. Goh? Ms. Valencia? Mr. Hazelwood?" We turn to see a woman in a suit and shoes wholly unsuited to the beach heading toward us in the sand. Despite the late hour, her hair is neatly pinned in a perfect bun low on her head. She shows us a badge: FBI. "I'm Agent Moore. Would you please follow me?"

Luke studies her badge, as if it might be fake. "The FBI can't operate outside of the US."

"We can with permission from the host country, and Colombia seems eager to cooperate on this matter." She puts her badge away and gives us a grim nod. "The medical crew has cleared all three of you. I'm here to take you home."

Home.

There were moments over the past couple of days when I thought I'd never see home again. I should be relieved. I should be ecstatic. Instead, I am numb.

"The missing persons' report lists several other American citizens who disappeared with you, but we haven't yet made contact with Holden Wainwright, Genesis Valencia, or Ryan Valencia." Agent Moore's gaze narrows on me as we head for the water. "Genesis and Ryan are your siblings?"

"Genesis is my cousin," I tell her.

Agent Moore pulls a notebook and a small pen from her pocket. "And do you know where they are?"

"They're still in the jungle. They didn't make it out." The reality is a bit more complicated than that, but this truth is enough for now.

"You should be out there looking for them!" Penelope shouts, tears standing in her eyes, and all across the beach, people turn to look.

"Ma'am, we already have agents out there, working alongside local law enforcement. I will let them know immediately that we're still missing three of the hostages."

"Two of them." I cling to the numbness, holding it in front of me like a shield. "Ryan was shot during the kidnapping. He's buried at the army bunkhouse where we were taken."

Agent Moore's step falters, the only sign that she's shocked by my brother's death, while rescue workers are still laying out the other casualties in a long line on the beach. "I'm so sorry to hear that."

"Agent Moore?" I ask as we climb into the small boat she's been leading us toward, where a Colombian soldier is seated behind the wheel. "Where did they take Indiana? What hospital?"

She frowns and looks at her notebook again. "Indiana?"

"He . . ." I push through the numbness, trying to think. "There was another guy in our boat. One of the hostages. He hit his head during the explosion and lost consciousness."

"There was a lot of blood, and his breathing was irregular," Luke adds. "One of the EMTs was working on him on the beach, but we lost track of him when they started pulling people from the water."

"And his name is Indiana?"

"I don't know his real name," I tell her. "That's just what we called him."

She scans several pages of handwritten notes. "Ms. Valencia, I don't have anything here about another missing American. Do you know if his parents filed a report?"

"I'm not even sure they knew he was here. He's not in high school."

She shrugs as Luke helps me onto the boat. "It's possible he was mistaken for one of the cruise ship passengers. We'll get it sorted out. For now, let's get you all home."

As our boat takes off down the shore, carrying us away from the nightmare of the past few days, I hold Luke's hand and stare back at the helicopters and rescue boats still lighting up the dark waters of the gulf, pulling screaming people from the water.

Their nightmare has just begun.

I love her.

GENESIS

"We thought you might like some company." The sound of Sebastián's voice makes my stomach churn. If I'd eaten anything, I'd be vomiting all over the floor, but I haven't been fed since they locked me in this dark, empty room. Since hours before the other hostages escaped the jungle on a speedboat stolen from a terrorist.

I know better than to answer. Instead, I sit in the grimy corner, deciding exactly how I will disable him when he comes through that door.

I'm the only one left, and I have no idea where I am.

A metallic squeal cuts through my thoughts, and I recognize the front door of the cabin as it creaks open. I scoot toward the front wall and peek through the crack in the boards. The front door stands open, but outside the cabin, there is only a yawning darkness.

The sun isn't up yet. I can't have been here for more than a few hours—unless I was unconscious for a full day.

"—your filthy hands off me. Do you have any idea who I am?" a familiar voice demands, and I sit up straight, suddenly alert in spite of hunger, exhaustion, and a concussion that makes the world spin every time I turn my head.

Holden.

Minutes before the rest of us fled the terrorist base camp toward the beach, Holden had grabbed a gun, shot a guard, and run off into the jungle. Abandoning the rest of us as we fought.

I knew he wouldn't make it out of the jungle on his own. My ex has the survival skills of a brain-damaged kitten. Still, in spite of everything he's done to me, I'd hoped he *would* get away, if only to deny that victory to Sebastián. And to his boss—my uncle David.

"We know who you are, *mano*," Sebastián tells Holden at the front of the cabin. He's in his element. In power. In control. "And we hope your semiprivate accommodation is to your liking."

Holden struggles as they drag him toward my room—I recognize his ugly grunt of effort and the scrape of shoes across the floor. Sebastián slides back the dead bolt and I stand, fighting nausea. My moment has come. But when he opens the door, light from the front room blinds me. I blink, and his pistol comes into focus.

I know how to take the gun from him. I've trained for this very moment, thanks to my father's ~~paranoia~~ full knowledge that his illegal activities were putting my life at risk. But my thoughts refuse to focus. I can't fight Sebastián while I'm weak from hunger and exhaustion, and unsteady from the concussion.

Holden stands in the doorway. His shirt is torn. Dirt streaks his face, and I can smell him from across the room. A night in the jungle has not been kind to my ex-boyfriend.

A man I don't recognize shoves Holden into the room with me. He stumbles, then catches himself against the rough wood plank wall. The door slams shut behind him, and the dead bolt scrapes home again. I am alone with Holden for the first time in a week.

The last time we were alone, there was a bed, and flattering lighting, and an open bottle of expensive vodka.

"We could blow off the Bahamas and just stay here." Holden kisses his way down my left side, and I arch into his touch. *"Naked."*

I squirm as his lips trail over the point of my hip, drawing goose bumps to the surface of my skin. "Why would I spend spring break in your pool house when my dad's private jet is at my disposal?"

"No one ever comes in here. It'd be like our own private island," he murmurs against my stomach. "Besides, you've been to the Bahamas a dozen times."

I shrug. "So we'll go somewhere else. Name your pleasure."

"This is my pleasure." He grabs my hips, and his sexy growl makes my pulse leap in anticipation. "Tell your dad you're going to Cartagena to see your grandmother, and he'll be relieved that you actually shacked up with me all week, safe in Miami."

"Or we could actually go see my grandmother."

He lifts himself to frown down at me. "I am not going to Colombia."

Holden blinks, and for a second, I'm not sure he can see me in the dark. Then his brows furrow and his gaze gains focus. He pushes away from the wall. His palms are full of splinters—I know that from experience—but he doesn't seem to notice. He's preoccupied with the greater insult.

Sharing a room with me.

He turns and pounds on the door behind him. "Sebastián! I want to talk to your boss!"

"This isn't the Ritz, Holden," I snap at him. My head is killing me, and I want him to stop shouting. "They're not going to give you an upgrade."

Finally he turns, and I can feel his scowl. "What, they didn't have a jaguar to throw me in with? Sebastián is a sadistic bastard."

"Agreed. But there's no one else for them to put you with. Everyone else got away."

"So what happened? You trip over your ego and get left behind?"

"Speaking of left behind, how could you do that to Penelope?"

He'd slept with my best friend for the same reason he'd hooked up with all the girls who came before—because he could. But Penelope had thought they had something real. Until he'd run off into the jungle without her.

"I didn't *leave* her. She just stood there blinking like an idiot."

"She was in shock." Because he'd just shot someone right in front of her.

"I was going to come back for her. I love her."

I roll my eyes. "Joke's on you. She got out, and you're stuck here with me."

Holden sinks into the corner farthest away from the one I've claimed. "I'd rather die of malaria."

"At least we agree on something." I'd rather he die of malaria too.

9 DAYS, 12 HOURS EARLIER

We want Holden back.

MADDIE

Lydia Reed leans forward in her chair, legs crossed at the knee and tilted to one side to preserve the flattering angle for the cameras. Studio lights glint off her perfectly styled blond hair. "We only have a few minutes left. So, tell me, how have your lives changed since you were rescued from the Colombian jungle?"

I glance at Luke on my left, but he's still staring at the camera as if it might grow a mouth and bite him. He was surprisingly adept at surviving in the wilderness, but in front of the lights and TV cameras, he looks young and lost.

Penelope should be used to this, yet she sits on Luke's other side twisting her fingers into knots. Waiting for me to answer.

She used to have guts. She'd have to, to perform back-flips across a four-inch plank of wood in front of an audience of millions. But she seems to have lost some piece of herself in the jungle.

What she *actually* lost was one hundred ninety pounds

of entitled blond asshole. Twenty-eight hours after we'd left the beach with Agent Moore, the Colombian army had yet to find any sign of Holden—or Indiana, for that matter.

"Well, first of all, we weren't really rescued." I turn back to the host and smile for the camera. I'm getting through this interview by channeling Genesis. My cousin has many flaws, but she knows how to stare down a challenge. "We rescued ourselves. We stole two speedboats and headed along the coast until we found help."

The talk show host's eyes widen, as if she hasn't already heard this part. "And that's when your kidnappers blew up the cruise ship?"

"That's when it exploded. Yes." I can feel a follow-up question coming, so I continue before she can pick apart my careful phrasing. "But that was just yesterday. We haven't had a chance to process any changes in our lives yet."

"I'm not sure I'll *ever* process this," Luke says with a glance around the live television studio, and Lydia laughs. She's charmed by his wide-eyed awe and by the sparse stubble he hasn't shaved yet, because he wants to look like the boy I fell for in the jungle, rather than the one I never noticed in fifth-period calculus.

Like the rest of the country, the host of *Rise and Shine Miami!* is also charmed by our narrative. By the story of the fifteen-year-old Boy Scout and the diabetic sister of a murdered hostage who fell for each other while they fought to make it out of the jungle alive.

Our story and the sudden national media attention is

all we have. I'm determined to shine this spotlight on Genesis, so people can't forget she's still out there. So the United States government can't forget that she still needs help.

"But the ship can't be coincidence, can it?" Lydia leans forward again, as if we are friends having an intimate chat. "The *Splendor*"—she glances at one of her note cards—"a twelve-deck, twenty-five-hundred passenger cruise ship—belonged to your uncle, Hernán Valencia. Your captors blew up the ship, killing more than *one thousand* people, within sight of the camp where they were holding you hostage. I can't be the only one wondering about that connection."

"I don't . . ." I clear my throat and start over. "Um . . . we don't have all those details, and the ones we do have, we're not at liberty to discuss. There's an ongoing investigation." I've said the same thing to every reporter who's dug up my home phone number, and I'm grateful for the legal shield to hide behind.

I know exactly what the victims and their families are going through, and the last thing I want to do is withhold information from them. But I can't tell them what really happened to the *Splendor*.

Family first.

"But surely there's *something* you can tell us," Lydia presses. "How did your captors get access to your uncle's cruise ship? Why blow it up at all? I would assume that was to make sure their ransom demands were taken seriously, except they never actually *made* any ransom demands, did they?"

"Um . . ." I clear my throat again, then Luke takes my hand, and the warmth of his palm against mine gives me focus. "Luke and I spent most of our time looking for the camp where the others were being held. We don't know what happened before we got there."

"And you?" Lydia fixes an expectant, bright-eyed gaze on Penelope. "Did you hear your kidnappers make any ransom demands?"

"No." Penelope looks like she's only half listening. "But they didn't tell us everything."

"I just don't understand that!" Lydia is like a dog with a bone. "Your captors had in their possession an Olympic silver medalist, the heir to a multibillion dollar pharmaceutical manufacturer, and the heiress to the largest freight shipping company in the world, yet none of your families reported being asked for a ransom. How do you explain that?"

Penelope's mouth opens. Then it closes. She has no idea what to say, because the truth—that their only demand was for my uncle to ship explosives into the US—is part of the FBI investigation into my family's ties to the people who kidnapped us. The people who still have Genesis.

Assuming she's still alive.

"Lydia, kidnappers don't typically reveal the details of their plans to their hostages, do they?" I point out in my most reasonable voice.

Our host frowns. "I would assume they don't." She glances at her notes again. "Okay, then, I have just one more question for you all this morning." Her expression softens as she glances from Luke to Pen, then back to me. "If you could say one thing to the hostages who didn't make it out, what would that be?"

I turn to face the camera directly—the one with the red "live" light shining. This is what I came for. "Just hang in there," I say to my cousin, a continent away. I know from experience that her captors might let her listen, even if only to torture her. "We're going to find you. We're going to bring you home, Genesis."

"And Holden," Penelope adds. "We're going to get him back too."

I would sleep just fine with the news that Holden Wainwright's corpse is rotting in the jungle. But the truth never makes anyone look sympathetic on live television, so I nod. "Of course we want Holden back too." Even though he ran off and left us all to fend for ourselves. "If you have any information about the kidnapping, please call 1-555-GENESIS. The number is international and toll-free." My uncle set it up the moment he found out his daughter didn't make it out of the jungle.

Lydia turns to face the camera. "That's all the time we have today on *Rise and Shine Miami!* I'd like to thank my guests, Maddie Valencia, Luke Hazelwood, and Olympic silver medalist Penelope Goh, for sharing their story of American courage and fearless spirit. We wish them and their families the best in this trying time. Our thoughts and prayers are also with all the *Splendor* cruise ship victims and their families, as the dust begins to settle after yesterday's early morning explosion. Please check out our website for ways you can help the survivors and their families."

Lydia's solemn expression stays frozen in place until the red light on the camera blinks out. Someone behind the bright lights announces that we're off the air, and our host thanks us again for appearing on her show, then disappears into her dressing room.

"I can't do that again," Penelope says as we make our way through the crowd of crew members going about their off-air duties. "We *do* know how and why those bombs were on your uncle's cruise ship," she whispers as I pull her aside with a tight grip on her arm. "And everyone who lost someone on board deserves to know it's because Gen's dad is a *drug trafficker!*"

"Was," I hiss into her ear, and I'm almost scared by how easy it's become to channel my cousin's ferocity. "He *was* a drug trafficker, and announcing that won't help the victims, but it will impede the FBI investigation and turn people against Genesis. Which will make it harder to keep public pressure on the government to find her." I take a deep breath and let her go before someone other than Luke notices tension between two of the rescued hostages. "You lied to your best friend for weeks about sleeping with her boyfriend," I whisper fiercely. "You can *damn well* tell this lie to save her life."

I'm glad you're here.

GENESIS

Holden sits across the room from me, trying to pluck splinters from his palm. He hasn't said a word in hours. Normally, I'd consider that a blessing, but this silence is unnerving and I need a distraction from the cramping vacuum my stomach has become.

And Holden might have information I want.

"Do you know where we are?"

"We're in the jungle, Genesis. Beyond that . . ." Shadows shift as he shrugs in the dark. "What am I, a human GPS?"

"I woke up in this cabin, but *you* walked here. What direction did you come from? Could you hear the ocean? How long were you alone in the jungle?" I demand. "Did the sun rise before they caught you?" Have I been here one day, or two?

"Why does it matter?" Holden goes back to his splinters.

It matters because the real cage I'm trapped in isn't this room; it's my own mind.

I can see through the crack into the main cabin, but

the front windows are boarded up and the door is closed. I don't know how long I've been here. I don't know if I should be asleep or awake. I don't know how many meals I've missed. I don't know whether or not my friends got away. If I hadn't seen the door open when they brought Holden in, I wouldn't even be entirely sure that the world outside this cabin still exists.

But saying any of that would make me sound desperate.

More interminable minutes drag past in silence, but for the scrape of Holden's fingernail against the pad of his palm.

I'm too hungry to think straight. I haven't been fed since I got here, and though I have no way to track time, my stomach insists that's been at least two days.

"Are they going to feed us?" Holden suddenly demands. "Or do they expect us to battle to the death, then eat the dead one? Because my money's on me."

He's bluffing again. Holden plays lacrosse at school, and a week ago, he outweighed me by seventy pounds. But I have a black belt in Krav Maga. I know how to use his weight against him. What's left of him anyway.

When they shoved him into the room, his cheekbones looked like they might slice through his skin. Even in the dark, I can see his hands shaking. I can hear exhaustion in his voice.

I'm exhausted because Sebastián's been starving me. What's Holden's excuse?

"When was the last time you ate?" I ask.

"The last time they fed us at the base camp."

"Why didn't you eat in the jungle?"

"What was I supposed to do?" he demands. "Wave my magic wand around?"

"You were supposed to look up! Fruit grows from trees, Holden! Even if you couldn't catch fish or rabbits, you could have had bananas. Avocados. Mangoes." I huff at him in disgust. "I was in here starving, and you were walking right by a virtual buffet!"

"I heard the explosion," Holden says, an edge of cruelty in his voice. "I was really hoping you died in the blast."

Hoping I died . . . ? Oh. He thinks I blew up a tent full of bombs on the beach. Which had still been the plan, when he'd abandoned the rest of us.

A familiar scraping sound comes from the front room. Like a chair being dragged across the floor. "I have news," Sebastián calls, and wood creaks as he sinks into the chair.

There's nothing in the world—short of freedom and food—that I want more than news from outside this room, but I know better than to admit that. Everything I say to Sebastián will later be used against me.

"The American media says your father's been arrested. One of your friends must have turned him in. Maybe your cousin?"

"Bullshit," I spit into the dark. "Maddie wouldn't do that." We might not be best friends, but family comes first. She believes that as much as I do.

"She would if she thinks it'll help them find you." Holden sounds practically gleeful. "Or if they threatened to charge her with obstruction of justice."

"They've frozen your *papi*'s assets." Sebastián's laughter scrapes along my spine like nails on a chalkboard. "There's no one left to ransom you, *princesa*. You better pray David finds some other use for you."

A new ache begins deep in my chest, rivaling the pain in my empty, cramping stomach. "You're lying."

"I have no reason to lie. And there's more, *princesa*. Your friends were on TV this morning, talking about their 'ordeal.'" His voice drips with sarcasm. "They're celebrities now. Everyone wants to talk to them. But you know who wasn't with them?"

I won't take the bait. It's all bullshit anyway.

"Your new boyfriend. The news says he's dead." Sebastián laughs again as he drags the chair away.

Indiana.

The last time I saw him, he was unconscious in the bottom of a boat still rocking violently from the explosion.

Sebastián's lying. Indiana can survive a head wound. I survived mine. But what if his was more than a concussion? I've spent hours—days?—trying not to dwell on that possibility, but now I can't shake it from my thoughts.

"You got your new boyfriend killed," Holden says. "Damn. Dating you ought to come with hazard pay."

"Indiana's not dead." He *can't* be. "But *you* would be if Sebastián hadn't saved you from starving in a jungle full of fruit."

Hatred rolls off him like heat from a blaze. "I'm glad

you're here," he announces after a few minutes. "If anyone deserves this, it's you."

I don't care what he thinks. So why do his words sting?

Because they're true.

Holden cheated on me with my best friend. He tried to get our captors to execute me. Then he abandoned Penelope and escaped on his own. But is any of that worse than what *I* did?

Does it even matter that I was trying to save lives, if I wound up taking them instead?

9 DAYS, 2 HOURS EARLIER

That was totally a compliment.

MADDIE

"Tell me again why we're doing this?" I whisper as Penelope rings the doorbell to the right of a massive set of iron-and-glass doors.

"Because Neda's a friend."

"She's *your* friend. Why do Luke and I have to be here?"

Penelope turns on me, dark brows drawn low. "You said we should use our celebrity to get Genesis and Holden back." Before I can remind her that I never said a *word* about getting Holden back, she rushes on. "When we were kidnapped and Neda went on the radio, her old beauty vlogs went viral. *Millions* of views, in just a few days."

Luke shoves his hands into his pockets. "And you really think the US government will feel pressure to continue an international search effort because of what some beauty vlogger says online?"

Pen frowns up at him. "I think this is an avenue of exposure we can't afford to turn down. For Holden and Genesis. Besides, Neda knows us. This is *friendly* media."

She doesn't seem to understand that there's no such thing.

The right-hand door swings open, and Penelope whirls around just in time to be pulled into Neda's embrace. "I can't believe you bitches did *Rise and Shine Miami!* before you did my show!" she scolds me and Luke over Pen's shoulder.

"You don't go live until five," Luke points out, as if logic plays any role in Neda's complaint. Or her life. "*Rise and Shine Miami!* filmed at seven this morning."

"Whatever." Neda waves us into the house, and the click of her three-inch heels echoes from the walls and tall windows of her two-story living room. "Come on. It's right through here." She turns without missing a step on the glossy marble tile, and I notice that her ankle has made a complete recovery from the injury that got her airlifted out of the jungle the night before the rest of us were taken hostage. "We just finished the remodel yesterday. My mom said that if I was going to host one of the most popular webshows ever, I should do it right."

"I don't suppose there's any chance she was talking about journalistic integrity?" I ask as she throws open a set of double doors with a dramatic flourish.

"Holy shit," Luke breathes.

"Damn." Penelope glances around in awe. "I've been interviewed in television studios that didn't look this good."

"It used to be a spare bedroom, but we have, like, six of those, so my dad called in a favor and they put this little studio together for me in under a week." Neda steps into the center of the room and spreads her arms, her brown eyes sparkling in the blinding light from overhead. "What do you think?"

I think we've reached a new pinnacle in the art of illusion.

The actual walls, darkly paneled, of Neda's new web studio have been hidden from view of the professional webcam by a seven-foot-tall, three-walled studio facade, painted in broad horizontal strokes of pink, blue, and green to look like a cotton-candy-colored living room.

Or, more accurately, a girl-cave.

"The teleprompter, I get." Luke waves a hand at the table-mounted hooded mirror connected at a ninety-degree angle to an iPad attached to the camera. It's already displaying text ready to scroll for the broadcast. "But why did you need fake walls?"

"Because wood paneling only makes an effective backdrop for old white men smoking pipes and talking about the 'good old days.' And it's easier to light the smaller space." Neda points overhead at a small but impressive system of studio lights mounted from bars attached to the ceiling. "Have a seat." She glances at her phone screen, then shoves it into the back pocket of a snug pair of white designer jeans. "We have about ten minutes."

Luke blinks at a pair of overstuffed pink couches artfully angled toward each other on a shaggy white patch of carpet. He doesn't sit until I tug him down next to me.

"I've been hyping this interview all day, and I sent out

the reminder blitz an hour ago. There are already eighteen thousand people signed in to watch live, and the views will grow exponentially once I post the recording."

I'm pretty sure her understanding of exponential growth is no more accurate than her habitual abuse of the word "literally," but the size of her audience suggests I may be the only one on the planet who cares. Except for Luke.

Neda takes her seat next to Penelope on the other couch and picks up a small remote control from a blue table, where expensive bottles of sparkling water are waiting for each of us. "You're my first-ever live guests, so I'll be improvising on the format. But what I really need from you guys, if I'm going to make a name for myself, is the juicy stuff."

"The juicy stuff?" Why is Neda looking at Luke and me? She doesn't even like us.

"Yeah. Something you didn't say on *Rise and Shine Miami!* Or in that interview with the *Herald*. Everyone loves the 'geeks in love' angle, so—"

Suddenly I understand why we're here. Neda wants to be famous, and Luke and I are her ticket.

"Did you just insult us *while* asking us for a favor?" he says, and I slide my hand into his grip. I love the confidence he gained in the jungle.

"That was totally a compliment. Geeks are hot now, right?" Neda presses buttons on her remote, and the camera whirrs as it focuses. "Are you guys ready? I'm going to start with an endorsement, then we'll get right to the story."

"Endorsement?" I raise my brows at Penelope, but she only shrugs.

"Five, four, three . . ." Neda winks at us, and suddenly I feel like a mouse lured into a trap. ". . . two . . . one!" She smiles at the camera, waits a beat, then launches into her opening monologue.

"Hi, this is Neda Rahbar, and you're watching *Survival Mode*. Today I have an exclusive interview with three members of the Miami Six, my personal friends and survivors of last week's Colombian jungle kidnapping, which I only narrowly missed myself. But first, this episode of *Survival Mode* is brought to you by Diorshow Black Out waterproof mascara." Neda holds a black tube next to her face and blinks for the camera, showing off thick, dark lashes. "Because your makeup should survive, even when you're not sure you will."

I laugh out loud, then slap my hand over my mouth.

Neda's smile never fades, but there's anger in her eyes when she turns to me. "So, Maddie, let's start with you and Luke. I *have* to ask the question all of my viewers are *dying* to know. What *do* you do when you and your boyfriend are trapped in the jungle with no condoms?"

But they're perfect for each other!

GENESIS

Footsteps thump outside the door, and I look up. *Please be dinner.* My head hurts and I can't stand without getting dizzy. My hiking boots are starting to look appetizing. Leather comes from cows, right?

A shadow appears in the line of light beneath the door.

"Please, can we get some food and water?" At first, I refused to beg. I told myself I was imagining more hunger than I actually felt because I had nothing to do in the dark but think about my empty stomach.

But I can't even pretend that's true anymore.

"What's the point of starving us?" I demand through the door. "If you're going to kill us, just shoot us and get it over with."

Starving is its own special brand of hell. My lips are cracked and my throat is so dry it's difficult to swallow. My arms weigh a ton apiece, and my feet feel like they're encased in concrete blocks. My thoughts won't focus, and every now and then I realize I've been staring into the dark, thinking about nothing at all. As if my brain has turned itself off to preserve energy.

No answer comes from beyond the door, but there's a single soft tapping sound, like the click of a computer trackpad.

"So, when I was airlifted out of the jungle because of my injury . . ." Neda's voice is like a slap to the face, and suddenly I'm wide-awake, after hours—days?—of existing in a timeless, nearly sleepless fog. ". . . you guys were about to party campfire-style at that army bunkhouse."

I don't realize I'm crawling toward the door until a splinter from the wood plank floor bites into my left knee.

"What happened after I left?" Neda asks.

"We celebrated your departure," Maddie says. A guy—Luke?—laughs, and I get lost in the bounce of each note. They sound happy. They are not hungry or in pain. They're probably not sitting in the dark, desperate for proof that the rest of the world still exists.

This is what I wanted when I made my cousin get on that boat. Maddie, safe at home.

So why do I suddenly feel so hollow?

"Screw them," Holden whispers, and the sentiment resonates so easily inside me that I decide this is a defense mechanism. Captives do whatever they have to do to survive. Resenting those who escaped is nothing.

I can't help it.

"We partied, then collapsed in our tents," Penelope says, and I can imagine Neda's nostrils flaring as she tries to roast Maddie alive with her glare. "The next morning, we woke up to armed men pulling us out of our sleeping bags. They took our phones and jewelry. Then they separated us into two groups and marched our group deeper into the jungle."

"Tell me about Genesis and Holden," Neda says. "How did they get left behind when you guys escaped?"

"Most of us ran down to the beach to get the speedboats ready," Luke says. "Maddie and Genesis stayed at the camp to . . . make sure no one got left behind."

We stayed to find a detonator. But Luke left that part out. Or maybe he doesn't know we actually found one. If he doesn't know I'm the one who triggered the explosion, it's because Maddie hasn't told him—or anyone else.

Relief washes over me, lifting a tiny bit of the weight that's been sitting on my chest. She's trying to protect me, all the way from Miami.

"Maddie made it to the beach first," Luke continues. "Then Genesis came running out of the jungle. But before she made it to us, the cruise ship exploded."

"After that it was chaos," Maddie adds. "We were all half deaf. Indiana went flying into the boat's dashboard, and he just crumpled right there at my feet with a huge gash on his head. He was bleeding in the bottom of the boat. So much blood."

How much blood? Where's Indiana? Why isn't he talking?

Sebastián was lying. He *had* to be.

"And Genesis . . . she . . ." Maddie clears her throat. "I looked back at the beach and she was fighting with one of the kidnappers. She yelled for us to go, before we lost our chance. To leave her there. She sacrificed herself so we could get away."

"Damn." Neda sounds stunned.

My eyes water. I blink, and tears roll down my face. I'm *so* tired. *So* hungry. But they're safe. That's worth *anything*.

"Penelope, what about you and Holden?" Neda obviously doesn't know that Holden left us before the explosion. Are they protecting him too? From what? Public opinion?

"I . . ." Pen hesitates. "I was already gone. I left on the first boat with Domenica and Rog."

"That random old guy we met on the beach?" Neda asks.

"Yeah, no one knows his real name."

"So, Rog stayed in Colombia, but where is Domenica?" Neda asks, and I crawl closer to the door, heedless of more splinters.

"What about Indiana?" I ask before I realize that she won't hear me. Why aren't they saying anything about him?

"Domenica's been 'detained' until the US government can clear her of involvement in the whole thing." I can practically see Maddie's air quotes as her pitch ramps up for a sermon. "Which is *total* bullshit. That's profiling. They can't assume she was involved in our kidnapping just because she's not American. *That's* what you should be using your platform for, Neda. Putting pressure on the US government to get Genesis back and set Domenica free."

"I don't have a platform," Neda says. "I have a *webshow*."

"If they were profiling, wouldn't they have detained you too?" Penelope says. "You're half-Colombian."

"I'm of half-Colombian descent," Maddie corrects her. "My parents were born in the US. But your point stands." A soft creak tells me she's shifted in her chair. Probably sitting up straighter, like she does when she's ready to drive a point home. "If the US government is going to detain Domenica, they may as well detain me too."

"She doesn't mean that," Luke says.

"Yes I—"

"So, back to Genesis and Holden," Neda interrupts, reclaiming control of the interview. "I know they're still trapped in the jungle, but at least they have each other. Right? Like lovebirds sharing a cage?"

Holden isn't moving. The air between us feels thick, as if gas has leaked into the space and a single spark will torch us both.

"Yeah . . ." Penelope hesitates. Is she reluctant to derail Neda's story or afraid that the truth will make Holden and her look bad?

"Lovebirds?" Luke laughs again. "They broke up. *If* they're stuck somewhere together, they're probably at each other's—"

"They *what*?" Neda's shock is almost palpable. "But they're perfect for each other! What the hell happened? I want *all* the dirty details!"

"What matters is that they're still missing." Penelope's voice is shaking. "And that twelve hundred thirty-four people died when that cruise ship blew up."

I choke on nothing as all the air is sucked out of my lungs. *Twelve hundred lives.*

My fault . . .

"Cruise ship?" Holden's voice is weak with exhaustion, but clear.

"Maddie's right," Penelope adds. *"That's* what your story should be about. The people who died. And the ones who are still missing."

"Genesis, if you can hear this, know that we haven't given up on you," Maddie says, and the darkness around me blurs beneath fresh tears. "The entire country is behind you and we *will* bring you home."

There's another soft tap, and the webcast ends. The sudden loss of connection to the outside world makes me feel like I've been kidnapped all over again.

"Do you think they'll still want you back when they find out who really blew up the *Splendor*?" Sebastián asks from the other side of the door. He chuckles as his footsteps recede.

"Who blew up—?" Holden's expression is hidden by darkness, but I hear comprehension dawning in his voice, and when it comes, it's like a knife to my gut. "I thought you blew up the tent on the beach. But you blew up a *cruise ship*?"

"It was an accident." My voice is hardly a whisper. "I thought the bombs were on a mini-sub." But he's not listening.

"Holy shit, Genesis. You have a higher body count than any terrorist since September eleventh!"

I'm doing exactly what she would do.

MADDIE

Neda presses a button on her remote control, and the red light on her camera blinks out. "And . . . we're clear." She turns on Penelope. "How could you not tell me that Gen and Holden broke up?" She shakes her head, and her dark curls bounce on her shoulders. "Wait. I'm glad you didn't. I don't think I could have faked surprise when you dropped that on me during the video."

Never mind the fact that it was actually Luke who dropped that on her.

"That was the perfect bombshell for this episode." Neda stands and plucks her iPad from the teleprompter rig. "They're not lovers leaning on each other under horrible circumstances. They're exes, forced to contend not just with their captors, but with each other!"

"One of your best friends is at the mercy of a multi-national terrorist organization." I glance around Neda's "studio," disgusted by the waste and excess. Thousands of dollars that could have gone to charity, spent on an effort to further inflate a vapid heiress's ego. "They have machetes, and guns, and *bombs*, and all you can think about is how juicy her breakup was?"

She cracks the top on a bottle of sparkling water. "Genesis understands manufactured drama. I'm doing exactly what she would do if she were here."

Genesis doesn't need to manufacture drama, online or in person.

Neda shrugs. "Of course, you'll have to come up with something new for the next episode. Something personal, yet *explosive*."

"Next episode?" Luke stands. "I'm not going to sit on your stupid pink couch and tell thousands of strangers about kissing my . . . Maddie." He glances at me, and suddenly I realize that we've never really defined what this is between us. And this is neither the time nor the place for that. "Unless you do an episode of my Let's Play."

"Your what?" Neda sinks into a chair behind her table and opens a sleek, thin laptop.

"My Let's Play. You come to my house and play the video game of your choice on camera for my next episode, then I *might* think about letting you exploit me again on your channel."

I blink at him, surprised. Impressed. "You have a channel?"

Luke shrugs. "Live-play video games. It's fun." He glances at Neda, who's hardly even listening as she archives the live broadcast on her channel. "But for her, it'll be an exercise in empathy. Through humiliation."

"Yeah." Neda rolls her eyes. "Because playing video games is so hard." Before Luke can respond, she turns to me. "Have there been any calls on the hotline?" We'd read the number again on Neda's . . . show.

"Only prank calls." My mother and Penelope have already asked me the same question, and every time I have to answer it, another little piece of me dies. "Who prank calls a hotline set up for hostages?" I sigh. It's hard to stay positive when I have nothing but bad news. "I should never have left Colombia. I should have stayed with Abuela until they found Genesis."

Luke wraps one arm around my waist. "Maddie, that wasn't an option."

He's right. I couldn't refuse to come home. Not after Ryan . . .

My eyes close. I can't stand to think about my brother still lying in a shallow grave in the middle of the jungle.

"Any updates from your uncle about Genesis and Holden?" Neda sets her iPad down, and finally I have her full attention. And, strangely, her sympathy. "Or your brother?"

"They've finally got the coordinates of the bunkhouse," I say, though Luke's already heard this. "There are several of them in that area, so it took them a while to figure out which one we were kidnapped from. But my uncle's hired an exhumation crew to go get Ryan tomorrow. They're going to bring him home."

So we can rebury him, next to my father.

"What about Indiana?" Pen asks.

"We haven't heard anything from Agent Moore," Luke says. "But Maddie and I have called every hospital in Colombia that took victims from the cruise ship explosion. There are three who fit Indiana's general description, but . . . they all died of their injuries. Head wounds."

"The hospitals won't send us pictures," I add. "So we're stuck waiting for relatives of the still-missing victims to identify them in person, so we can eliminate all three as possibilities."

That will happen. I *refuse* to believe Indiana survived the kidnapping only to die during the rescue. When we find Genesis, I *will* have good news for her.

"What if none of them are Indiana?" Neda asks, and though she looks both fascinated and horrified by that thought, I can't shake the suspicion that she's already planning another big reveal for her webshow.

"If he's not in any of the hospitals, I think the FBI is going to have to classify him as the third still-missing American hostage," I tell her. "But without a name or a picture, they can't even confirm that he was there in the first place."

"That is *so* screwed up," Neda says. "Like he's some kind of ghost."

"But he was in your boat, right?" Pen asks. "We're sure he got out?"

"Yes. And he was unconscious, so he couldn't have just walked away."

"You think someone *took* him?" Luke frowns at me. "With the FBI and the Colombian army crawling all over that beach?"

I shrug. I'm not sure what to think yet. "The beach was chaos. One of Sebastián's men could have come in dressed like a soldier and just carried him off into the jungle during the confusion."

"Oh my God." Pen sinks onto one of the pink couches, stunned. I know exactly how she feels. The idea that Sebastián could have had someone watching us—waiting for a chance to recapture us—*while we spoke to the FBI agent* was enough to make terror pool in the pit of my stomach.

If he can operate right under the nose of the authorities in Colombia, what's to stop him from getting to us anywhere, even here, in the States?

He will never get the jump on me again.

GENESIS

I slide down the rough plank wall, hardly noticing that friction drags my shirt up and the wood skins my spine. Holden is saying something, but I can't focus on his words. *Twelve hundred thirty-four people.*

One minute they were fine—partying on my dad's cruise ship—and the next . . .

It doesn't matter that I didn't *mean* to blow up the *Splendor.* That I thought I was blowing up mini-submarines full of drugs and bombs, to keep Sebastián from hurting anyone with them. What matters is that I killed half the passengers, and probably injured most of the others.

My father is a drug trafficker. My uncle is a terrorist. My ex is a backstabbing asshole of *massive* proportions. But *I* killed more than twelve hundred people with the press of a single button.

And I can never, ever undo that.

Was Indiana one of the casualties? Right or wrong, thinking about Indiana's death hurts even worse than thinking about the twelve hundred others.

"Do they know?" Holden asks, and finally I hear him. "Do the rest of them know what you did?"

I shrug. "Maddie knows I had the detonator and she knows the ship blew up. I'm sure she's put the pieces together, but it doesn't sound like she's told anyone else."

"How are you dealing with that? I mean, what's the point of even trying to escape this time? It's not like you can go home." There's a joyful cruelty in his voice. "When everyone else figures out what you did, you'll never see the outside of a prison cell again."

"It was an accident, Holden." My words sound brittle. As if they might crumble. "No one would ever believe I intended to kill all those people."

"Yeah. I'm sure the terrorists will come testify on your behalf."

I'm ready for him to start ignoring me again. "I'll worry about that once we get out of here."

"My parents will ransom me as soon as they have proof of life, but you . . ." Holden's shrug is an eerie blurring of the shadows from his corner of the room. "They'll never unfreeze your dad's bank accounts. You may have to buy your own way out of here." His pause is heavy with sarcasm. "What *on earth* will you sell?"

I hate him like I've never hated anyone in my life. Fortunately, I also understand him like no one else ever will.

"You still haven't figured it out." I force a laugh from my parched-sore throat. "We're not being held by Silvana and the Moreno cartel anymore. Sebastián's boss is my uncle

David, and if he wanted me dead, he'd have already put a bullet in my head. If he wanted money, he'd have already ransomed you. What he wants is to teach the US a lesson."

"Uncle David?" Holden says. "Maddie's dad's dead."

I shrug in the dark. "Turns out we were wrong about that."

"Holy shit. Where is he?"

"He's not keeping me up to date on his social calendar. All I know is that he's not going to kill his own niece. But if he doesn't get whatever he wants from *you*, he has no reason to let you live." I let that sink in for a second. "Money won't help you now, Holden."

"Then why am I here?" The new fear in his voice energizes me almost as well as food would.

The naked bulb overhead lights up, and I squint against the sudden glare. For a second, my eyes refuse to focus. I've been in the dark for far too long.

I blink over and over, and gradually my eyes remember how to function. The world has color again, though that color is mostly the faded gray of aged wood.

My gaze falls on Holden. I couldn't see him very well, backlit by light from the front room when he was tossed in with me. But now I can see his black eye and split lip. There's a large bruise on the left side of his jaw and a gash in his forehead.

Maybe he fought Sebastián's men. Maybe they remembered that he shot one of their friends before he ran into the jungle.

Either way, the whole thing is my fault. Holden wouldn't

be in Colombia if not for me. He wouldn't have been kidnapped. He wouldn't have been recaptured and beaten if I hadn't dragged him into the jungle in the first place.

He wouldn't be staring at me with such consuming hatred if I hadn't chosen Indiana's life over his, when our captors had knives to their throats.

I blink, stunned. I have made him what he is.

Sebastián opens the door. He has a pistol in one hand and a paper plate holding a sandwich in the other. Peanut butter on whole wheat. My mouth waters. "Tonight we're going to play a game. Two prisoners. One meal. Winner takes all. Ready?" He sets the plate on the floor, then slides it a few feet into the room. "Go!"

Holden and I lurch into motion at the same time. A wave of nausea washes over me with the sudden movement, and my head spins.

He's closer. Before I can even grasp for the plate, he's shoved half the sandwich into his mouth.

Sebastián laughs, and I wish I'd never left my corner. If he gets the reaction he wants, he'll play this game again.

Still chuckling, he closes the door and slides the bolt home.

Holden needs food worse than I do, I tell myself as I retreat across the rough floor.

My ex moans around a huge mouthful. "Crunchy peanut butter. Grape jelly."

He will *never* get the jump on me again.

I'll be fine.

MADDIE

"Maddie!" When Luke and I come through the front door, my mother jogs across the small kitchen and living room to pull me into a rum-scented hug, as if she wasn't sure she'd ever see me again.

I swallow my frustration and hug her back. Her fear makes sense. She thought Ryan and I were in the Bahamas with Genesis until the police came to tell her we were missing—from Colombia.

She never got to say good-bye to Ryan. She still hasn't gotten to bury him.

"Hi, Luke," my mother says as she lets me go, and there is tension in her voice. She likes him, but she wants to talk to me about Ryan. Alone.

I told her he died protecting me. That's all I've got in me right now.

"Hey, Mrs. Valencia." Luke gives her a formal nod, then seems at a loss. He's uncomfortable here, surrounded by pictures of Ryan. Faced with a mother in mourning.

That makes two of us.

"I just made coffee," my mother offers, though from the scent, her mug is at least half full of rum. "Or I could brew some tea." A week ago, she would have told me it was too late in the day to drink caffeine. But since I've been back, she hasn't said *no* to me once.

"Thanks anyway." With an awkward smile, Luke holds up the paper cups we got from the coffee shop down the street.

"I just spoke to your uncle." My mom sinks into her chair at the table, where her mug is still steaming. Ryan's baby photo album is spread across the plastic placemat. "He says you won't take his calls. He's been very good to us, Maddie."

Uncle Hernán got us kidnapped. He got Ryan killed. But if the FBI hasn't told my mother that, I'm not going to either. Not yet anyway.

"They found the bunkhouse where you were all taken," she says, but I already know that from the texts I haven't returned. "Hernán is going to personally oversee the . . . disinterment."

My hand closes over the medallion hanging from my neck.

I pick up the first clod of dirt, then I'm digging, frantically tossing handful after handful over my shoulder. Soil cakes beneath my nails. Bugs land on my neck, but I hardly feel the bites.

Eighteen inches down, I scrape a muddy swath of cotton.

I claw at the dirt now, sniffling, and each bit I remove exposes more of a blood-and-dirt-stained shirt.

My finger scrapes metal, and I freeze.

No.

I brush the dirt away. My hand trembles as I clutch the medallion. Ryan never took it off.

I left him there.

"Do you want to . . . ?" My mother gestures at the album.

"I can't." I swallow the lump in my throat. "I'm sorry."

She looks disappointed as Luke and I head down the short hallway. But staying won't make her happy. Not even if I sat at the table and stared at old pictures of Ryan with her. That would only make us both cry.

"Sorry about that," I say as I close my bedroom door.

"No reason to be." Luke sinks onto the edge of my unmade bed, and I sit next to him. He hands me one of the cups of coffee so he can wrap his arm around me.

"Thanks for coming over. The coffee shop was too public." People were staring, because we're front-page news. America's sweethearts—survivors in love. At least, according to the headlines. And this morning, someone called my mom with an offer to buy the rights to my "story" for a book. Or maybe for a movie. I didn't ask for details.

The media doesn't seem to care how much pressure the attention is putting on my brand-new, forged-in-fire, as-yet-undefined relationship.

"We can cancel tomorrow's talk show," Luke says as I lay

my head on his shoulder. "We could just go to school like normal people."

As if none of the past week even happened. "School may be the perfect place to hide from the media. But I can't let the world forget about Genesis. We have to keep pressure on the government until they do something."

"I know. We—"

Someone knocks on the front door, and we both go quiet as we listen to my mother's steps cross the living room. Reporters have come to our apartment twice since we got off the plane. My mother says something to whoever's at the door, then her voice rises. "Madalena, you have company! She's in her room. Go on back."

I open my bedroom door just as Kathryn Coppela is raising her hand to knock. "Hey." Her hand hangs in the air for a moment. Then she drops it and glances at Luke over my shoulder. "Sorry, your mom didn't say . . ."

"It's okay. Come in." I close the door behind her and sink onto the bed next to Luke. After a second, she sits in my desk chair.

"Hey, Luke."

"Hey," he says.

Kathryn isn't my best friend in the television sitcom BFF way. We had a rocky friendship in middle school that stuck mostly because we kept getting put into all the same classes. Then, last year when my father died and my brother wound up in rehab, I kind of pushed people away. Including her. Not on purpose. It just happened. But she's the only one who's tried to check on me since the jungle, not counting a bunch of Instagram and Snapchat messages from people who haven't spoken to me in person in years.

"I saw you guys on TV," Kathryn says. "And there were vigils while you were gone. I can't believe . . . Are you okay?"

I glance at Luke, and his shrug seems to say it all.

No, I'm not okay. But no one ever knows what to say when you respond to a polite question with the truth. "I'll be fine," I tell her.

Kathryn sets her keys in her lap. She looks really uncomfortable. "I'm so sorry about Ryan. It doesn't seem real."

"I know." Though the truth is that nothing feels real right now. Going from a jungle terrorist camp straight back to school, and friends, and home feels like turning the page in a sci-fi novel and suddenly finding myself in a western. These two worlds don't fit together. How can I possibly exist in both?

"Anyway, I just wanted to see how you are. You didn't miss much school, but I have notes from history and calculus, if you want." Kathryn brushes her long, pale brown hair back from her face as she stands.

Obligatory condolence received. I guess this is over.

"Well . . . Thanks." I start to stand, but she waves me off.

"You guys don't have to get up. Is it okay if I use your bathroom on the way out?"

"Yeah. Second door on the right."

"I remember. Thanks."

"That was weird," Luke whispers when I close the door.

I shrug. "Some people don't know how to deal with someone else's grief." I don't know how to deal with my mom's. "It was like this after my dad died too. People mean well. But they don't know what to do."

Luke scoots back to lean against my pillows, and I lie down next to him, my head on his shoulder. "So your mom doesn't know about your uncle?"

I shake my head, and my hair catches on his sparse chin stubble.

"So, what's going on with him? Are they going to arrest him?"

"In Cartagena? I doubt it. And if they don't arrest him, he's not subject to extradition, so . . ." I shrug.

"So as long as he stays in Colombia, he's free?"

I nod. "Freedom is the greatest privilege afforded by wealth."

Everything *is negotiable.*

GENESIS

The cabin's front door opens with a squeal I know well, followed by firm, heavy footsteps. "How are they?"

My head pops up at the familiarity of the voice. "It's my uncle," I whisper as I crawl across the floor toward the crack in the front wall. I haven't seen him since they threw me into this room.

My empty stomach insists that was days ago.

Holden pushes his back against the wall, while I press my face against it, peering through the hole. It takes a second for my eye to focus. The rest of the cabin is lit by lamps, and after so much darkness, the light hurts.

"They're breathing." Sebastián's blurry form begins to solidify through the crack. The windows are still covered and the front door is closed. But he's holding a beer bottle dripping with condensation. Does that mean this is afternoon? Or does he drink in the morning?

They're speaking in English, which can only mean they want Holden to understand. But why? They've been denying us information—along with food, water, and the bathroom—since we got here. With the exception of certain instances clearly meant to torture us. Like the peanut butter sandwich. And Neda's webshow.

If they're letting us hear this, there's a reason.

"Have you fed them?" My uncle sets a backpack on the floor of the cabin with a heavy thud. He's wearing mud-coated boots and casual hiking clothes. He looks rested, well-fed, and healthy.

I want to kick him in the gut.

Sebastián shrugs. "I tried to teach them to share, but they're selfish, spoiled brats."

"They still need to eat." Uncle David stomps toward our room.

I scramble back from the wall as he unlocks the door and pushes it open. He flips a switch outside the room and the bulb overhead lights up, blinding me again.

Holden blinks against the glare.

"Damn it, Sebastián," my uncle growls. "They look like skeletons."

Sebastián grumbles and I look past my uncle's towering silhouette to see him heading toward a small kitchen.

"Genesis, how are you feeling?" Uncle David squats on the balls of his feet next to me.

I look him in the eye and force my thoughts into focus, fighting vertigo. "I'm concussed, malnourished, dehydrated, and I probably have a vitamin D deficiency from the lack of sunlight, so I'll give you one guess."

He chuckles, as if he finds my suffering—or maybe my willingness to express it—entertaining. "Well, let's see what we can do to fix at least a couple of those." As if he weren't responsible for everything that's happened to both of us.

He turns to Holden. "You must be the boyfriend."

"No," Holden and I say in unison. That's the first thing we've agreed on since . . . ever, maybe. "Your niece dumped me," he adds.

Uncle David glances at me, his nauseating smile still firmly in place. "And I'll bet she made a scene of it. Even when the girls were little, Genesis had a flair for the dramatic."

"You know what else is dramatic? Kidnapping. Wrongful imprisonment. Assault and battery. Extortion. Arms trafficking. Faking your own death. Most of those are also felonies."

"As is mass murder . . . ," Holden adds. But he's looking at *me*.

"I didn't make those bombs," I remind him. "I didn't put them on a cruise ship full of innocent people. I didn't even know they were there."

"You'll have to excuse her." Uncle David turns back to Holden. "She's always found taking responsibility for her actions distasteful. I blame her upbringing. The rampant overindulgence of a child rarely produces a productive and responsible member of society."

"The irony here is *absurd*," I snap. Holden is the poster child for entitlement. "He's never even heard the word 'no.'"

"Is that right?" My uncle pulls a cell phone from his pocket and opens an app I don't recognize, then taps on the triangle play symbol.

An audio file begins to play. I recognize Sebastián's voice.

"Mr. Wainwright, we're prepared to return your son to you tomorrow. If you're prepared to pay the ransom."

"Just give me an account number." Holden's dad's voice is scratchier, as if reception over the satellite line isn't great.

"We don't want your money," Sebastián says. "In fact, we're prepared to pay *you*."

"You're going to pay me to take my son back?"

"We're going to pay you for your shares in Wainwright Pharmaceuticals. Through a shell corporation, of course. I believe that's a fifty-one-percent stake in the company. We'll give you one-third the current value of the stock. That, and we'll return your only child to you, alive and well. And largely unharmed."

Silence stretches over the staticky line and across our small room. Holden stares at the phone. He's holding his breath, every muscle tense.

"No," his father finally says.

Holden's jaw clenches.

"No?" Sebastián sounds skeptical, but not truly surprised.

"I'll meet any monetary demand," Mr. Wainwright says over the recording. "Name your price. But I won't let you fund your terrorist organization with profit from my company."

Sebastián snorts. "Mr. Wainwright, this isn't negotiable."

Holden's father huffs over the line. *"Everything* is negotiable."

Uncle David stops the recording and slides the phone back into his pocket. He turns to Holden, who's staring at the floor, grinding his teeth so hard I can hear the friction. "Looks like you're going to be with us for a while." My uncle pushes Holden's dirty blond hair from his forehead and studies a gash near his hairline. "We're going to get you fed, showered, and patched up. And since my brother's *princesa* has been indulged her entire life, this time we're just going to let her wait her turn."

8 DAYS, 10 HOURS EARLIER

Telling the truth won't change anything.

MADDIE

"We're so glad to have you back, Maddie," Mrs. Wilkins says as I take my seat. AP English Language is half over, but I don't care. No one even expects me to be here, two and a half days after I escaped from captivity in the jungle. After my brother was killed. While my cousin is still missing.

I'm only here because Luke's parents made him go straight to school after our interview this morning, because they think normalcy is what he needs. And because, as it turns out, the school *does* have a no-tolerance policy on reporters.

While I'm in school, I won't hear my mother cry or our home phone ring. What I didn't count on was the attention.

I can feel everyone watching me. Last week I belonged here, but now I feel like a zoo exhibit, on display behind glass.

Ryan had more friends in this school than I do, and my phone is full of unreturned text message condolences from seniors I hardly know. Yet there are almost none from my own friends. The school sent flowers, but no one other than Kathryn has actually spoken to me.

Mrs. Wilkins drones on, reviewing the essay standards for the AP Lang exam. The practice test is this weekend.

Exams feel about as relevant to real life as the possibility that I might leave school today in a levitating car. How am I supposed to care about exams when my brother is lying in a shallow grave in Colombia?

What if Genesis died two days ago, and no one's found her body yet? What if we never find her? My heart races and the backs of my knees feel damp. I can't spend the rest of my life wondering what happened to her. Knowing she'd be alive and well if she hadn't pushed me toward safety.

I can't spend the rest of my life lying to the world about what happened to the *Splendor*. The secret already feels like a parasite lodged in my heart, slowly eating me alive. But telling the truth won't change anything.

My phone buzzes against my hip, and when I pull it out of my pocket, I'm surprised, for a second, to be holding the latest model, in a brand-new, unscuffed case. Because my last phone was used as a detonator by the terrorists who kidnapped us.

I glance at the screen beneath my desk and find a text from Sara Brown, who sits two seats to my right.

Hey, are you okay? What did the terrorists do to you out there? Is it true you hooked up with Luke Hazelwood in the jungle?

I haven't spoken to Sara since freshman year. I didn't even realize she still had my number.

People are dead.

Maybe coming to school was a mistake.

I open my browser and search for information about the *Splendor* explosion. The first result includes photos of the victims—images of the faces I would have seen if I'd pulled back the blankets covering the bodies lined up on that Colombian beach.

I'm not hiding my phone anymore. Today, I could probably flip off the principal. But for several seconds, I sit frozen, staring at the text preview instead of clicking the link.

Amber and John McLean, both thirty-two, died on board the Splendor *yesterday, where they were celebrating their tenth wedding anniversary. They are survived by three small children . . .*

Oh, God. As I scroll through the links, a panicky pressure builds in my chest. Each comes with a picture and a text preview. Most of the victims were in their twenties and thirties. Most had kids. Many died alongside their spouses or significant others.

And their families still have no idea how and why they died.

Then I come to the word "survivor." I tap the link feverishly, desperate for good news.

Pamela Mathis, single mother of four, survived the explosion of the Splendor *off the coast of Colombia early Wednesday morning. She has been airlifted to a hospital in Miami where she is recovering from the loss of both lower legs and a spinal fracture that has left her paralyzed from the waist down. Doctors expect her recovery to take months . . .*

The words blur, and when I blink, tears land on my phone. I feel sick.

This wasn't supposed to happen. Genesis pushed the button, but if she hadn't, I would have. We were trying to save people. Instead, we killed hundreds and injured hundreds more. We made orphans and widows. We—

I jump up, still clutching my phone, and run for the door. Mrs. Wilkins's surprise bleeds into sympathy as I pass her podium.

In the bathroom, I stand with my hands braced on the sink. I don't even recognize the girl staring back at me in the mirror. The girl who's gone on camera three times now and let the whole world believe a lie.

I hope Holden's okay.

GENESIS

Holden has been gone for hours. I think. It feels like forever. And somehow, being alone in the dark is actually worse than being with him.

He's not in the cabin. Uncle David has taken him somewhere, and Sebastián won't tell me anything.

I can't focus.

I think I'm losing my mind.

With one breath, I hope Holden's okay. With the next, I hope he's suffering at least a little, because he cheated on me with my best friend. He tried to get Sebastián to execute me at the base camp. I hope he's hungry and exhausted because *I'm* hungry and exhausted, and I may deserve everything that's happening to me right now, but Holden deserves what's happening to me too.

Right?

Maybe we're two halves of the same screwed-up coin. Maybe we both belong here.

My thoughts are tangled like a string tied in knots, and

I can't follow the threads. I'm too hungry. Too tired. But I can't sleep, because every time—

The overhead light blinds me again, and I throw one arm over my eyes. Hinges squeal and I squint, trying to focus.

Holden steps into the room. He's wearing clean clothes. His hair is wet. He smells good. And as I watch, simmering in jealousy, he licks a red smear from one finger.

Barbecue sauce. My stomach clenches at the scent. My mouth waters.

I got a bathroom break, a granola bar, and a damp wash-cloth. He got a shower, fresh clothes, and a hot meal.

The light blinks out and the door slams closed. The bolt slides into place with a soft grinding sound.

Holden settles onto the floor in the dark. "Your uncle's not a bad guy." He sounds smug, and if it wouldn't be a waste of what little energy I have left, I would punch him in the face.

"If he gives you something, it's because he wants something." The envy in my voice probably undermines my point. "Nothing here is free."

"You're just pissed because—"

The light flares overhead and the door opens again. Sebastián's blurry outline takes up most of the threshold.

I stand, blinking furiously, and the small room spins around me. That granola bar was nowhere near enough.

Sebastián bends to set a plate on the floor, then pushes it into the room. "You know the drill."

"Wait!" I cry as Holden stands. But Sebastián slams the door and slides the bolt home. He leaves the light on.

I blink at the plate. Another peanut butter sandwich.

Holden dives for the food. I dart forward, but he's closer. He wins. Again. Even though he *just* ate.

Despair crashes over me. I can't miss another meal.

I lunge forward and sweep Holden off his feet. The effort exhausts me, but he thumps to the ground. The sandwich bounces off the plate onto the floor, and I grab it.

I back away, clutching my prize so hard that peanut butter squishes between my fingers. "Stay back," I growl. I sound feral.

I'm not hungry.

MADDIE

Nothing has ever felt less relevant to my life than the choice between mass-produced chicken Parmesan and soybean burgers. I'm not hungry. But if I don't eat, my blood sugar will drop, and the last thing I need is to pass out in front of the entire cafeteria.

No one's really noticed me yet, so I head for the nearest food line with my head down, passing table after table full of classmates who didn't spend their spring break in a terrorist base camp.

". . . tour of French wine country. My dad's obsessed with drinking wine within twenty kilometers of where it was bottled. *So dull.*"

"And I'm starting to freak out about the AP German test. I'm fine on the written, but my accent isn't—"

"My mom said there's nothing wrong with the shoes I wore to prom last year. Which means I have to wear red again."

A loud crash rings out from the other side of the room,

and I jump. My pulse races and I start to duck behind the nearest table. Then the cafeteria breaks out in applause as the poor freshman who dropped his tray begins to shovel sauce-drenched pasta back into its compartment.

Eyes down, I step into the queue for my lunch, but I'm not sure which line I'm in until the woman behind the sneeze guard drops a burger on my tray and hands me a paper boat of fries. I give my student ID number to the cashier, and as I wander out of the line, my gaze finds the table where I've sat all year with Kathryn Coppela.

I can't sit there today.

The Maddie Valencia who left for spring break a week and a half ago—the Maddie who ate here five days a week for three straight years—is gone. She never made it out of the jungle.

This Maddie has no clue how to be here right now.

You're a fraud.

GENESIS

"You really think you deserve that, after what you did?" Holden drops the paper plate and pushes himself to his feet. His jaw is tight, muscles tense.

I rip a bite from the peanut butter sandwich, ignoring the grit of dirt between my teeth.

He grunts as he lurches at me, hunched over, head low; he might as well *tell* me he's going to tackle.

Still chewing, I step aside and he crashes into the rear wall headfirst. Stunned, Holden collapses.

I bite off a full quarter of the sandwich and chew rapidly, holding his focus.

He stays huddled in his corner, stubbornly refusing to rub the lump rising on his forehead while I tear another hunk from the sandwich. I recognize the cold glint in his gaze, and it isn't hunger. It isn't anger. It's hatred. Holden doesn't just want to take my food. He doesn't just want to win, or to humiliate me, or to gain the upper hand.

He wants to hurt me.

"I'm going to testify at your trial. You and your drug smuggling father are going to get exactly what you deserve," he spits. "And I doubt a six-by-eight prison cell comes with an ocean view, *princess.*"

Prison. Holden is threatening me with *prison?*

"This coming from a guy who sells his dad's pharmaceutical samples at parties." And it's not like Holden needs the money. He sells because it puts him in demand. Makes him feel important.

His dismissive huff fills the small room. "You're a fraud, Gen. Your uncle told me the truth. You may not have known those bombs were on a cruise ship, but you knew they were on one of your *dad's* ships. You blew them up to destroy evidence linking him to the drug trade."

"Holden, that is *not—*"

"That's obstruction of justice. Another felony." He pushes himself to his feet again and stalks toward me with newfound confidence. "If you ever get out of *this* cage, I'll make sure you spend the rest of your life in another one."

I see nothing but the red haze of rage. I lunge at him and hook my arm around Holden's neck, dragging him off balance. He hits the floor on his back. The entire cabin shudders.

I drop with my left knee on his rib cage and unleash on his face, fury making up for what I currently lack in strength. Blood bursts from his nose. His lip splits. His teeth cut my knuckles.

Sebastián pulls me off of Holden.

I twist out of his grip, snarling, but the pistol pointed at my face ends my protest.

Uncle David appears in the doorway as Holden pushes himself to his feet, wiping his bloody face on his clean shirt. "I'm sorry." He waves Holden forward. "Krav Maga. My brother created a monster."

"You started this," I remind Holden as they escort him from the room.

And suddenly I'm in the dark, alone with my rage.

This will be okay.

MADDIE

I turn and am heading for the exit, still clutching my lunch tray, when my name echoes across the cafeteria. All around me, chatter fades into silence. I can feel them staring at me. My body tenses, my grip on the tray almost painful.

Then he says my name again. "Maddie." I exhale when I recognize the voice and turn to see Luke jogging across the cafeteria toward me, as if hundreds of people aren't staring at him. At us. As if he doesn't see a damn one of them.

I never even noticed that he and I had the same lunch period before we were taken hostage together. But then, I hadn't really noticed Luke himself before that either.

"Hey." He stops a foot away, and there's something fragile in his expression. Something hopeful but unsure. As if I might ignore him here, at school, after spending twenty-four hours a day with him in the jungle. After clinging to him when the plane landed in Miami, and my mother stood with the small crowd, expecting to hug both of her kids. And finding only one.

"I can't do this," I whisper to Luke as Penelope heads for the fold-down staircase that will lead us off the small plane. I'm standing in the narrow aisle, with nothing between me and the exit but my own fear, yet I can't make my feet move. "I can't tell her that I lived and he didn't. That I left him there . . ."

I can't tell my mother that Ryan died because I was stupid. Because we went back for my lost insulin. Because I got caught and he was trying to defend me.

"You didn't leave him," Luke whispers. "You survived. Come on. I'll be right there with you." His hand slips into my grip, fingers intertwining with mine.

I follow him down the aisle and off the plane. My mother's face lights up when she sees me. Then she looks past me, waiting for Ryan. When we step onto the tarmac, someone folds the stairs up behind us. Understanding crashes over my mother's face. Her hands steeple over her mouth and nose. She starts to cry.

Tears fill my eyes. Luke's hand is a warm, firm anchor holding me steady in a churning sea of grief. . . .

"Do you . . . um . . . want to sit with me?" Luke asks, and I shake off the memory to find him watching me in equal parts concern and . . . anxiety. As if I might say no, now that we're back at school and I have other options.

"Yes." Relief echoes in my voice, and he stands straighter. "Thank you."

His smile is the warmth of the sun on my back and the

crash of the waves over my feet—everything good and beautiful about our trip to Colombia. He takes my tray in one hand and wraps his other arm around my waist, guiding me across the room toward his table, while everyone in the cafeteria watches us. While curious whispers rise all around us.

As I pull out the chair next to Luke's, Kathryn's gaze catches mine and she smiles with a glance at him. She looks happy for me. For us.

Luke sets my tray down at his table and introduces me to his friends. Landon Johnson and Jayesh Bhatt are fellow Eagle Scouts and Luke's known Michael Tu and his girlfriend, Emma, since day care.

"So," Jayesh says as I sit down across from him, "Luke tells us you roast a mean marshmallow."

I blink at him. Then I laugh. Maybe this will be okay. I mean, it's still really weird to be here, after being out there, but maybe—

My phone buzzes in my pocket. I pull it out and read the text from an unidentified number. My smile dies as chill bumps rise on my arms.

I know you're lying.

I'm not daring him.

GENESIS

A door squeals open outside my room and light leaks from a crack I hadn't noticed in the left-hand wall. I crawl across the floor and peer through the crack into another small room next to mine. On the floor lies a bare mattress.

Holden limps into the room looking healthy, clean, and well-fed, aside from the bruises and split lip I gave him. The light in his room stays on, even after the door closes, and when I squint, I can make out a switch by the door.

Uncle David has given him food, clean clothes, water, *and* light.

I want to bang on my door and demand food, but the thought of standing is overwhelming. Exhausting. Which is why I shuffle forward on my hands and knees. I can't afford to be too tired to ask for food.

"Hey!" I shout, but my voice is weak. Which pisses me off. "Hey!" This time I pound on the door to make sure I'm heard. "If you're not trying to kill me, you need to feed me now."

Footsteps thump toward my room and I scramble away from the door as it opens. My uncle's silhouette is backlit by blinding light from the main room. "You are definitely your father's daughter."

"And my uncle's niece," I tell him as I shield my eyes from the glare. For a moment, I think he's going to yell at me. Then he laughs instead. "Uncle David . . ." I try to swallow, but my throat is too dry. "If you're going to kill me, just do it." I'm not daring him. I'm calling what I hope is his bluff. "Don't let me die like this. I'm still your blood."

He stares at me as if he's trying to decide something.

"You're not going to let us go, are you?"

His eerie calm makes my stomach pitch. "Holden's release is already being worked out."

I blink, so startled by his answer that I hardly even register the slice of afternoon jungle I can see through the open window over his shoulder. "Why not mine?"

"Because I can't trust you."

"But you can trust *him*? He killed one of your men!"

"*You* blew up my arsenal! I had plans for that shipment, but now I've had to move on to plan B, and that's your fault, Genesis."

Plan B? I feel like I've been punched in the chest.

"No. Please!" I stick my foot in the doorway when he tries to close me in again. The door hits my boot. "Don't leave. What's plan B?"

He pushes my boot out of the way with his own, and when he starts to close the door again, to leave me alone and starving in the dark, tortured by the knowledge that he's planning another attack I won't be able to stop, I say the only thing I can think of that might truly hurt him.

"Didn't you ever wonder why Ryan looked more like me than like Maddie?" My uncle turns on me, and I fight the urge to step back as rage storms behind his eyes. "Ryan thought you died a hero, building houses for the poor in Colombia. You must be *so relieved* he never found out you were actually a terrorist."

My uncle slams the door in my face and locks it.

I laugh out loud, to be sure he can hear me.

Then I retreat into my corner and wipe silent tears from my face.

8 DAYS, 1 HOUR EARLIER

I'm sorry.

MADDIE

Fifteen minutes after I texted him, Luke knocks on my front door. I let him in with a kiss, then tug him past my mom and the funeral planning station she has set up on the table. She doesn't look up.

"What's with all the catalogues?" Luke asks as I close my bedroom door behind us.

"Ryan's funeral is on Wednesday. Uncle Hernán told her not to worry about the cost." He's throwing money at another problem, because he won't come back to the United States for the funeral while Genesis is still in Colombia. "And now she can't decide whether Ryan would prefer marble or granite. A flat marker or a headstone."

I'd rather think of him grinning as he dumps salt into my lemonade than lying under *any* kind of gravestone.

"At least she's staying busy." He sinks onto the end of my bed and I sit in my desk chair facing him. The room is so small that our knees nearly touch. "That's probably among the healthier coping mechanisms."

"I guess," I say as I dig my phone from my pocket.

"Okay, let me see it." He holds his hand out.

I open the text and set my phone in his palm.

He frowns at the screen. "Maddie, this came in seven hours ago. Why didn't you say anything then?"

"I didn't want it to be weird at lunch. With your friends." Also, I'm not sure which lie my mystery stalker is referring to: the one about my uncle (which Luke knows), or about my cousin (which Luke doesn't know). "Any idea how someone can send a text from a blocked number?"

"There are instructions online." He looks up from the phone. "You think this is about your uncle?"

"What else could it be?" But as soon as I've said it, I feel bad about lying to Luke. Even indirectly. "Is there any way to find out who sent it?"

"Not that I know of." He hands me back my phone. "There are some third-party apps that can help you trace a blocked message, but they have to be already installed when you get the message. Want me to set one up for you, in case it happens again?"

"No, that's okay. It's probably just some asshole messing with me. The downside of sudden fame."

"I'll research a few tonight, in case you change your mind." He stands, and I stand with him.

"You don't have to leave," I say. Luke's brows rise when I go up onto my toes and slide my arms around his neck. I press my mouth against his, but he's too stiff to give in. "What's wrong?"

"Your mom's right down the hall."

"I don't think she's even noticed I'm home." On the bright side, she hasn't asked about my blood sugar levels even once since the night we got back.

"Maddie, we're not going to make out in here just to get your mom's attention."

"That's not what this is." I kiss him again, and this time his arms slide around my waist, pulling me closer. His hand slips beneath the back of my shirt, warm against my skin. But he still feels a little . . . distant. "You make me feel good." I press closer to whisper against his neck, and his whole body tenses against mine. "I need to feel good right now. Please don't make me justify that."

Luke leans down to kiss me, and I block out everything else. I feel only his mouth against mine. His hands on my skin. I open my mouth to deepen the kiss, and he groans. I slide my hands beneath his shirt, dragging the material up as my fingers skim the lean, surprisingly well-defined lines of his stomach, and—

He steps back and his shirt falls into place. "We should stop." He's trying to do the right thing, but he doesn't really want to stop.

I don't want to stop either. He's the only thing keeping the world from crashing in on me, and the urge to cling to him is so strong that I can't see past it.

"You're thinking too much." I sit on the bed and try to pull him down with me, but he can't be moved.

"Not with your mom down the hall, Maddie. Honestly,

I don't think either of us is in a place to make a decision like this right now." His conflicted gaze begs me to understand.

"You're right. I'm sorry." I suddenly feel awkward, and I'm not sure where to look, but he only smiles and takes my hand.

"Don't be. And I'm not saying no. I'm just saying 'not yet.'"

Not yet.

I can work with that.

You can't keep us here forever.

GENESIS

"What's the plan, Sebastián?" I demand when he opens the door. My uncle's gone, and I have no idea when he'll be back. "You can't keep us here forever."

He sets a plate on the floor, his pistol aimed at my face. "If it were up to me, you'd be dead. Just like your boyfriend."

Indiana. I push grief aside.

"You don't know the plan, do you?" I stand, one hand propped on the rough wall for support. "You have no idea what's going—"

An explosion rocks the jungle, and the entire cabin quakes around us. The floor trembles beneath my feet.

"*¡Hijo de—*" Sebastián spins toward the front room, where one of my uncle's men is peeling back the cardboard taped over the front window. Light pours into the cabin, but it's a jumping, flickering brightness.

The jungle is on fire. Again.

Adrenaline shoots through me. The explosion echoes in my head.

"*¡Vamos!*" Sebastián shouts. "*¡Llama a David!*" Sebastián turns back to me, cocking his pistol.

"Stay put, *princesa.*" He slams the door.

My pulse races so fast my head swims. I've forgotten about the sandwich on the floor. I scoot over to the crack in the wall and press my face against it, desperate for more information.

Sebastián stands at the front of the cabin, gun in hand, staring out the open door. What's visible of the jungle flickers with the reflection of firelight. Sebastián's posture is tense. He's sent everyone else to investigate the explosion.

I won't get a better chance to fight him. To escape.

"Sebastián!" I shout. "What's going on?"

"Hey!" Holden yells from his room. "Was that a bomb? Are we under attack?"

We? Which side does Holden think he's on?

Through the crack in the wall, I see Sebastián twist toward our rooms. But then his jaw clenches and he turns back to the jungle without a word.

"Answer me!" I stand and pound on the door. "How close is the fire?"

When he doesn't reply, I kick the door. The whole thing shudders, but again it holds. Then, out of desperation, I try the knob.

It turns.

I stare, stunned, as the door opens an inch with a soft creak. In the chaos, Sebastián forgot to lock it.

Through the slim crack, I see him staring out the front

of the cabin. He hasn't noticed that my door is open.

I take a deep breath, trying to assess my physical state. I've gone too long without real food and rest. It won't do me any good to sneak out of my room if I can't take him down. I need a weapon.

Heart thudding in my ears, I push the door open a little wider and scan what I can see of the cabin for a gun left unattended in the confusion. There aren't any, but Sebastián's folding chair sits against the wall next to my door. Lying on the seat is his satellite phone.

I hesitate for just a second. If I attack him and fail to get away, he'll lock me up again and I'll have lost my shot at the phone. But if the other men get back before I finish a phone call, I'll have lost my chance to escape.

My arms still feel heavy and I'm light-headed. I'm *going* to make a break for it, but I'm probably going to fail. So first, I grab the phone and slip back into my room.

I leave the door barely cracked open so that I can see out with one eye. Then I take a big bite from the sandwich still lying on the plate in the middle of the floor and chew as I dial the hotline number Maddie recited on Neda's webshow.

1-555-GENESIS.

He would never . . .

MADDIE

The phone rings, and I roll over to grab it from my night-stand as I try to shake off sleep, hoping it's Luke. Hoping he's changed his mind and wants to come over. I hate being alone in the apartment with my mom. It's too quiet. I can hear her crying.

My phone screen shows only the clock and the date—no incoming call. Yet something is still ringing.

Shock pulls me upright. I'm instantly awake. *The hotline phone.*

I scramble off my bed and grab the purse hanging over my doorknob. Pawing past ChapStick, tissues, and the keys to my mom's car, I grab the prepaid phone, and it vibrates in my hand. The number on the screen is international; there are way too many digits for a US number.

I press the button to accept the call. "Hello?"

"Maddie?"

"*Genesis?*" I clutch the phone so tightly I can't feel my fingers. "Where are you? Are you okay? Are you free?"

"No. I'm in a cabin somewhere in the jungle. Sebastián's here, and his men caught Holden too."

"Your dad has men ready to go on a moment's notice. Where in the jungle are you?"

"I don't know." Her words are rushed, each syllable clipped short and so soft I can hardly hear her. "But something just exploded, and I can see flames through the window. I'm gonna run."

"Okay. Flames should be visible from the helicopter. I'll tell your dad. Let me get my other phone—"

"Wait!" she snaps in another fierce whisper. "Your dad's here."

"What?" I've misheard, obviously. So why does my chest suddenly feel so tight?

"He's alive, and he's here, and—"

"He's alive?" My legs fold beneath me, and suddenly I'm sitting on the floor of my bedroom, staring at nothing. At everything. "Sebastián took him? Has he been held captive this whole time?" For a *year*?

"No—"

"Oh my God." My brain feels like an engine revving up, thoughts flying too fast to truly sink in. Could I really get my dad back? "Let me talk to him. I *swear* we're going to get you both out of there."

"Maddie." Genesis is still whispering, but now she sounds . . . strange. "Your dad's not a hostage. He's . . . a terrorist. Sebastián's boss." She clears her throat softly. "He's the one who had us kidnapped in the first place."

I blink, trying to understand. "What the hell are you

talking about?" She's delusional. Nothing else makes sense.

"Your dad faked his own death so he could make some kind of statement to the world. Those were his bombs on my dad's cruise ship. But I don't have time to—"

"No . . ." I want to laugh, because surely this is a joke. Only it's not funny. "No!" I shout into the phone, and now I want to throw it. "What is wrong with you?" Maybe she's been brainwashed. Maybe Sebastián's making her say this, with his machete at her throat.

"Mad—" Her voice cuts off with a thud, then a gasp of pain, and I jump. A loud clatter splinters my thoughts as her phone hits the floor.

"*What have you done, sobrina?*" The new voice sounds distant, as if it's speaking from across the room. Except that it's not new at all. It's a voice I've known all my life.

"*Papi?*" I shout into the phone. My bedroom blurs as tears fill my eyes. There's no answer. I hear only a click, then the silence of a dead line.

I blink, uncomprehending. Then the truth crashes over me.

The phone slips from my hand. I scoot away from it until my back hits the far wall. I can still hear the voice echoing in my head.

That man may have sounded like my father. He may even have Genesis fooled. But I know better. My *papi* would never.

He would never . . .

He would *never* . . .

I should beg for my life.

GENESIS

"What did you tell her?" Uncle David demands.

"The truth." I have no idea how much Maddie understood. Or how much she's willing to believe, considering that she *idolized* her father.

The weight of his rage feels like a boulder poised to crush me. I scoot away from him, my shorts snagging on the rough floor. Whatever frayed family bond has been keeping me alive has snapped. Today I've taken his son *and* his daughter from him, and he suddenly seems willing to do the same to my father.

I should apologize. I should offer to call her back and swear I was lying. I should beg for my life.

"She deserves the truth." I don't know where the words are coming from. "She wanted to be just like you."

The blow comes fast and hard. Pain explodes in my face, and I crash to the floor in a heap of bruised limbs, but I'm up in an instant.

I can't even *remember* how to back down.

My uncle takes one heavy step forward, and even if I wanted to retreat, I have nowhere to go. "You—"

Sebastián bursts into the room. "Joseph went for the Jeep. We have to go, David. That explosion will bring the army down on us like a hammer."

Uncle David turns to him, still clutching the satellite phone. His brows rise in silent question.

Sebastián's focus flicks from his phone to me. Understanding dawns, and he steps back, jaw clenched. "I don't know—"

My uncle follows him out and latches the door. I block out the yelling and the angry thuds while I scarf down the rest of the sandwich—Sebastián deserves whatever he's getting—and when they stop, I look through the crack in the wall. The front door of the cabin still stands open, and now I can hear the blaze crackling.

"Pack up fast," Uncle David says. "Then tie up our guests and get moving. I'll meet you there." He storms out of the cabin. A second later, Sebastián follows, clutching his side with one hand and stuffing a rag to his bloody nose with the other.

"Holden!" I shout as I head for the wall our rooms share. "Did you—"

Glass shatters as I press my eye to the crack in the wall between us. Holden stands in front of a broken window—I hadn't even realized he *had* a window—with several hunks of broken glass scattered around his feet, though most of it has fallen outside. He's studying the window as if he'll crawl through it, but I can tell at a glance that he won't fit.

Footsteps approach my room. I go still. Sebastián *can't* be back already.

My heart thumps as the dead bolt slides free. The door swings open and a backlit figure stands in the doorway. He reaches for the switch outside my door, and the overhead light blinds me. But I would recognize his blurry silhouette anywhere.

"Indiana!" I throw myself at him. "What are you doing here?" I push hair back from his forehead, where a large gash at his hairline is swollen in the center of a huge purple lump. My chest aches with relief, my thoughts swirling in confusion.

"I came to rescue the princess."

You're all we have left.

MADDIE

My uncle's phone rings five times, then goes to voice mail. *Damn* it. "Uncle Hernán, Genesis just called the hotline phone. She said there's been an explosion in the jungle and she's going to run. Send your men in *now*. Have them look for fire."

I hang up and stare at my phone. I *just* spoke to her. *How can there be no way for me to help her?*

Dad.

I crawl across the floor and clutch the hotline phone to my chest. I could call the international number back. I could talk to my father.

I could demand answers.

I *need* to know why he spent my entire life lying to me about who he was. Why he chose terrorism over Ryan and me. Why he had us kidnapped at gunpoint.

My stomach roiling with nerves, I tap the international number to call it back. My head spins while the phone rings in my ear. I'm about to hear my dead father's voice. I'm going to yell at him until I lose my voice, then hope to

God he calls me Maddie-cakes and explains how this is all a huge misunderstanding and he's not actually responsible for hundreds of deaths.

That somehow, despite the evidence, he's still the man who took Ryan and me to serve at soup kitchens and build houses for the poor. An activist trying to make life better for those who can't stand up for themselves.

But then the ringing in my ear becomes a jarring, discordant series of notes, followed by an automated voice telling me that the number I'm calling is no longer in service.

He disconnected the number.

He disappeared *again*. I don't even get a good-bye.

I throw the hotline phone across the room, where it thumps off the far wall. For several minutes, all I can do is inhale calm and exhale rage, trying to spit out the poison churning in my gut.

Somehow, knowing he's still alive somewhere in the jungle hurts worse than thinking he was dead. When he was dead, he was my hero. He was a martyr who died trying to help people. I wanted to be just like the man I thought he was. But that man was a lie.

The truth is that my father is a monster.

Frustration and adrenaline firing through me, I head out of my room and down the short hallway. I don't realize I'm holding my breath as I pass Ryan's door until I exhale. The headstone catalogues are still spread across the kitchen table, pinned in place by a half-full cup of straight rum, but my mother is gone.

Then I hear her voice. She's on the phone in her room. I can't tell her about my dad.

Yet somehow, I'm standing outside her door, my right hand raised to knock, the hotline phone once again clutched in my left. I don't even know how I got here.

"Hernán, *please* answer your phone. It's not about the money." My mother isn't so much speaking as sobbing into my uncle's voice mail. "We need you here. You can't miss the funeral."

My hand falls to my side.

"Please. You're all we have left." She's begging now, and I feel sick inside. "Come home."

I turn and go back down the hall. Before I even realize what I'm doing, I have her glass in my hand. I throw the rum back in one swallow. It burns going down. But it's not enough.

The bottle is at the top of the coat closet, where Mom started keeping it when Ryan went into rehab. As if having to reach up high would stop an alcoholic. I grab it on my way back to my room.

I drop the hotline phone on my nightstand and curl up on my bed with the bottle. I wish Luke were here. I wish I could lay my head on his shoulder and breathe him in and think about the jungle.

Strange, that I would think about being stuck in the jungle with a murderer on my heels with any sort of nostalgia, but things were clear out there. I knew who I could count on and who was trying to kill me.

I dig my cell from my pocket and call Luke. While the phone rings, I turn the bottle up and take another burning gulp of rum.

"Hello? Maddie?" Luke sounds sleepy. "What's wrong?"

"Can you come over?" I take another swig. "Please."

Springs creak as he gets out of bed. "I'll be there in ten minutes."

We can't leave him.

GENESIS

"But I seem to have forgotten my shining armor."

I laugh, because the only alternative is crying. "I thought you were dead!"

Indiana winces as my fingers brush his injury. "We both will be, if we don't get out of here. Come on." He tugs me out of my prison cell, and over his shoulder I see another familiar form and a scraggly man bun I would recognize anywhere.

"Rog?" He's holding a pistol, and he looks comfortable with it.

"Time to go." Rog gives me a fierce grin. "Sebastián's men are crawling all over this corner of the jungle, and the explosion won't keep them occupied for long."

"That was you guys?" I gape at Indiana.

"Rog has a surprisingly broad skill set," he says as he tugs me toward the front door. "Come on. The explosion should bring the army running, and we need to find them before Sebastián's men find us."

"Wait!" I turn back as Rog tries to usher me out the door. "Holden's in that other room. We can't leave him."

Rog scowls, and I can practically see the argument forming on his tongue. But then he rolls his eyes and shrugs. "I'll get him. Go."

I grab a protein bar from the table near the door while Rog unlocks Holden's room. As I shove it into my pocket for later, Holden's door swings open. I hear a grunt, then a pained strangling noise.

Rog goes stiff with his back to me. His pistol clatters to the floor. He stumbles back, clawing at his own throat, and Holden blinks at him from the doorway, clutching a large, bloody shard of window glass.

"What did you *do?*" I shriek as Rog grasps at his own neck, blood pouring between his fingers.

"Shit! I thought . . ." Holden blinks again, his focus narrowing on Rog. "I thought he was one of Sebastián's . . ."

I grab a rag from the table and kneel over Rog, pressing the cloth to his throat. He blinks up at me, his mouth open. There's *so* much blood. It soaks through the rag in seconds.

"Genesis, we have to go." Holden's arm lands on my shoulder, but I shove him away.

"We can't just leave him."

"It was an accident," Holden insists, though no one's claimed otherwise. "There's nothing we can do for him, and if Sebastián catches us trying to escape, he'll kill us. No matter what your uncle's orders are."

"What? Your uncle?" Indiana looks confused.

"I'll explain later," I promise.

Indiana nods. "Holden's right, G." His voice is tight with regret. Thick with anguish. "Besides, I think Rog is gone."

I turn back to Rog and find him staring up through sightless eyes. The blood flow has slowed.

It happened *so fast*.

"Come on." Indiana takes my hand and I let him pull me up, tears blurring the cabin around me. "He came to help me get you out of here, and that's what we're going to do."

It's okay.

MADDIE

After I hang up the phone, I take one more drink from the bottle, then I sneak it back into the closet. My mother is crying softly in her room. She doesn't hear a thing.

I brush my teeth so Luke won't smell the rum on my breath, and by the time I hear a soft knock on the front door, I feel a little dizzy. When I stand to answer it, the room looks unsteady.

"Where's your mom?" Luke says as I lead him toward my bedroom.

"Asleep." She stopped crying a few minutes ago. I close the door behind us, then wrap my arms around his neck and lay my head on his shoulder. This is what I wanted.

"Maddie?" Luke pulls back to look at me. "Have you been drinking?"

"A little," I admit.

He leads me to the bed and turns back the covers. "Lie down. I'll get you some water."

"Stay." I pull him down next to me.

"Maddie, I can't . . ." He looks so conflicted, as if his

body and his head want different things. I know the feeling. "You're drunk."

I blink up at him, and his face blurs as tears fill my eyes. "I think my dad's a terrorist."

His frown deepens, and now he looks worried. "I don't even know what that means. What's going on?"

I lean back on the bed and pull the covers up to my chest, like a shield. "Genesis called the hotline number. She said my dad is Sebastián's boss. That he faked his own death."

"Genesis called the hotline? Wait, what?" He frowns, clearly trying to process the new information. "Your dad . . . ? That's crazy." He looks as skeptical as I felt during the call. "She was probably speaking under duress."

"I heard him." I take a deep breath, then spit out the words I've been trying to come to terms with from the moment I heard his voice. "I think he's *holding* Genesis in the jungle. I think everything that happened to us is his fault."

I can't tell whether Luke believes me, but finally he nods, then pulls his shirt over his head. He leaves his shoes on the floor, then slips under the covers with me, still wearing his pants.

"Go to sleep," he says as he turns off my lamp. Then he slides one arm over my waist, his chest pressed against my back. The warmth of Luke's arms and the rum buzz begin to pull me toward sleep. "It's okay. We'll figure this out in the morning."

7 DAYS, 18 HOURS EARLIER

No one could possibly blame you.

GENESIS

Tears burn my eyes and blur my vision. My hand is shaking. My legs are unsteady as I descend the cabin's single front step, but I hit the ground running, and I can't stop.

"Wait!" Indiana calls softly as he bursts through the front door behind me. To our left is a second cabin—presumably where Holden showered and ate—and to the right, the jungle is *on fire.* Holden is ahead of us, already running in the opposite direction of the flames. "We need to head west." Indiana gestures toward the blaze. As if the path to freedom includes walking through fire.

"Why?" But I stop, fear undulating through me in overlapping waves, urging me to *run.* In *any* direction.

There's blood on my hands. Literally.

Holden stops, but doesn't return. As if he wants to hear Indiana's idea before he makes up his mind.

"Because the army bunkhouse where they dragged us from our tents is due west of here. That's how Rog and I came in." Indiana wraps his arm around my shoulders, which is when I realize I'm shaking uncontrollably. Surrounded by trees and fire, all I can really see is blood.

And those unseeing eyes, staring up at the ceiling.

Indiana rubs my bare arm. "There's a much more direct route from the bunkhouse back to Cabo San Juan than the one we took last week."

Because last week, the bunkhouse wasn't our destination; it was a detour after Neda twisted her ankle.

I blink, trying to draw my thoughts into focus. Trying to put what just happened behind me. We've all seen enough death. There's no reason to dwell . . .

"If it's that close, Sebastián must know that," Holden says as he finally turns toward us. "That'll be the first place he looks."

"We don't actually have to go to the bunkhouse," Indiana tells him. "The army is looking for you guys, and they'll be drawn this way by the explosion. We just need to make sure they're the ones who find us. Which means heading toward the soldiers, not away from them."

"Assuming they're not in on this like the last bunkhouse soldiers. I'm not trekking through the jungle just to get caught again," Holden snaps.

"Do what you want." Indiana dismisses him and tugs me toward the west, clearly eager to get away from the cabin. That same urgency makes my legs ache to run, in spite of my exhaustion. "We need the bunkhouse as a point of reference, at the very least. Otherwise, we may never make it out of the jungle."

"Lead the way," I say. With a relieved smile, Indiana takes off through the jungle on a path that will lead us around the fire, pushing aside branches and stepping over roots as quietly as we can.

I follow him and, cursing beneath his breath, Holden thrashes his way through the brush after us, despite his protests.

My pulse pounds in my ears with every step. The fire roars, drowning out my thoughts and any attempt to speak. My head spins, and the trees seem to be dancing around me. I try to focus on what's ahead of me, rather than what's behind me, but I haven't eaten enough for this kind of exercise.

Indiana is a blur in front of me, stumbling through the sweltering jungle. Grabbing branches for support. He touches the healing gash on his head, then runs his hand through his hair to disguise the motion, but I can see that he's struggling. I've hardly eaten in days, and he's still recovering from a head wound. I can't believe we're even on our feet.

We have no supplies, except my protein bar and whatever Indiana has in his backpack. If not for the fire, we wouldn't be able to see where we are going. And with every step I take, I'm terrified that I'll hear boots on the ground behind us. Voices shouting through the jungle. When Sebastián realizes what happened, he *will* come after us.

We should have grabbed Rog's pistol. In that moment, I couldn't bring myself to loot his still-warm corpse, but now . . .

I can't be this close to freedom only to watch it slip

through my grasp. Not again.

Determination and fear sharpen my focus. *One step at a time, Genesis.* Just think about the next step. Then the next.

When we've safely passed the fire, Indiana's pace slows while he swings his backpack off his shoulder and begins digging in the bag. I catch up with him as he pulls out a compass and a flashlight. "Hold this for me?" He hands me the light, and I shine it on the compass.

Indiana makes a correction to our course, now that we've gone around the blaze, and we head due west. "Water?" He pulls a plastic bottle from a pouch on the side of his bag and offers it to me.

"Thanks." I take several gulps, then pass it to Holden before I remember that he had water in his room in the cabin.

I pull the stolen protein bar from my pocket and eat as we walk, hoping to steady my legs and ease the fierce ache in my head. Malnutrition and dehydration have taken a heavy toll on me. Everything hurts, and the jungle has a blurry, unreal quality that has nothing to do with the fact that little moonlight filters through the thick canopy overhead.

"How long has it been?" I whisper, pushing a branch out of my path. I don't hear anyone following us, but that doesn't mean my uncle's men aren't out there. "Since that night on the beach? The cruise ship."

"That was early on Wednesday morning," Indiana says.

"This is Friday." He hesitates. "Well, it's probably early Saturday by now."

Three days. "If Uncle David wasn't trying to kill me, he was certainly trying to break me."

"Maddie's dad? I thought he died," Indiana says.

"Turns out he'd just rather be a terrorist than a father. The bombs were his."

"Damn."

"Yeah." I step over a dimly lit root arching from the earth. "How long have you and Rog been out here looking for us?"

"Since Wednesday morning. After the explosion, I woke up in a boat on the beach with no idea what was going on. I stumbled around for a few minutes, trying to remember what had happened, and Rog found me. He said you never made it out of the jungle. He wanted to take me to the hospital, but I was afraid that if I went, they'd hold me for questioning, and I . . ." He shrugs, a shifting of the shadows to my left. "I couldn't leave you out here. So when the authorities started showing up, we got back in the boat and headed down the coast to find some supplies."

"So you never went to the hospital?"

"I only lost consciousness for a few minutes."

"You could have a skull fracture! You've been hiking for nearly three days with a head wound, *looking* for armed terrorists!" I stop for a second to study him in the distant flicker of flames. Then I press myself against Indiana and go up on my toes to kiss him. We have time for that.

Holden makes an angry noise as he stomps past us, but Indiana holds me for a second. Then takes my hand and leads me forward again.

"Rog was army special forces," he says as we settle back into the hike. "He knows first aid. He wouldn't let me head back into the jungle until he was pretty sure it was just a concussion."

Special forces. A vet. And he died at the hands of the spoiled rich kid he was trying to set free.

Though I hadn't thought it was possible, I hate Holden a little more.

I let my focus wander back to Indiana, and an isolated ray of moonlight shines on his injury. "That was still dumb."

His smile reminds me of the night we met, on the beach at Cabo San Juan. "As dumb as refusing to rescue yourself so you can blow up a terrorist's arsenal?"

Indiana wouldn't joke if he knew about the *Splendor*, and I'm not surprised that he doesn't. The explosion is what knocked him unconscious, and afterward, he didn't speak to Maddie and the others or to the authorities. "The bombs weren't on a mini-sub, Indiana. They were on a cruise ship."

"She killed twelve hundred people," Holden says from the shadows to my right. "She's a mass murderer."

Indiana blinks at me in the dark, clearly stunned. Then he shakes his head and turns to me, brushing a strand of dirty hair back from my face. "No. G, you didn't kill *anyone*. You didn't put those bombs on the ship. You didn't know they were there. No one could possibly blame you for that."

But he's wrong. The world will be looking for someone to blame, and Holden is ready to point the finger right at me.

7 DAYS, 17 HOURS EARLIER

It's probably too late.

MADDIE

My eyes fly open in the dark and I sit straight up in bed. *My dad's alive.* The sudden realization wakes me up like a bucket of cold water thrown over my head.

Genesis!

"Maddie?" Luke says, and I gasp, surprised to find him in my room. In the middle of the night. "What's wrong?" His voice is husky with sleep. The bed creaks softly as he sits up next to me, and finally I remember.

I called him. And I drank rum. Which would explain why my head feels . . . heavy. Why the room looks a little unsteady.

I'm still kind of buzzed.

I reach over Luke to fumble for my phone on the nightstand, and I find myself pressed against his bare chest, nothing but my shirt between us. His body goes utterly still against mine. He even stops breathing. Then he hands me my phone.

"Sorry," I mumble as I press the home button. Light

from the screen illuminates his face while I scroll through my messages. Nothing from my uncle.

Genesis called two hours ago. If they haven't found her yet, it's probably too late.

Please, God, let them find her.

I have to tell my uncle the rest. Even if the words kill me.

Genesis said my dad's alive. That he's there. That he's behind this whole thing.

If Uncle Hernán wants more information than that, he's going to have to call me.

"How do you feel?" Luke strokes hair back from my face.

I drop my phone on the comforter and turn back to him. "I—" My mouth is dry, and suddenly that seems to have nothing to do with the rum and everything to do with the fact that Luke's in my bed. Under the covers. We shared a tent and a hammock in the jungle, but somehow this feels a million times more intimate. "How did you get here?"

"I took my mom's car." He leans back against my headboard, and the vertical lines of his abs stand out with the movement. "But I should probably get it back before she notices it's missing."

"You don't have a license." He won't turn sixteen for another month.

"You were upset." He bends to pick up his shirt from the floor, then pulls it over his head. "Are you sure you heard your dad over the phone?"

I crawl out of bed, straightening my pajama shirt. "I *know* his voice, Luke."

Still sitting on the edge of the mattress, he pulls me closer until I'm standing between his thighs, both my hands in his. "Okay, so what do we do?"

I shrug and sit next to him. "I guess I'll have to tell my mom." And maybe . . . the police.

What if they think my mom and I *helped* him?

My eyes fall closed as the reality hits me. I'm the daughter of a terrorist.

But how can I not turn him in?

"Do you want me to stay?" Luke takes my hand. He looks worried.

"No, that's okay. Take your mom's car home before she reports it stolen." She already blames me for "luring" her son into the jungle, where we were kidnapped. Even though, technically, Luke was never actually kidnapped. "Thanks for coming."

Dazed from both the rum and from psychological whiplash, I walk Luke to the door and lock it behind him. Then I grab my phone from my room and realize I don't know who to call to turn my father in.

Can you call 911 to report a terrorist a continent away?

We cannot *be caught.*

GENESIS

We've been walking forever.

It's probably only been a couple of hours, but with freedom taunting me like a glimmer of light at the end of a dark tunnel, every step feels like a mile. Every second feels like a month.

And I am *so* tired.

The bouncing beam from Indiana's flashlight threatens to hypnotize me. Branches seem to be reaching into my path just to smack me in the face, while roots pop up to catch my boots. The possibility of falling and impaling myself on a stick is the only thing keeping me awake.

Until I hear the faint snap of a twig behind us.

Adrenaline races through me and I freeze. Indiana goes still.

Another snap echoes from somewhere at our backs.

Indiana clicks the flashlight off. A couple of steps ahead of us, Holden turns, and too late, I realize he hasn't heard. And we can't warn him without making more noise.

"What the hell?" he demands.

"Genesis!" Sebastián roars from somewhere behind me, his voice an echo of rage and resolve.

He found Rog's body.

He knows how we got away.

Fear gives me a fresh burst of energy and I lurch forward, Indiana's arm still in my grip. We *cannot* be caught.

I can't spend another day in the dark. Another night in the jungle.

Holden starts to run, stumbling over roots and foliage he can't see very well, and I hope we aren't following him just because he's in the lead.

"Over here!" Sebastián shouts.

I don't know how many of my uncle's men are chasing us, but I know they have more energy. More strength. More resources. More experience beating their way through the foliage.

"This way," Indiana hisses when Holden veers to the right.

My ex groans, but corrects his path. I follow them, trying to ignore how heavy my legs feel. How indistinct the trees and roots and brush look as they fly past.

A bright light appears ahead, and I stumble to a startled halt. "Indiana." I grasp for his arm again. "What's that? Did they get ahead of us?"

"I don't think so," he says as Holden turns to look back at us. "I think that's the base camp."

Holden scowls. "That light's too bright to be—"

"Come on!" Indiana grabs my hand. "I think that's a searchlight! The army could be looking for us!"

Brush rustles at my back. "I've got them!" Sebastián shouts. I look over my shoulder to see him pointing a pistol at my back. He lunges toward us, grabbing for my arm.

Indiana pulls me forward, and we're running again, toward the light. Toward the bunkhouse. Toward the Colombian army, which, according to Indiana, has been looking for Holden and me for three days.

Footsteps clomp closer. A hand catches in my hair. I scream as I'm pulled to a stop and strands pop free from my scalp.

Indiana turns. "Let her go!"

Holden stops and spins toward us, but says nothing. His eyes are wide and watchful, as if he's waiting to see how this will play out.

I spin and swing my right fist up. More hair pulls loose from my head. My punch lands on Sebastián's jaw.

He staggers back, more angry than hurt by my weak blow. I lurch forward, but I'm exhausted and my steps are erratic. My foot lands on a thick branch and folds beneath me. Pain shoots through my ankle, and I scream again. I push myself to my feet as an Indiana-shaped blur flies past me. He tackles Sebastián. They hit the ground, and the gun goes off with the soft *thwup* of a suppressor.

Fear blazes through me like a bolt of lightning. "Indiana!"

7 DAYS, 16 HOURS EARLIER

I know what to expect from this.

MADDIE

"Mom!" I bang on her bedroom door with both fists, even though it's the middle of the night. If I don't tell her now, I'll lose my nerve.

There's no answer.

"Mom! Wake up!" I try the doorknob, but it's locked. "I need to talk to you!"

She mumbles something from behind the door, but I can't understand her. She's always been a light sleeper. In fact, after my father ~~died~~ faked his death, she hardly slept at all.

"Mom!"

When she doesn't answer, I march into the kitchen and rummage through the junk drawer until I come up with a nickel. In the hall again. I stick the nickel in the slot on the back of her doorknob and twist to unlock it. The door swings open.

My mother lies facedown on her pillow, on top of the covers. Her pajama pants are twisted around her legs, and there's an empty glass on her nightstand.

I cross the room and sit on the edge of her bed. My father's half is undisturbed. He's been gone for nearly a year, but she never even rolls onto his side. The pair of jeans he tossed over the back of the chair near the closet before he headed to the airport on his last trip to Colombia is still where he left it.

"Mom." I shake her shoulder, and she mumbles something in her sleep. The empty glass on her nightstand smells like rum, but I can't really criticize her for that. At least, not until my own headache goes away. "Mom!" I shake her harder, and finally her eyes flutter open.

"Maddie?"

"Yes. Wake up. I have to tell you something."

My mother blinks. Then she sits up and smooths hair back from her face. "What's wrong, *mija*?" Her lips are dry and cracked. I should get her a glass of water. But I have to say this before I chicken out.

"Dad's alive."

She frowns and blinks at me. "What? Did you have a dream?"

"No. Mom, he's still alive. He's in the jungle." Too late, I realize that she's still half asleep, and I'm not making any sense. Because what I have to say makes no sense.

"Madalena, are you okay? Do you want me to make you an appointment with Dr. Hillard?"

"No, Mom, I don't need a counselor. I know this sounds crazy, but Genesis called the hotline. She said my dad is still alive."

"Maddie . . ." Her voice is soft with sympathy. She thinks I've lost my mind.

"Mom, I'm not crazy. She's still in the jungle, and Dad is with her. He's not dead. *I heard his voice.*"

My mother's eyes widen as she assesses my state of mind. Finally she decides I'm telling the truth. Or at least that I believe I am. "In the jungle . . . ?"

"In Colombia. He's alive."

"Oh my God . . ." My mother covers her mouth and nose with both hands. Her eyes water, and too late I realize that she's happy. Because I haven't told her the rest of it.

"No. Mom, this isn't good news. He . . ." There's no easy way to say this. "Mom, Dad is the one who had us kidnapped. He's the reason Genesis is still a hostage. The reason Ryan died."

Her hands fall into her lap. "Maddie, that's—"

"I *know* it's ridiculous. But that doesn't mean it isn't true. If you don't believe me, call Uncle Hernán." He'll believe me. And he'll convince her.

My mom's eyes fill with tears again, and we've now swung the full range on the emotional pendulum. She looks like I just put a pistol to her chest and pulled the trigger. I should feel terrible for putting my mother through this, when she's already been through so much, but I can't feel bad for her. Not right now. I can't feel much of anything.

I feel numb. Like when you sit on your leg for too long, and your foot goes to sleep. Only the leg I've been sitting on is actually my own heart, and it's so damaged that it can't register any more pain.

But I know what to expect from this. When you hop on your foot, the first feeling that comes back is that hellish walking-on-nails sensation. A pain that makes you want to cut your own foot off.

My mother's in that hell right now.

And I know that no matter how blessed I feel for my numbness at the moment, I'll soon be in that hell with her.

Again.

It's over.

GENESIS

Time slows as Indiana and Sebastián struggle on the ground. The suppressed gunshot wasn't loud enough to be heard from more than a few feet away, but it echoes in my head like an explosion.

Finally Indiana gets up, holding Sebastián's gun in one hand, clutching his head in the other. There's no blood that I can see, but he looks dazed. "Stay down." He aims the pistol at Sebastián's chest. I don't know if he's ever fired a gun, but in that moment, he looks perfectly willing to shoot.

"You think you're free, *princesa?*" Sebastián spits, staring up at us from the ground. "David can use you in the States as easily as he used you in the jungle. You and your friends are going to push another button for him. You'll never be free."

My pulse spikes painfully. What does that mean? Is he talking about my uncle's plan B?

"Go!" Indiana shouts at me and Holden as he backs away from Sebastián, still aiming the gun at him.

I turn to run again—the light from the bunkhouse is just a few hundred feet away now—but my ankle folds beneath me.

Indiana kneels to help me up, but then he begins to wobble and has to grab my shoulder for balance.

"Holden!" he shouts. Holden reluctantly slows and looks over his shoulder. "Help her. I can't . . ." He wobbles again when he stands.

Holden glances at me, then in the direction we're fleeing, and I can see his thoughts as they flicker over his face. I'll slow him down. He wants to leave us.

Indiana aims the gun at Holden's foot. "Either we all get out, or none of us get out."

I can't tell whether he's bluffing. Neither can Holden.

Anger draws his brows low as he snaps at Indiana. "You two are *not* going to get us caught again." He sweeps me up in both arms, bandaging his wounded pride with a blatant show of strength, and takes off.

I cling to Holden for balance, and over his bouncing shoulder I see Indiana racing unsteadily toward us. Sebastián starts after us, favoring one leg, but alive and well.

A motor grinds to life from the bunkhouse ahead, and I can't hear anything else. The light gets brighter as we get closer, blinding me through the tree branches. People are shouting, but I can't make out any of the words.

My heartbeat is a cadence of uncertainty and fear. For all I know, my uncle could be herding us into a trap.

Holden bursts through a clump of brush into the

clearing, and I blink, trying to take it all in. The bunkhouse looks just like it did last week, when we were led away from it at gunpoint, but this time there are no tents set up. This time, a crowd of men stands around the base of a tree on the edge of the clearing. Most of them wear camouflage and carry automatic rifles.

Exactly what our kidnappers wore.

My chest feels so tight my lungs won't expand.

One of the men sees us. He shouts, and the motor dies; it's a generator, powering the bright light. The soldiers turn, lifting their rifles. A camera flashes in my face.

A man in khakis and a dark polo shirt pushes through the crowd. "Genesis!" he shouts as he races toward us.

Tears blur the base camp in front of me as Holden sets me on my feet. It's over. Finally the whole thing is over.

The man in the polo wraps his arms around me, and I inhale the familiar scent of his shampoo.

"Dad."

7 DAYS, 13.5 HOURS EARLIER

Everything's going to be okay.

MADDIE

"Mom! Breakfast is ready!" I slide her fried egg—over medium—onto a piece of buttered toast, then top it with two slices of bacon. Next come two tomato slices, a sprinkling of chopped cilantro, and a drizzle of hot sauce. Then the top piece of toast.

We used to have egg sandwiches for brunch every Saturday. Back when my dad was ~~alive~~ still here. Back when Ryan was around to steal my bacon and drink from my juice glass. Reviving the custom now could make us both sad. But I've decided it won't. I'm reclaiming the tradition for what's left of our family.

It's just me and Mom now, and I've already half lost her. I have to get her back.

"Mom!" I set her plate on the table, then make a sandwich for myself. I get open-faced, for fewer carbs—screw you, diabetes!—plus a sprinkling of cheddar cheese.

We each get a cup of coffee. Black. And a big glass of water with lemon. Because rum hangover.

I take a bite of my open-faced sandwich and chew as I walk down the short hall. "Mom!" I call again with my mouth full. My voice is relentlessly cheery, because my mother will wallow. After my father ~~died~~ faked his own death, she wallowed so thoroughly that she didn't notice my brother's descent into alcoholism. She's been wallowing ever since she found out about Ryan. And since bad news seems to come in sets of three, I fully expect that finding out her husband is a terrorist will push her over the edge into bed-ridden, TV-watching, quietly drinking Mom.

Her bedroom door is locked again, so I open it with my trusty nickel, but she's not in bed. "Mom?" I call, but there's no answer.

The door to the tiny master bathroom is also closed and locked, but again my nickel prevails.

My mother is sitting on the floor, leaning against the side of the tub. At first, I think she's asleep. Then I see the pill bottle in her hand and the glass of water on the edge of the tub, still cloudy with toothpaste residue around the rim.

I stumble backward. My open-faced sandwich hits the linoleum. Then I fall to my knees on the floor next to her and grab the bottle. "*Damn it*, Mom!"

I fumble for my phone and dial 911.

"This is 911, what is your emergency?"

"I just found my mother unconscious on the floor with an empty pill bottle. They were prescription sedatives." My voice sounds so much calmer than I feel. "She's still breathing."

"Good. I'm sending you some help. What's your name and address?"

I give the operator the necessary information, and I'm relieved, in spite of the circumstances, when she doesn't seem to recognize my name. Evidently not everyone watches the news.

"The ambulance is headed for you now. You should hear the sirens in a few minutes. While we wait, I want you to stay on the phone with me and give me some additional information. Can you do that?"

"Of course," I say into the phone as I watch my mother's chest rise and fall slowly. I take her hand. "Everything's going to be okay," I tell her, though she can't hear me.

"What did she take?" the operator asks.

I pick up the bottle again and read her the label of the pills the doctor gave my mother a few days ago. After Ryan died.

"Do you know how many she took?"

"No." The bottle shakes in my grip. "The label says there were thirty pills, and the prescription's three days old. It says to take one per day. So she might have taken as many as twenty-seven today." Thinking about that—about the numbers, the probability—is much better than thinking about what's actually happening here.

About the fact that my mother would rather die than live in this sad half-family with just me.

I'm not ready.

GENESIS

My father's embrace lifts me off the ground, and for a moment, all I can do is breathe him in. I'm furious at him. I may actually hate him. But I've known this scent all my life. His shampoo. His cologne. Even his sweat. In some strange, confusing way, I feel like I'm home, even though I'm still standing in the middle of the jungle.

Then Indiana bursts through the brush, carrying Sebastián's gun.

Rifles swing toward him. One of the soldiers begins shouting in Spanish.

"*No!*" I pull free from my father's grasp and step in front of Indiana, my arms spread, my pulse rushing fast enough to make me dizzy. I am his human shield. "*¡Esperen! ¡Está conmigo!*"

"*¡Suelta el arma!*" one of the men shouts.

"Drop the gun," I translate for Indiana, without turning around. The pistol thunks to the ground at my feet.

"*Está bien,*" my father says, his hands outstretched as if

to soothe the soldiers. "*Es uno de nosotros.*"

He's one of us. My father doesn't know Indiana, but he's willing to vouch for him if I am.

"Dad!" I spin toward the jungle again, flinching as my ankle refuses to support me. "Sebastián was right behind us!"

He shouts an order in Spanish to the soldiers, and half of them take off into the jungle carrying their rifles. Eager to apprehend the fugitive.

"*Princesa . . .*" Tears stand in my father's eyes. He holds his arms out to me, and some part of me wants to step into his embrace again. To accept the love and comfort he's given me my whole life. But I can't. Nostalgia and relief can't make me forget the lie my entire existence has been built upon. The felonies that paid for every cent I've ever spent and every thread I've ever worn. Or the fact that this whole thing is his fault.

His, and his brother's.

Hurt flickers over his features when I reject his hug, and though I saw him a week ago, the fine lines around his eyes and mouth suddenly seem deeper. I missed him. I still love him. But I don't even know who he is anymore.

"*Mija?*"

"Dad, this is Indiana."

My father tilts his head slightly, but accepts the sudden subject change. He holds his hand out, and Indiana shakes it. "Indiana. My niece and her friends have been frantic about finding you. The FBI has been stumped."

"Well, I'm happy to have been found, sir." Indiana even

manages a smile, in spite of the circumstances.

"He escaped with Maddie and Luke, but went back into the jungle to find me." No matter how angry I am at my father, I *need* him to respect Indiana. To like him. To understand the sacrifice he made for me, after knowing me for less than a week.

"You have my *deepest* gratitude," my father says. "And a standing invitation to our home."

Holden shoots us all a disdainful look as he stomps past on his way to one of the picnic tables, and my father turns to me with one arched brow. "And Holden is . . . ?"

"History."

"I can't say that I'm sorry to hear that." It's no secret that he never liked Holden.

"Dad." I pull him away from the crowd, deeper into the clearing. I'm not ready to talk about his criminal history, but this other family secret—one of them, anyway—can't wait. "Did Maddie call you?" As mad as I am at him, I don't want to have to say the words.

"She left a message on my cell. I forgot to give her the new satellite number. *Mija*, I had no idea David was . . . alive. Much less behind all of this. I'm so sorry he used you. All of you." His agonized gaze tracks to the left, and I follow his focus to see that two of the men who came here with my father are still standing beneath a tree on the edge of the clearing, where the bright light hanging from one of the lower branches would be shining on them, if someone hadn't turned off the generator.

Both men are holding shovels.

"You're here for Ryan . . ." My words carry very little sound. The clearing blurs as my eyes water.

"I'm here for you both. But I promised Daniela that I'd bring him home." He studies me closely, his eyes still damp. "*Princesa*, I know that saying I'm sorry is nowhere near enough. But I'm hoping it can be a start. I'm so happy to have you back." He reaches for me again, as if he can't quite process my rejection of his hug.

I can't really process it either. It's been the two of us against the world since my mother was murdered. But I can't pretend nothing has changed, when the truth is that nothing will ever be the same again.

"I—" I turn away from him without offering any explanation, fighting the urge to let him hold me and make everything okay. "Call the helicopter. I want to go home." With that, I head for Indiana and Holden, who sit on opposite sides of one of the picnic tables. It's strange to see them there, where we shared bottles of beer with our fellow campers hours before Uncle David's men kidnapped us at gunpoint.

Someone has given them each a steaming paper cup of coffee and a protein bar.

I limp over and slide onto the bench next to Indiana. His arm settles around my waist and I lay my head on his shoulder, flexing my foot as the pain in my ankle begins to fade. I only met him a week ago, but in that time we've seen each other at the lowest of lows. Injured. Starving. Threatened with dismemberment. Nearly blown up.

In that time, everything I thought I knew about my life—including my father—has turned out to be a lie.

Maybe it's time for something new. Something sweet, and—

A loud rustling at the tree line draws my attention. The soldiers who left the clearing a few minutes ago are back, and two of them have Sebastián by the arms, his hands cuffed at his back.

As they march him past our table, he holds my gaze with an unsettling smile.

"It's over," Indiana whispers as I snuggle closer, clinging to the only person on the continent who hasn't let me down.

"Maybe for you," I say. "For me, it's just beginning."

7 DAYS, 12 HOURS EARLIER

This is my fault.

MADDIE

"Maddie!" Luke jogs past the nurse's desk, his worried gaze trained on me. He's still in the same shirt he was wearing when he came over last night. The shirt he put on when he woke up in my bed early this morning. "What happened?"

"I made egg sandwiches," I say as I stand from the chair in the hospital waiting room. I know that's not what he's asking, but for some reason, it's what my brain keeps bouncing back to.

He folds me into a hug. "I mean, what happened to your mom?"

"She made a long-term residential decision in favor of a box in the ground. With a bottle full of Ativan."

"Is she going to be okay?"

I shrug as I sink back into the padded green chair I've been sitting in for the past hour and a half. "The doctor says that, like, ninety-eight percent of suicide attempts by pill overdose are unsuccessful."

"Ninety-eight point two," Luke corrects, and I'm not surprised that he knows the actual numbers. "Though survivors sometimes have long-term organ damage from the attempt."

I frown, and he takes my hand. "Sorry. I guess you don't need all the details right this moment."

"I told her, Luke. This is my fault. I told her about my dad, and she tried to kill herself."

"That doesn't make it your fault. You can't blame the messenger for the content of the report."

"You're right." Anger blazes through me as the truth of what he's saying sinks in. "It's *my dad's* fault. All of this is his fault." Yet I can't help chafing over the knowledge that my mom was happier with the lie about his death than with the truth about his life.

And the supersecret truth is that I can't really blame her for not wanting to live in a world where everyone will know she's married to a mass-murdering terrorist. I don't want to live in that world either. But the alternative—death—holds no appeal.

I've spent the past hour and a half sitting here in the waiting room trying to figure out how my father, a spirited activist I knew and loved, became a man willing to kill thousands to make a point.

I suspect that what happened to my father was apathy.

Not his own. Everyone else's.

I think people got tired of hearing what he was saying— and really, he only ever spoke about one thing. He was obsessed with his cause, and the less they listened, the louder he shouted. Looking back—knowing what to look for—I can see that.

Parties where someone's casual xenophobia would send

him into a half-hour diatribe. Dinners when my mother couldn't get a word in around his railings against the US policies that contributed to the decline of the Colombian farming economy.

Eventually, I think, he realized that his voice wasn't loud enough to reach people who were determined to turn a deaf ear. So he decided to say something they couldn't refuse to hear.

The truly terrifying part is that I understood his frustration with the willfully ignorant. We shared that frustration. At least, I *thought* I'd understood. . . .

"I wonder if he'd care. My dad, I mean. If I told him about my mom." I pick at a ripped seam in the vinyl upholstery. "I wonder if he ever loved her. Or me and Ryan. I mean, how could he have, if he—"

"Maddie." Luke's voice sounds strange. He's staring at something on the wall over my shoulder. "Look."

I turn and see that the television mounted in one corner is tuned to a news station. A ticker at the bottom shows a never-ending loop of headlines, and the volume is muted, so I can't hear what's being said. But at center screen, to the right of the news anchor's head, is a still photograph that sucks the breath right out of my lungs.

It's Holden. In a jungle clearing. Carrying Genesis in both arms.

The caption reads:

Holden Wainwright rescues heiress girlfriend from armed terrorists.

You can't believe anything they told you.

GENESIS

The soldiers drag Sebastián across the clearing and he fights their hold, straining to turn and look at me. "This isn't over, *princesa*! You will never be free!" he shouts.

I flip him off as they haul him into the bunkhouse. Then I take the protein bar Indiana offers me and I exhale. Long and slow.

The man who kidnapped us has been caught.

We *are* free. But even if the world never finds out that I blew up the *Splendor*, they will find out about my father. According to Sebastián, they already have.

Two men with shovels are digging up Ryan's grave as the sun finally climbs high enough to be seen through the jungle canopy. They're being very careful. Very respectful. And they haven't said a word so far, except to answer my father's questions.

I wonder if they know who they're digging up.

Ryan stares at me through sad, half-focused eyes, his legs splayed out in front of him on the spotless white carpet. I pluck

125

the glass from his hand before he can spill his whiskey, then I toss it back myself. He's had enough.

"I'm so sorry about your father." I sit against the wall next to him and let my head fall onto his shoulder. "But you and Maddie don't need to worry about money. My dad will take care of everything. Family first."

Ryan lets his cheek rest against the top of my head, and for a moment, we just sit like that. Leaning on each other. "It's more complicated than that, prima. Hermanita," he says at last. "But you can't tell Maddie. . . ."

Ryan and I never talked about it, after that first time. I always felt like acknowledging the truth would have driven a wedge through our family. Pulling us apart, rather than bringing us together.

But now that he's gone . . .

I can't watch them pull him from the ground, yet I can't make myself turn away. So I watch Ryan from the corner of my eye. In death, as in life, he exists on the edge of my awareness. Always there. Yet never my focus.

That's only one of a million things I would do differently, if I could go back and talk to the girl I was a year ago. But it's too late for so many things. . . .

"Genesis." My father's standing at the end of the picnic table, and he's probably said my name several times. He's finally off his satellite phone. "The helicopter's on its way."

"Good." I stare at the cracked picnic table, trying to pull myself out of a fog brought on by malnutrition, sleep deprivation, and shock. "Where's Indiana?" I don't remember him leaving the table.

"He and Holden are getting cleaned up in the bunkhouse."

Indiana and Holden, alone in a bathroom. I can't help thinking I should go in there, to stand between them, but I'm too tired to move. To even think.

My father sinks onto the empty bench across from me. He hasn't tried to touch me since I shrugged out of his hug. "Here." He sets a bottle of SmartWater with electrolytes on the table between us. I've already had three of them, and I still haven't needed to use the restroom. "I've ordered a steak for you on the jet. But I have another protein bar for now, if you're hungry."

I'm starving, but the thought of eating makes me feel sick. I suspect I'll have to go slowly until my stomach adjusts to normal meals again.

I blink and force my gaze to bring my dad into focus. "So there's still a jet? Sebastián said your assets were frozen."

My dad reaches across the table for my hand, but I pull it out of reach, and the fresh pain that flickers across his face actually hurts me too. Why is it so hard to be mad at him? "Genesis, *no*," he says. "You can't believe anything they told you. Our assets are intact."

"But should they be?" I demand softly. "Silvana and Sebastián didn't make up the part about you trafficking drugs for twenty years, did they? So everything we have is profit from illegal activity?" How am I ever supposed to

127

accept another dime from him, knowing that?

He glances around to make sure no one's listening, but the diggers are still carefully digging, the soldiers are speaking on a radio to colleagues out in the jungle searching for Sebastián's accomplices, and the photographer—*why* is there a photographer?—is sitting on a log near the fire pit, scrolling through the images on his digital camera while he holds it toward the sky, searching for a stronger signal.

My gaze slides from the dark patch of dirt where Ryan died to the bare spot where we all pitched our tents last week. I can't believe we're back here. Where the whole thing started. Couldn't Uncle David's men burst into the clearing again at any moment and start shooting?

Panic spikes my pulse. My leg bounces beneath the table. We have to get out of the jungle. *I can't be here anymore.*

"*Princesa*, this isn't the time," my father says. But I don't understand his answer, because I've forgotten what I asked.

Oh yeah. Drug trafficking. Illegal profit.

"When will the time be? When is it going to be convenient for you to explain to me how my entire life—everything I've ever had or done—has only been possible because my father is a criminal?"

He looks like someone's replaced his coffee with straight lemon juice. Like he wants to spit it out and rinse away the uncomfortable truth. But I can't let him do that. "We can discuss this in detail once we're home. Once you've had a chance to rest." Then he blinks, and suddenly he looks like there *is* something he wants to discuss now. "Genesis." He leans toward me over the table and lowers his voice even further. "What happened to Silvana?"

"Why?" I demand softly. "So you can resume sleeping with the enemy?"

My dad recoils as if I've slapped him, and I feel both guilty and justified.

"So I can make sure she pays for what she's done to you," he says through clenched teeth.

"I don't know where she is." I look into his eyes so he can see that I'm telling the truth. I don't want to answer any more questions about this. "I haven't seen her since I woke up in that cabin."

My father presses his lips together, but I'm too tired to try to figure out what he's thinking. Especially if it's anything other than "good riddance."

"What's going to happen to Sebastián?"

"The Colombians have agreed to hand him over to the US," my dad says. "But not until tomorrow. They have until then to interrogate him."

"And Uncle David? Dad, he's planning something else. A new target or a new weapon. Sebastián said he'd use *us* in his plan B."

"He also told you our assets had been seized and that Indiana was dead." My dad glances at the bunkhouse, where several soldiers are gathered in a tense discussion. "I told them everything you told me. Soldiers are crawling all over the cabins where you were held, looking for David and the rest of his men."

They won't find my uncle. A man with the resources to fake his own death and hide in the jungle for a year won't have any problem evading the authorities for as long as he wants. But . . .

I frown at my dad from across the table. "How do you know what the US and Colombian governments have agreed to?" That's more access than he should have, no matter whose pockets he's lining. "Who do you keep calling?"

"I have a contact at the State Department." He's speaking so softly I can hardly hear him.

"What kind of contact?" I whisper. His silence makes me nervous. "Dad. What's going on?"

He exhales slowly and glances around the clearing again. Then he looks me in the eye from across the table. "Genesis, I'm a witness for the State Department, in their case against Gael Moreno and his organization. For drug trafficking. I've been working with them for the past year."

"You're an *informant*?"

She'll be better soon.

MADDIE

I follow Luke down the sterile hospital hallway toward the elevators, sipping my coffee, but I don't truly register the buzz of voices until we round the corner and I can see the crowd.

My first thought is that something terrible has happened. Why else would so many people be gathered near the emergency room?

Then I realize they're all holding cameras and microphones.

"Maddie!" one woman yells, and the other heads turn our way.

Flashes go off in my face, and I flinch. "Is it true your mother tried to kill herself?" a thin man in a baggy T-shirt demands.

They're gathered between us and the elevator. Which puts them between us and my mother. I am frozen.

"Was this about your brother's murder?"

"Have you heard anything from Genesis and Holden? Can you confirm that he carried her out of the jungle, and they've been rescued by the Colombian army?"

"How is your mother, Maddie?"

"Is it true that she shot herself?"

A panicky feeling closes in on me—suddenly the hall-way feels much too narrow.

"Come on," Luke murmurs, wrapping an arm around my waist. "There have to be other elevators."

"Hey!" a sharp new voice shouts over the din, and it takes me a second to realize that the woman pushing her way through the crowd isn't a reporter. She's a doctor in a white coat, followed by a security guard. "You all can't be in here!"

"Everybody out!" the security guard shouts as he spreads his arms and begins pressing the crowd toward the sliding glass emergency room doors.

As soon as they've cleared the bank of elevators, Luke starts forward, ignoring the reporters as if he simply can't hear them. As if they don't matter. As if they aren't fighting one another for the chance to plaster the most difficult moment of my life all over the news and the internet.

I follow Luke into the elevator and press the button for the second floor. The doctor gets in with us just before the doors slide closed. "Do you know where you're headed?" she asks. She's not my mother's doctor, but thanks to me, my mom's a high-profile patient. Everyone in the hospital probably knows she's here.

"Yeah. We're good, thanks," I tell her.

When the doors slide open, she goes left and Luke and I

go right. My mother's room is three doors away.

The door before hers opens, and a woman in shorts and a pink tee comes out. She pulls her phone from her pocket and leans against the wall while she scrolls through whatever she's reading. I hope it's something funny. Something that helps her not think—just for a moment—about whatever sad thing is happening to whoever she's here to visit.

Then I push open the door to my mother's room and go in.

She's still unconscious, and she looks very small on the bed. She and I are the same height, but she's lost weight since both her children disappeared into the jungle. She'll be better soon.

I have to believe that.

"What did the doctor say?" Luke asks as I circle the bed to sit in the chair by the window.

"The nurse said he'll be in to give me an update in—" My phone buzzes with a new text, and I pull it out of my pocket. My focus narrows on the message and the rest of the room seems to fade around me.

The truth will set you free.

My face feels warm, my palms damp. It's another unidentified number. Or maybe the same one from before. I look up to find Luke watching me.

"What's—"

The door opens, and I turn, expecting to see a doctor or

a nurse. Instead, I find the woman in the pink T-shirt. She's aiming her phone at us, and I hear at least ten camera clicks before Luke and I recover from shock enough to yell at her.

"Out!" I shout while he closes the door in her face.

Ten minutes later, I find three of the shots on a tabloid website, with the caption:

America's sweethearts bond by mother's deathbed.

7 DAYS, 10 HOURS EARLIER

I'm stronger.

GENESIS

The roar of the jet engines is both isolating and intrusive, locking me inside my head, yet stealing my thoughts before I can truly focus on them.

I stare into the mirror in the rear bathroom as if I've never seen my own face. And the truth is that I haven't. Not like this.

It's not just the dirt smeared over my skin or the bruise from where my uncle hit me. It's not how tangled and filthy my hair is. It's not even the sharp quality of my cheekbones, after nearly a week with very little food.

This feeling that I don't know the girl staring back at me comes from my eyes. From something behind them. Something reflected in them.

I am not the same Genesis who hiked into the jungle more than a week ago. That Genesis is still lost out there somewhere, and I may never get her back.

But maybe that's not as much of a loss as it sounds like.

The old Genesis trusted too easily. She would have

sworn she was independent and skeptical, but she let a stranger lead her into the jungle. She failed to notice that her boyfriend and best friend were hooking up. She lived her entire life under the lie her father crafted.

This jet is a part of that lie. This bathroom, thousands of feet in the air, is a part of that lie. So are the clothes and makeup waiting for me in the bedroom beyond the small folding door and the car that will pick us up at the private airfield.

My entire life has been a lie, and the worst part is that I don't know how to live with the truth.

Disgusted, I turn away from the mirror and step into the shower. I don't really care about clothes and makeup at the moment—all I really want to do is sleep—but there will be cameras when we get off the plane, and I know I will care later. When I see the footage. When I hear myself described as unfashionably thin and washed out—an irony considering that most people think there's no such thing as being too thin or too white.

Ten minutes later, wrapped in a thick towel, I comb my clean, wet hair, then step into the bedroom. Through the open door, I see Holden and Indiana eating a steak dinner on satin placemats and a linen tablecloth. They've washed up and changed into the clothes my father's assistant bought for them while we were being airlifted out of the jungle.

"And they'll need new phones. Get whatever's newest and has the most memory. Make sure they're activated, and program Genesis's with all of the family numbers . . ."

My father's on the phone with another assistant, making sure that the moment I get off the plane, I can leave the jungle behind and step back into my life without missing a beat.

I close the bedroom door and put on the new clothes waiting for me. My dad's assistant knows what I like better than he does, so they fit, and somehow they seem to say "I've been through hell and I'm stronger for it."

Or maybe that's wishful thinking on my part.

Wearing a light layer of makeup, I emerge from my mile-high cocoon and take a seat at the table. Indiana smiles at me as he chews, but the look Holden gives me as the flight attendant slides my plate onto my placemat makes me want to shield my meal from him with one arm.

The attendant removes the stainless steel dome to reveal a still-sizzling steak, a baked sweet potato rolled in sea salt, and several thick sprigs of asparagus drizzled in hollandaise.

I smell the meal sitting in front of me, and my stomach growls. But what I see is a peanut butter sandwich on a paper plate.

I have no idea what to say.

MADDIE

The nurse comes in with a tray of Jell-O and a pitcher of water, even though my mother's still unconscious. She stares at me as she sets the tray on a table made to slide over the hospital bed, and I realize that she's not just being nice. She's curious. She knows who I am.

Everyone on the second floor knows who Luke and I are, after the incident with the paparazzi.

He comes into the room holding his phone, and the nurse stares at him as she slowly backs into the hall. As if she expects us to start making out, right there on the foot of my mother's hospital bed, for her entertainment.

"Is there anyone you want me to call?" Luke asks for the third time as the door closes behind the nurse. I get it. I feel like someone else should be here too. But my mother's parents died years ago, and Abuela is in Cartagena.

Does she know my dad's alive? Does she know what he's done? Does she know about Ryan? I should call her. But I have no idea what to say.

"There's no one else," I tell Luke, and he looks as sad about that as I must sound. His family's normal. His parents love him, and they love each other, and neither of them has ever pretended to be dead or tried to make that fantasy a reality. "Are you sure it's okay with your parents that you're here?"

He grins. "I didn't ask them. Did your uncle text you back?"

"Not yet." I'm beginning to think that if Genesis really has been found, I'm more likely to hear about it on the news than from Uncle Hernán. He still doesn't know what my mom did. . . .

I stare at the television so I don't have to see her closed eyes and pasty skin. Her cracked lips. She's breathing on her own, but the doctor says we won't know whether there's any long-term damage until she wakes up and they can run some tests.

But there's already long-term damage. That's why she took the pills in the first place.

There isn't room for me in the vinyl-covered recliner, but I dig my phone from my pocket and squeeze in next to Luke anyway. "I changed my mind. I want the app."

Luke gives me a blank look.

"The app that will trace a blocked text." I'm still scared that if we find and confront whoever's sending them, Luke will figure out that Genesis pushed the button. That it could just as easily have been me. But I'm *more* scared of the fact that there's a stranger out there in possession of that same information. "I got another message." I open it to show him.

"Oh. Okay." He takes my phone and types while he speaks. "According to Michael Tu, this is the best one." He hands my phone back to me with the App Store open to a call-tracing app.

"You and Michael just happened to be talking about third-party number-tracing apps?"

He shrugs. "I thought you might change your mind. It works on calls and texts. The next time this happens, follow the directions and the app will show you the phone number or email address the texts are coming from."

"No name?"

He actually smiles a little at what's evidently a stupid question. "No, we'll have to do a little detective work of our own from there. But a phone number is a good starting point."

"Okay. Thanks." I tap the button to download the free app.

And for the first time since we landed back in Miami, I feel like I am in control.

We're happy to have you.

GENESIS

"Indiana, we're happy to have you," my father says as the jet taxis toward our private hangar at the private airport. "Please stay with us for as long as you like." But he's being polite. He'd rather be alone with me. So we can talk.

"Thanks, but I don't want to be in the—" Indiana's polite protest ends in a surprised sound as he slides up the airplane window shade on his side. "Who're all those people?"

I lean forward to look out his window and Holden crosses the aisle to bend over me—much too close for comfort—with one hand on the back of my chair. "Paparazzi," he declares, sounding satisfied.

My father takes a look. "Security has them cordoned off."

"First time?" Holden asks Indiana, and I want to punch him.

"Just keep walking." I close the window with a decisive click. "No matter what they ask. Dad has a car waiting."

A shadow falls over the plane through the other open

windows as we roll into the hangar, and a minute later, the attendant opens the door. I file down the steps behind my father, with Indiana at my back. Holden takes up the rear.

As the press shouts questions from behind the barricade, out on the tarmac, Indiana follows my father and me across the hangar toward a black limo. After the dark jungle and the narrow plane, the Miami sun feels too bright, the hangar too broad and echoing. I feel . . . exposed.

The driver is already loading my dad's bags into the trunk.

Indiana and I don't have bags. The supplies we hiked into the jungle with are long gone, and the luggage I took with me to Colombia is still at my grandmother's house in Cartagena. She's promised to bring it with her when she comes for Ryan's funeral on Tuesday.

My father was in such a hurry to get me home that he wouldn't even wait for his mother to join us on the jet, and I can't help wondering if that's because he doesn't want her to find out about his criminal past.

Or because he isn't ready to find out whether she knew that Uncle David is still alive.

I'm not ready for that either.

My dad's assistant stands next to the car, holding a bag from the Apple store. My new phone.

A week ago, the inability to communicate with the world was nearly as difficult to get used to as the guns constantly pointed at us. Genesis from a week ago would be itching to rip open that box and tell the world that she was back, and that she'd arrived in style. She would have texted all her friends and posted dozens of pictures of tropical drinks and Caribbean sunsets.

But with the paparazzi shouting my name and the *Splendor* haunting my memory, that phone feels more like a noose than a lifeline. I don't want to go anywhere or see anyone.

I turn when I reach the car and realize that Holden hasn't followed us. The car his parents sent is parked outside the hangar—which gives him an excuse to march right past the gaggle of photographers.

"Holden! How many terrorists were there?"

"How were you treated?"

"What was it like to be held at gunpoint?"

"Why weren't you and Genesis brought home with the others?"

I scowl when he begins answering their questions, holding court with a somber but obliging air.

"Wow," Indiana whispers from my right, half shielding me from the cameras with his body. "It's like he feeds on the attention."

"Like gasoline tossed into a fire," I agree.

My father has hardly noticed. He's scowling at his phone as he scrolls through messages he was too busy to check on the plane. "Maddie texted," he says as he takes the rear seat, next to his assistant. "Daniela's in the hospital."

I slide onto the bench seat facing him, the paparazzi forgotten. "What happened?" How much more could life possibly throw at Maddie?

My father is still reading his messages as Indiana climbs into the car next to me. As he closes the door, one last question from the reporters follows me into the car, shattering this safe space like a hammer through a sheet of glass.

"Holden, tell us how you rescued Genesis from the terrorists and carried her to safety!"

6 DAYS, 23 HOURS EARLIER

I actually prefer it.

MADDIE

"Do you want more juice? Or some soup?" I ask as I back away from the hospital bed.

My mother shakes her head with a small smile. "I'm really fine, hon."

It's ridiculous of me to treat her like she has the flu, but I don't know what else to do. Feed a cold, starve a fever, but how do you help someone who took an entire bottle of pills?

She regained consciousness about half an hour after Luke went home, but she's been fading in and out of sleep ever since, and as terrible as it sounds, I actually prefer it when she's asleep, because I have no idea how to talk to her now. I'm so mad at her, but I'm terrified that telling her that will send her into another tailspin. So I keep finding reasons to leave the room until she passes out again. Or at least pretends to.

I don't think she knows what to say to me either.

"Okay, well, I'm going to get a bottle of water." I turn toward the door just as it opens, and for a second I can only blink at the thin, pale face staring back at me. "Genesis!"

Our hug is more like a collision in the middle of the room, and suddenly I'm crying. "When Silvana tackled you on the beach, I thought you were dead!" My words all run together, and I'm not sure anyone else can even understand them. "Then the news ran this picture of you and—" Over her shoulder, I see her dad follow her into the room, and behind him is . . . "Indiana!" I hardly know him, but I let go of my cousin to throw my arms around him. "I thought you were dead too!" After the past week, this feels almost too good to be true.

Indiana laughs as he returns my hug.

"There's a whole story," Genesis promises me. "I'll tell you tonight." She lowers her voice as her father sinks onto the side of my mother's hospital bed. "Is it okay if we stay with you?"

She's pissed at her dad. I get that like no one else possibly could.

"Of course." My cousin the heiress and her hot vagabond boyfriend. Crashing in my eight-hundred-square-foot apartment.

No problem.

"A pallet on the floor?" Genesis looks at me as if she doesn't understand why I'm rolling out the sleeping bag next to my bed. But she knew there was no guest room before she asked to stay over.

I shrug. "Or you can sleep in my mom's bed while she's

gone." Indiana's already making a place for himself on the couch. "But you'll have to wash the sheets yourself." We don't have a spare set of full-sized sheets, and I doubt Genesis has ever been within a few feet of a washing machine.

My cousin shrugs, and I'm almost impressed when she takes the bundle of spare blankets from me, studying my sleeping bag as if she's made a decision of more significance than a single night spent on the floor. "I haven't slept in a bed in a week. One more night won't hurt."

She must *really* not want to go home. But what I can't figure out is why she doesn't just stay at a hotel. She probably has the Four Seasons in her contacts list.

"Thanks for letting us crash. I'm not ready to forgive my dad, though he seems to think that testifying against the Moreno cartel makes up for working with them in the first place."

"Your dad's going to testify?"

Genesis nods. "That's the only reason they haven't frozen our assets."

I sink onto the edge of my bed and watch her make her pallet. "So where's Rog? He and Indiana blew up the jungle to rescue you, and he what? Stayed in Colombia?"

"Um . . . yeah." The stiff way she unfolds the last blanket says there's more to it than that, but she won't talk until she's ready. So I change the subject.

"Did Holden really carry you out of the jungle?"

She grabs a pillow from my bed and puts it at the head of the sleeping bag. "Of course not. I twisted my ankle right before we got to the bunkhouse and he only picked me up because Indiana threatened to shoot him in the foot if he didn't help me. He seriously carried me for, like, a few feet out of a two-hour hike. And that stupid picture has gone viral."

"The world wants a hero. Even if he's really an asshole. How's your ankle?"

She shrugs. "I iced it on the plane and it's fine now."

"If Neda were as persevering as you, we wouldn't have been at that bunkhouse in the first place." We'd detoured from our sightseeing goal so she could be airlifted out of the jungle. "We would never have been kidnapped."

"That's not true. We were targets." Genesis doesn't mention that the whole thing is my father's fault, but I know that's what she's thinking. It's what *I'm* thinking. "If they hadn't gotten us at the bunkhouse, they would have gotten us wherever we camped."

I know she's right. But blaming Neda feels good. Beyond that, it feels fair. "Your dad said they caught Sebastián?" That was all he'd been willing to say at my mother's bedside, other than that he was bringing Ryan home.

"Yeah." Genesis pulls herself up to sit on the end of my bed, and all the joy and relief of being home is suddenly gone. "Maddie, I don't think this is over. Your dad told me he has a 'plan B.' And Sebastián said he can still use us from here—from *home*. He said we'd 'push another button' for Uncle David."

I sit up straight on my bed, chills rolling up my spine.

"Oh my God! Is that real? Or is he trying to scare us? I mean, Sebastián could just be trying to ruin freedom for us, right? Making sure we're looking over our shoulders for the rest of our lives?"

"Maybe. But what if he's not? What if this is real? We can't afford to ignore that possibility. Right?"

Genesis has literally never asked me for advice. I'm pretty sure this is one of the signs of the Second Coming.

"Maybe we should tell someone. Has the FBI interviewed you yet? They talked to Pen, Luke, and me for hours. Separately."

"Not yet, but my dad got a call from them on the way to the hospital. They're going to schedule something." She lies across the end of my twin bed, propped up on one elbow, her eyes dull from exhaustion. "What did you tell them?"

"That I was already on the escape boat when the cruise ship blew up. Genesis, I didn't tell them you had the detonator."

"I know. Thanks." She rolls onto her back with her eyes closed. "But they have Sebastián now. He'll tell them. Or Holden will."

I take a deep breath and lie back on my remaining pillow so that I won't have to look at her as I ask my next question. "So . . . what happened to my dad?"

For a long time, she doesn't answer, but I can tell from the rhythm of her breathing that she's still awake.

"Please." My voice is so soft that at first I'm not sure whether I'm asking her or silently pleading in my own head.

All I know is that I can't handle any more lies.

"He's gone, Maddie."

An odd mixture of fear and relief washes over me. "Gone, as in . . . ?"

"I don't think you'll ever hear from him again. That's the way he wants it. That's why he faked his death. Sometimes we're better off without the truth."

The final sound of her statement tells me that's all I'll get out of her, but that's not good enough.

I want to ask her what he said to her. If he's the reason she's so much thinner than she was just a few days ago. If he gave her the bruise on her cheek. I want to know how he could possibly do what he's done. I want to know why my father chose terrorism over me.

What Genesis leaves unsaid resonates in the air between us. My father is in hiding, presumed dead, possibly carrying out a second twisted terrorist agenda that might cost even more innocent lives. *Her* father is across town in a mansion on the beach, bought and paid for with profits from the drug trade that has killed thousands and sent thousands more to prison.

And thanks to his deal with the feds, he's going to get away with it.

Somehow, the cousin I used to hate has become the only member of my family I can trust.

I don't know why I'm asking.

GENESIS

When Maddie falls asleep, I tiptoe into the dark, silent living room. The green glow from the digital clock on the microwave is just enough light to keep me from tripping over a backpack leaning against the end of the couch.

The backpack is Ryan's. It's still here, waiting for him to come home and pick it up, even though he's currently in the possession of the Miami-Dade County Medical Examiner.

The thought of him lying all alone in a refrigerated drawer brings fresh tears to my eyes. And makes me want to punch someone.

I need to forget everything that happened in the jungle, but the harder I try, the more fiercely the memories dig in.

I back away from the body. From the blood pooling on the floor. Indiana looks concerned. Holden is . . . angry. Guilty. Shocked. He wipes his bloody hands on his shirt and stares at the body, his expression a destructive blend of rage and . . . relief.

"Genesis?" Indiana whispers. "Are you okay?"

I shake off the memory, and instead of answering, I round the couch and stretch out next to him. He scoots back to make room for me, and we lie face-to-face. His arm slides around my waist. My hands rest on his chest. We're sharing a pillow.

No moment in my four-year relationship with Holden ever felt this intimate.

"So, what are your plans?" The question feels formal—at odds with how closely we're pressed together—but I'm not sure how else to ask. "I don't know what you were planning to do after Colombia, but . . ."

But he struck off into the jungle with a possible skull fracture to rescue me. That's not the kind of thing a person does if he's just planning to hit the road a few days later. Right?

I'm trying not to care either way. I really am. Everyone I've ever trusted has betrayed me. Except for Maddie. And I'm not about to climb into her bed and cuddle.

"All year, my plan has been to go to new places and meet new people," Indiana whispers.

"Is this the first time that plan has led to you crashing on a stranger's couch?" I ask, and my nose brushes his.

"No. And Maddie's not really a stranger anymore, but Miami is a new place for me, so technically I'm sticking to my plan."

"How long can you stay?" I don't know why I'm asking. I only have six weeks of high school left, and after that, I'm off to either NYU or Berkeley. I *always* have a plan, and that's been the plan since I was a sophomore.

But nothing feels certain anymore. I'm not sure I can use my father's dirty money for tuition. I'm not sure when Holden will out me as a mass murderer or whether the inevitable death threats will keep any good school from taking me, for the safety of the other students.

I don't know how Indiana fits into the chaos my life has become. I don't even know if he wants to.

I just want to know if it's possible.

Indiana brushes hair from my face, over my shoulder. "The beautiful thing about a nomadic existence is that my plans are somewhat flexible. And by somewhat, I mean entirely."

I press my mouth against his to keep him from noticing my *stupidly* big smile. Indiana kisses me back. His hand spreads out against my lower spine, pressing me even firmer against him. I slide my hand into his hair and lift myself onto one elbow, giving myself better access to his mouth.

"The floor can't be very comfortable," he murmurs against my neck when we pause to catch our breath. "You're welcome to share the couch with me."

"I thought you'd never ask. . . ."

6 DAYS, 21.5 HOURS EARLIER

This is enough for now.

MADDIE

I'm still awake when Genesis sneaks out of my bedroom. I could have guessed she wouldn't make it more than an hour on the floor, but I still don't understand what she's doing here.

Is she reluctant to spend her father's money on a hotel, now that she knows where the money came from? Or does she truly want to be near me?

The walls of my apartment are thin and the springs in our old couch are loud. When I hear them groan, I sit up and dig in my nightstand drawer for my earbuds. But when I grab my phone, I realize I don't want to hear music.

I want to hear Luke's voice.

The phone is already ringing before I notice that it's nearly midnight. He's probably already asleep. I should hang up.

But I don't.

"Hello?" His voice sounds sleepy and intimate in my ear, and suddenly I'm so jealous of Genesis that it's hard to draw my next breath. I've never wanted her money, or her big house on the coast, or her private prep school that costs more than most colleges. But I want what she has right now.

I want Luke to be here, curled up next to me in my bed.

"Hey," I whisper into the phone. I'm pretty sure Genesis and Indiana wouldn't hear me even if I started shouting, but this feels like a whispering moment. "Sorry. I didn't realize how late it was until the phone was already ringing."

"Late-night call from a beautiful girl?" Luke says, and I can hear the smile on his face. "Not a problem. What's up?"

"Nothing. I just . . . wanted to hear your voice."

Silence echoes over the line, and I close my eyes. Was that too much? Am I freaking him out? A week and a half ago, I wouldn't have noticed him if we passed each other in the school hallway, and now I'm terrified that I'm more into this than he is. That I'm clinging to him because everything else in my life has fallen apart. And I'm worried he might not understand that that's not because of how solid and dependable he is, but because of how good he makes me feel, even during the worst week of my life.

"Do you want me to come over?" he asks, and I exhale in relief.

"No, that's okay." The fact that he's willing to is all I really need to know. "I just . . . this is enough for now."

"Is Genesis there? Is she listening?"

"No, she's on the couch with Indiana."

Luke's bedsprings creak over the line. "I'm glad they're keeping you company, with your mom still in the hospital."

"If this were just about keeping me company, Genesis would have invited me to her house. She's pissed at her dad." A sentiment I completely share. "And I think there's something she's not telling me."

"Like what? You think she's lying about something?"

I shrug, though he can't see the motion. "Right now, I think it's more like . . . withholding."

"You sure you don't want me to come over?"

"No thanks. Just get some sleep. I'll talk to you tomorrow."

"Okay. Text me if you change your mind."

"I will. Night." I hang up the phone, and for several minutes, I can only lie in bed trying to make my thoughts stop racing. Trying not to picture my father in the jungle, ordering the kidnapping that cost my brother his life. My mother in her hospital bed, dark circles beneath her closed eyes. Ryan lying in the grave Luke dug for him at the army bunkhouse.

And when it's clear that I cannot sleep here, in a room that's too quiet for all the noise in my head, I get up and pad barefoot into the little square of hallway outside my room.

Genesis and Indiana are . . . occupied. So I turn in the other direction and find myself in Ryan's room.

Everything is just like he left it. There are drumsticks and cleats on the floor. A cookie wrapper on his bedside table. Two of his dresser drawers are standing open. And the whole room smells vaguely like sweat and soap.

Tears fill my eyes as I cross the carpet toward the bed.

I lie down, intending to inhale the scent from Ryan's pillow, just for a minute. But when I wake up hours later, early morning sunlight shining into my swollen eyes, I realize that I cried myself to sleep in my brother's bed.

6 DAYS, 13 HOURS EARLIER

I'm not going.

GENESIS

The buzzing of my phone wakes me up. Indiana shifts beside me, and the blanket we're sharing slides down to expose my back. The rest of the room is cold compared to our naked couch cocoon.

I roll over and grope on the floor for my cell. Daylight peeks through the vinyl mini-blinds over Maddie's living room window, but it's still pale and weak. Early morning light.

I resent the wake-up text. Whoever it's from.

I check the screen.

Put on something nice and meet me at the local ABC station. We're going live via satellite on Good Morning America Weekend Edition at 9 am.

There's no name associated with the phone number, but I know it's Holden. No one else would talk to me like that.

I slide out from under the blanket and pull on my clothes, and as I head into the kitchen, I add him to my contacts list, then text him back.

I'm not going on TV with you!

His reply comes as I open the first of three cabinets in Maddie's tiny galley-style kitchen, in search of coffee.

Viewership of 3.5 mil. people. Love the pic and want to hear our story, Gen. If you don't show up, I'll tell it my way.

Translation: If I don't tell the world he's the hero that stupid picture made him look like, he'll tell everyone I pushed the button that killed twelve hundred innocent cruise ship passengers.

Exhaling my frustration, I text him back.

You can't be serious.

His reply comes within seconds.

Stop being selfish, Gen.

Then:

Play nice, or . . .

Chill bumps rise over my arms in a frigid wave. He knows what really happened to the *Splendor*. He knows about my father. He knows about my uncle.

This is why he hasn't outted me yet; he's going to blackmail me. But for what? A PR opportunity?

Knowing Holden, it's bigger than that. A book deal. A movie. A chance to transform his image from wealthy, entitled prick to national hero.

Or this could just be revenge for me choosing Indiana's life over his.

When the truth is that Indiana and Rog are the heroes.

I could go on *GMA* and tell the world the truth—that he's a coward and a liar, at best; a murderer at worst—but if he goes down, he'll take me and my whole family with him.

Groaning softly to myself, I reply.

Fine. But Indiana's coming with me. Send a car to Maddie's apartment in an hour. I'll text you the address.

Maddie's cabinet holds a stack of plates on one shelf and on the other, a mismatched collection of brightly colored glasses our grandmother sent from Colombia last Christmas. I find a nearly empty bag of pre-ground generic brand coffee in the fridge, but there's nothing to put in it but whole-fat milk or expired soy.

With another sigh, I text Holden one last time.

I want two bottles of water and two VENTI caramel lattes waiting for me in the car, or there's NO TELLING

what I'll say in my sleep-deprived state. And you better have hair and makeup standing by.

Holden understands diva demands. He practically invented the concept.

His reply comes a second later.

Whatever. Just be here. And turn on the charm.

I shove my phone into my back pocket and take a second to breathe.

Three and a half million people. Live national television. With Holden.

I'd rather get Botox with a crack-house needle.

I tiptoe into Maddie's room and grab my toiletry bag, then shower as quickly as I can in a bathroom that doesn't look as small as I remember it being, after a week of sponge bathing with a questionably fresh rag. The hot water runs out before I can rinse my hair, and I shiver as I shave my legs. But I love every second of it.

When I open the bathroom door, I smell coffee. Maddie is in the kitchen stirring milk into a mug. She holds out the pot to offer me some.

"No thanks," I say, and she replaces the pot. The circles under her eyes say she didn't get much sleep. The ones looking back at me in the mirror told the same story.

"Good morning." Indiana pads into the living room on bare feet, his hair still wet from the shower and partly covering the puffy gash on his forehead. He must have used

Maddie's mother's tiny bathroom.

His chest is bare and still beaded with water. The urge to touch him is suddenly overwhelming, and for the first time in my life, I'm unsure how to handle that.

With Holden, there was a lot of posturing. Being with him was like playing chess—there was a purpose behind every move each of us made.

But with Indiana . . . ?

"Good morning." I let my gaze linger on his chest, indulging the moment and a memory from last night. Holden was my first and—until last night—my only, and no matter how many revenge-hookups I'd indulged in when he cheated, I'd had no plans to change that as long as we were together. But Indiana is . . .

The way Indiana looks at me makes my skin flush and my stomach flip. My hands want to reach for him all on their own, and that impulse scares me in the best possible way.

I give him a smile, then I head for Maddie's bedroom to grab my makeup, and I'm totally *not* running away from an overwhelming urge to touch him and the fear that I won't be able to let him go.

Indiana intercepts me on the way and slides his arms around my waist. He kisses me, and a little bit of the tension from Holden's demands eases inside me. I sink into the kiss as if I'm not standing in the middle of my cousin's tiny apartment. As if we're alone, and nothing else in the world matters.

His hand slides up my back as he steps away, and a soft, satisfied sound slips from my throat. I should be embarrassed about how much that reveals, but strangely, I'm not.

Holden only kissed me when he expected that kiss to lead to something more. Or when there was an audience around to appreciate the gesture. But there's no audience here, except for Maddie, and she doesn't care what we do.

"What's the hurry?" Indiana says with an amused smile.

"Holden just threatened to call me a mass murderer on national television if I don't go on *Good Morning America* with him and make him sound like a hero."

"Wait." Maddie sets her coffee mug down with a harsh clack against the countertop. "Indiana searches for you for three days with a head wound and you're going to give Holden credit, on national television?"

Indiana tenses, his smile fading into a rare glimpse of anger.

Guilt washes over me. Protecting my family means denying Indiana and Rog the credit they deserve. "I—"

"I don't care about that," Indiana says, and he seems to mean it. He doesn't care about cameras or attention. Or credit. "What I care about is that he killed Rog and now he's blackmailing you."

"*What?* Holden killed Rog?" Maddie's focus flickers between us.

"It was an accident," I explain. "He thought Rog was one of Sebastián's men."

But Indiana's jaw tightens. "Even if that's true—" And

163

it's clear from the deeply furrowed line of his brow that he doesn't entirely believe it. "The *Splendor* was an accident too."

"Yes, but he knows that if both of those come to light, people will care *way* more about the *Splendor*." About the twelve hundred innocent people I killed and the hundreds more I injured than the one man who died on a rescue mission he knew from the start would be dangerous. "And there's more than that. He knows the truth about my dad. And about Maddie's."

"That *bastard*," Maddie breathes. Then she sinks into a chair at the table, blood draining from her face. "He's threatening the whole family. My mom . . ."

"He says if I make him look good, he'll make me look good. He'll keep his mouth shut."

"Do it," Indiana says through clenched teeth. "That stupid picture has already done most of the work, and you can probably say what he wants without actually lying. And if that'll keep him from dragging your whole family through the mud . . ."

If I don't cooperate, he won't just drag the Valencia name through the mud—he'll bury us all alive. But . . .

"It may be a moot point, once the FBI talks to Sebastián." He has no reason to out Maddie's dad, but he also has no reason to protect me.

"But if your dad's working with the government, it won't be in their interest to let any of that come out," Indiana responds.

"So if I keep Holden happy, this might all just go away." And right now, all he's asking for is a little flattering press coverage. "I can do that." Not just for myself. Not just for my dad. But for Maddie and her mom. They've been through enough.

I look up at Indiana. "Do you mind coming with me?"

He actually manages a smile as he pulls me close. "I'd kind of hoped not to have to share you with your ex and a national audience today, but sure."

In the kitchen, Maddie stares blankly into a bowl of Ryan's favorite sugary cereal. Which is definitely not on the diabetic-friendly list of foods. "Why don't you come with us? We'll go out for a real breakfast and some decent coffee afterward." I owe her that, at the very least. For letting me and Indiana crash with her. For being the only member of my family who's never lied to me. That I know of.

"No way." Maddie takes a bite of her cereal and speaks around it. "I've had enough of live television for one lifetime. And I don't care if I never see Holden again."

That makes two of us.

We're going to get through this.

MADDIE

There's no press at the hospital when I arrive, and I don't know whether that's because it's not even eight a.m. on a Sunday, or because Genesis and Holden's rescue has over-shadowed the media's obsession with Luke and me as the forged-through-hardship All-American romance. And I don't really care which it is.

My mom's door is ajar, but I stop outside when I hear a male voice from inside, assuming it's a doctor or a nurse who might not speak as freely if he knows I'm listening. But then I recognize the voice.

Uncle Hernán.

"Did you see him?" My mother's voice sounds nasal, like it gets when she's been crying.

I should go in. But if I do, they'll stop talking about my father, to shield me, and I'm not going to settle for that anymore. Not after sixteen years spent idolizing a man who turned out to be a monster.

"Briefly. Daniela, this is only going to upset you," Uncle

Hernán says. "We can talk about something else."

"No," my mother insists. "I want to know. I *need* to know."

I ease closer to the door until I can peek through the slim opening, and I see her pushing herself upright on the mattress. The tray next to her bed holds an untouched plate of pancakes, sausage links, and the ubiquitous hospital lime Jell-O.

"Daniela . . ." My uncle sinks into the chair next to my mother's bed. He takes her hand, and something about the gentle way he holds it—how badly he obviously wants to comfort her—makes me wonder if I've been too hard on him. I don't know the story behind his connection to the Moreno cartel. I don't know why he ran drugs for them, or how long that lasted. For all I know, he did it to keep Gael Moreno from hanging Genesis from a bridge, as he did with several of his enemies back during the height of the cartel's power.

Maybe it was never about the money. Maybe it was always about family.

"We're going to get through this," my uncle whispers, and I have to ease closer to the door to make sure I won't miss anything. "We still have Maddie and Genesis to think about. We have to be there for the girls right now. They lost him too."

They?

Genesis was never very close to my father, and I doubt being taken hostage by him improved their relationship.

They're not talking about my dad. The understanding sneaks up on me, like a sound you don't even know you're hearing until you realize you can't hear anything else.

They're talking about Ryan.

I have one hand on the lever, ready to push the door open and go in.

"I know. They lost a brother. I just don't know how . . ."

They lost a brother? I don't hear the rest, because I can't stop hearing what she's just said.

Genesis didn't lose a brother. What the hell is my mother talking about?

"We need to be there for them, but no one's going to begrudge you this one day. Take care of yourself today, Daniela," Uncle Hernán says. "Or let me take care of you. This is our loss too." His voice cracks, and his next words rip me open like a knife to the chest. "We lost a son."

It'll be like old times.

GENESIS

"Are you ready?" the woman in the headset asks me. She's an assistant producer. Or a production assistant. I wasn't really paying attention when she introduced herself. "We're going live in five minutes."

It's not like I've never been on TV. I've been on camera at fashion shows in Paris and Milan with Neda and her parents. I've been filmed at the Olympics with Penelope. Twice. I've been at three movie premieres and two fifty-thousand-dollar-a-plate charity dinners with Holden and his family. I've been photographed in the hottest Miami night-clubs and backstage at all the best concerts. I've had my hair and makeup judged by Jared, and once *People* magazine declared that I wore it better than Selena Gomez.

They were not wrong.

Also, it should be noted that I wore it *first*.

But I've never actually been in a television studio, on a live feed. I've always planned to be famous someday, so this moment was inevitable, but I never thought I'd be doing it with Holden. *For* Holden.

Although, negotiating with him for our mutual benefit did feel frighteningly familiar. Somehow, though we've broken up, we're still jockeying for position. For dominance.

"She's ready," Holden says from my left, before I can answer for myself. I glare at him. It used to be easier for me to let him believe he's running things. I used to be happy pulling his strings from the sideline, because it was enough for *me* to know who truly had the upper hand. But we're not together anymore, and this time he *actually* has the advantage. Because he's willing to destroy me and my family to get what he wants, and he has the ammo with which to do it.

"May we have a minute?" I ask. I've been trying to get Holden alone since we got here, but he's managed to dodge my every attempt at a private conversation.

The woman with the headphones frowns with a glance at her watch. "You can have two and a half minutes. Exactly." Then she heads over to talk to the cameraman.

The studio is smaller and quieter than I expected, and a lot more . . . empty. There are only a handful of employees, including a single camera operator and a tech guy who tests and adjusts the microphones and the bright overhead lights.

There's no news desk or snack table. There're no hair and makeup artists. This isn't where they broadcast the local news. This is a small space set up for exactly what we're about to do: transmit a local feed to a national network.

Looking around, it's hard to imagine that millions of people will be staring at me in just a few minutes. A month ago, I would have loved every second of this, but now I just want to get it over with and get Holden off my back.

"What's the plan?" I whisper. "You actually expect me to lie for you on national television?"

Holden shrugs. "I expect you to tell truths that will make us both look good. And if you play nice, so will I." The threat in his tone is as cold as the glint in his brown eyes. This isn't just about making him look like a hero.

He's angry. He wants me to suffer.

I want to press him for more details, but I'm not going to say anything I don't want picked up by my microphone. In case it's already hot. "So this is it? One interview, and we're done?"

"I never said that. Raina has several more lined up for us."

It turns out that while I was visiting my aunt in the hospital and trying to make up for several days of near starvation, Holden and his parents were hiring a publicist. If I'd known he was going to drag me on camera, I'd have done the same thing.

"Holden . . ." I groan through clenched teeth.

His jaw tightens. His eyes narrow. His voice is a hard-edged whisper. "You told Sebastián to kill me and save that cowboy drifter. Is it *really* so hard for you to pick me this time, Gen?"

"That's not how it happened," I whisper, but he's not listening.

Holden pastes on a smile like flipping a switch, and

suddenly there's *no sign* of the vengeful asshole who's threatening to destroy what's left of my family. "The spotlight loves us. It'll be like old times."

Except that I'm ready for some brand-new times.

The woman with the headphones returns just as Indiana and Neda get back from the vending machine with a bottle of water and some kind of wrapped snack.

"I mean seriously, who's even going to be up to watch this early in the morning?" she complains.

Indiana shrugs. "You're up."

"I'm working." She has her phone out, filming "behind the scenes" footage of our interview for her webshow. But what she's really hoping to capture is a throw-down between my ex and my next.

I almost hate to tell her that I'm here to *avoid* drama.

"Sorry." Indiana smiles as he hands me a protein bar. "I'm sure you're tired of these, but it was this or an out-of-date cinnamon roll." He thinks I need to eat. He's not wrong. Unfortunately, the lady with the headset is gesturing to Holden and me, which means we're out of time.

"Camera off," I tell Neda.

She pouts, but shoves her phone into her pocket.

"You'll be great." Indiana runs one hand down my arm, then pulls me close for a kiss. "When this is over, you can put the whole thing behind you. Including Holden," he whispers.

Indiana was there when I found out Holden was cheating on me with Penelope. He was there when Holden suggested

I sleep with one of our jungle captors as a distraction so he could steal one of their guns. He knows exactly how badly I don't want to be seen with my ex on national television. Or anywhere else.

I don't have the heart to tell him that this interview is just the first in a series designed to punish me for choosing his life over Holden's.

The lady with the headset stares at us in surprise. I don't know what Holden told her before we arrived, but she clearly had no idea that Indiana and I are together.

Holden's phone rings, and he frowns at the screen. Then he answers. "Hello?" The voice on the other end sounds female. He listens for a second, then his gaze flicks toward me. "How did you get this number?" he demands softly. A second later, he hangs up.

"Reporter?" I haven't had any media calls yet, but Maddie and Luke both have.

"Yeah." Holden shakes his head as if to clear it. "Let's go."

"Indiana should go on with us," I tell Holden as the woman adjusts the microphone already clipped to my shirt. "He's part of the story."

Holden opens his mouth to argue, a storm brewing behind his eyes, but Indiana beats him to it. "No thanks. I'm allergic to the spotlight, but I'll be cheering you on from backstage."

"Who are you?" the production assistant asks, when Indiana steps back.

"No one," he says with a quiet smile.

"Okay, then, let's go." The woman guides me and Holden to a pair of chairs set up in front of a large green screen. "Just speak at a normal volume," she says. "The microphones will pick it up."

There's a voice in my ear, coming through the earpiece an assistant fitted me with, but it sounds like another producer running through a series of checks. I can't see Susan, the talk show host who's going to interview us, and I can't hear her yet either.

This is a strange kind of one-sided event from my perspective, but I know it'll look normal to everyone watching at home. I saw Penelope do a bunch of stuff like this after she won her Olympic silver medal.

"Okay, take a deep breath," the woman in the headset says. "It'll all be over in a few minutes."

That's probably exactly what they say to prisoners awaiting execution.

The battery pack rubs my back beneath the waistband of my jeans, and the little microphone clipped to my collar is ruining the lines of my blouse. But there's no chance to fix either of those, because by the time we sit in the chairs set up for us, the man behind the camera is already counting down. He gets to two, gives us a silent "one" with his index finger, then points in our direction.

We're live.

"Hi, Holden and Genesis, thank you so much for joining us!" Susan's upbeat voice says into my ear, and I smile for the camera. "The world is captivated with your story, and I wanted to start by asking about this picture of the two of you!" Her voice rises with every word until her delight rings in my ear like the high-pitched squeal of a trapped animal.

We can't see the picture, but I know damn well which one she's talking about. I can't escape that shot. Holden, who was willing to let Sebastián and Silvana blow up half of the United States rather than help me get rid of the bombs, carried me for less than the span of a city block, and now the world is hailing him as a hero.

"Can you tell us what was happening in that moment?" Susan asks in my ear. "It's such a moving story. Boyfriend and girlfriend taken hostage together. Escaping together. And the photo is so romantic. Like the cover of a novel . . ."

I open my mouth to tell her the truth—that my *actual* boyfriend was two steps behind us in the jungle—but Holden takes my hand and squeezes it. Hard.

"The truth, Susan, is that Genesis and I have had rough patches just like any other couple, and the roughest of those came while we were in the jungle. Having a gun held to your head is pretty stressful, and I said some things I'm not proud of. But then Gen got hurt while we were trying to escape, and I realized exactly how much she means to me. I couldn't leave her behind."

Holden gives the world a disarming shrug, then turns to me with a smile that I might actually buy, if I didn't know him. "So I picked her up and started running." I swallow revulsion as he lifts my hand to kiss my knuckles. "And it turns out nothing heals a wounded relationship like escaping certain death. Together."

I can only smile at the camera through clenched teeth.

Holden may think he's safe, now that he's out of the jungle, but he brought the biggest threat back with him.

I'm going to *kill* him.

Holden is a hero.

MADDIE

We lost a son.

My uncle's words echo through me like a bolt of thunder. My travel mug crashes to the tile. Coffee splatters everywhere. A chair scrapes the floor as Uncle Hernán stands, but I'm already running down the hall toward the elevator.

"Maddie!" he shouts as the door to my mother's room squeaks open. But I keep going. I can't even turn and look at him.

Uncle Hernán is Ryan's father.

Was. Uncle Hernán *was* Ryan's father.

The elevator is too slow, and I can hear my uncle's footsteps thumping toward me. So I take off for the stairs at the end of the hall. Pushing the bar on the door sets off an alarm, but I'm only one floor up. I hit the midpoint landing before the door closes behind me, then I'm on the ground level racing toward the nearest exit. Which is the ER.

The TV mounted in the waiting room is tuned to a news station showing that picture of Holden carrying Genesis out of the jungle. There's no volume, but I know what they're saying. Holden is a hero. Genesis needed to be saved.

The world no longer makes sense, and I can't get out of here fast enough.

I bump into a man in a white lab coat on my way down the hall. "Sorry!" I call over my shoulder as I run, and the apology costs me my balance. My hip hits a cart standing in a doorway, and something clatters to the ground, but I can't stop to look.

Tears blur my vision, and by the time I burst through the ER doors into the parking lot, they're rolling down my face.

In my mother's car, I start the engine and suck in several deep breaths until I'm calm enough to be behind the wheel. Then I slam the gearshift into drive and pull onto the street. I have no idea where I'm going. As I change lanes and take turns, blinking to clear fresh tears from my eyes, I realize that every single thing I thought I knew about my life has been a lie.

My father is a terrorist.

My brother is only my half brother.

My mother cheated on my father.

And she would rather be dead than be alone with me.

My phone buzzes on the passenger seat, but I ignore it. It's either my mother or my uncle, and I'm not ready to hear their explanations and apologies. All I can think about is that Genesis and Ryan were born six months apart. Which means that for the overlapping three months, my uncle had *two* women pregnant with his children.

Does my father know?

Does Genesis know?

Is this why Uncle Hernán has always thrown money at us? Why he paid for Ryan's rehab and my insulin pump? Because he felt guilty? Or obligated?

My phone rings again, then slides off the seat onto the floor when I take a sharp left turn. A minute later, I pull into a parking space and stare through the windshield at the ocean. I don't know how I got to the beach. I can't remember much of the drive. But this feels like the right place to be when my world is falling to pieces all around me.

Everything here feels normal. Here, parents sit under umbrellas and kids play in the sun with no idea that I'm hiding the sixteen-year lie that has been my life.

I get out of the car and shove the keys into my pocket. Leaving my sandals on the ground beneath the car, I walk barefoot onto the beach, waiting for the steady pulse of the waves to calm me.

My father. My mother. My uncle.

I sink onto the ground and bury my toes in the sand. If the people I love most—the people who *raised* me—have been lying to me for my entire life and I had no clue, how am I supposed to trust anyone else, ever again?

"Maddie?"

Startled, I look up to find Luke frowning down at me, one hand shielding his face from the sun. "What are you doing here?"

"Your mom called to ask if I'd seen you. I figured that

meant something was wrong." He drops onto the beach next to me, kicking up a tiny wave of sand with his sneakers.

"She didn't tell you what happened?"

"No, but she was crying."

Good.

I don't mean that.

"How'd you find me?"

"I made a good guess. In the jungle, you told me this was where you came after your dad's funeral. To think." He frowns, but looks more amused than anything. "It's weird to think about him having a funeral, since he's not actually dead."

"Weird doesn't even begin to cover it," I mumble. I can't believe he remembered this place. I must have told him a hundred random things about myself as we hiked through the jungle, to keep from having to think about Ryan, and about our infinitesimal chances of making it out alive.

Luke brushes a tear from my cheek with his thumb. "Wanna talk about it?"

"No. But I'll tell you, if you promise not to ask any questions."

"Okay."

"I went to see my mom in the hospital, and I overheard my uncle admit to being Ryan's father."

Luke's eyes widen. "Whoa. I mean . . . *wow.*" Then he frowns. "So—?"

"Nope." I shake my head. "You promised."

"This isn't about . . . that."

I'm skeptical, but I nod.

"So . . . ," Luke says again, and this time he's grinning. "Since that's clearly going to take a while to process . . . wanna go to the arcade?"

6 DAYS, 10 HOURS EARLIER

I don't care who sees.

GENESIS

"What the *hell*?" I demand in my fiercest whisper as soon as the voice in my ear says we're off the air. I jerk my hand from Holden's grip, and in that moment, I don't care who sees. I can't do this with him.

I won't.

"Just shut up and smile," he whispers back, as if we're sharing an intimate moment off camera. As if the crew members are just waiting to reveal our discord to the press.

"Go to hell." I leave him standing in front of the green screen beneath the lights, all alone.

Indiana gives me a questioning look—one eyebrow raised—as I march across the small studio toward him.

"I'm so sorry," I say as I pull the earpiece from my ear and the microphone from my shirt. The battery pack falls from my waistband, and suddenly the production assistant is there glaring at me as she picks it up.

Indiana shrugs. "Live television." He seems calm, but I'm sure that once we we're alone, I'll see the truth. He'll look hurt. Or angry. How could he not be?

Yet when we're outside, warm in the midmorning sunlight, he only takes my hand and threads his fingers between mine as if none of that actually happened. As if I didn't just pretend that my ex is still my boyfriend, and that he rescued me from the jungle like some kind of prep-school Tarzan, when the truth is that he nearly starved to death because he didn't have the sense to look up at all the fruit growing overhead.

"I'll fix this," I say as we head for the black car idling across two parking spots, where the driver is reading a comic book against the steering wheel. There has to be some way for me to tell the world that Holden and I *truly* aren't a couple anymore without provoking him.

Indiana shrugs again as he opens the rear passenger's side door. "Seriously, G. Don't blame yourself for what he did."

I slide into the backseat, and for a moment, my mind is totally blank. I can't process what happened in there. What Holden did.

But I can't process Indiana's lack of a reaction either.

"Why doesn't this bother you?" I ask as he sinks onto the bench seat next to me and closes the car door. "Holden just told the whole world that he and I are still a couple, and he did it just to be an asshole." He's forcing me to choose between being with Indiana and protecting my family as a twisted revenge against me for choosing Indiana's life over his in the jungle.

"What bothers me is that he's blackmailing you and threatening your family. But the specifics of his petty little lies don't bother me because I don't care what anyone else thinks, G." Indiana leans forward and kisses me, teasing my bottom lip until a new heat rivals my anger and I want to devour him whole. "I don't need the rest of the world to know about us or to see us together," he whispers as he slides one hand into my hair. "In fact, if it'll keep the press out of our business so I can have you all to myself, I say we put out a statement telling the world you've joined a convent."

His warm lips close around my earlobe, the short stubble on his cheek scratching my chin, and I have to bite back a moan.

"You are the best thing I've ever had," I tell him as I pull away just enough so that I can recapture his mouth with mine.

"Had? Past tense?" He gives me a mock frown. "I hope that doesn't mean you're done with me."

"We're just getting started. . . ."

"Where to, ma'am?" the driver asks, reminding us that we're not alone in the car.

"Just drive, please." I don't know what else to tell him.

As the car pulls out of the studio parking lot, a familiar form catches my attention from the sidewalk across the street. I can't see her face clearly in the shadow of the building, but her slim build and the silhouette of her hair . . .

Silvana.

No. I'm imagining things, which is no surprise,

considering the stress I'm under and the fact that one day of proper rest and nutrition isn't enough to make up for a week of physical and psychological stress and malnutrition/ starvation in the jungle.

My phone buzzes with a message from my father.

HOLDEN?!?

Clearly he saw the show and wants an explanation. But he's not getting information from me until he's willing to reciprocate. I dismiss the text.

"Genesis?" Indiana says as our car turns and I lose sight of the figure. Before I can decide whether or not to mention my hallucination, my gaze catches on the television in the back of the car. It's muted, but that stupid picture is on the screen again. I want to punch the TV. But mostly I want to punch Holden.

Indiana's hand settles onto my arm. "Let's go dancing."

"What?" My phone buzzes again before he can answer. Penelope's name and number are on the screen. She saw the broadcast. Holden pulled the rug out from under their relationship on national television, but *I'm* the one she'll hate.

I decline the call and shove my phone between my thigh and the leather seat. I don't know what to say to her yet. I haven't even officially told her that I'm safe and sound in the United States again, yet I've accidentally stabbed her in the back.

"G. Let's go dancing." Indiana turns off the television.

"Neda got a call and left in the middle of the interview, so it's just the two of us. There are good places to dance in Miami, right?"

There are *great* places to dance in Miami, but it's Sunday morning, and—

My phone buzzes again. It's Penelope. I decline the call again.

"What were you saying?" The world feels like it's spinning too fast. Like I can't even trust the ground beneath me.

Indiana takes my chin and slowly tilts my face up. He looks worried, but calm. Like a doctor in possession of a cure. "The interview's over. You're done with Holden, at least for today. So why don't you forget about him and show me—"

My phone buzzes again, and this time when I pick it up, I'm ready to hurl it out the window if I see Penelope's name on the screen. Instead, I find an unfamiliar number. I answer, because my frustration has reached a boiling point, and I'm eager to unleash on whatever unsuspecting salesman was unfortunate enough to pick my new number from his database.

"Hello?" I demand into the phone.

"Genesis, what the hell?" Neda asks. "Penelope's freaking out. Seriously. I'm going to have to medicate her, if you can't talk her down."

Damn it. "Neda, remember that time you took NyQuil instead of Tylenol?" Those don't even look alike. "Do *not* give Penelope any medication."

"Fine." I can practically hear her pout over the phone. "Then you talk to her and I'll pour her a drink."

"No! Neda. It's ten o'clock in the morning."

"So it's too early to talk to your best friend, but you'll tell the whole world you're back together with Holden before normal people are even awake?"

"It's not too early to talk, it's too early to drink. And normal people *are* awake."

Indiana gives me an amused look.

"Fine. I'll make her some chamomile tea," Neda says. "That's what my mom does when her sister gets hysterical." In the background, I hear Penelope sniffling, and my hatred for Holden seeps even deeper into my bones. "Charlotte, make Penelope a cup of chamomile," Neda says, without bothering to take the phone away from her mouth. "And I could totally use an espresso."

"Yes, ma'am," her housekeeper says, and when both the sniffling and the sound of running water fade, I realize Neda's gone into another room.

"So, what the hell happened with Holden?" she demands a second later. "If you two were going to get back together, live on the air, you should have done it on *my* show!"

"We're *not* back together. Holden's telling the story he wants to see in print."

"That sounds more like you," Neda says, and I can't exactly deny it. "Why did you play along?"

"Because he knows me well enough to destroy me and he never aims an unloaded gun." I don't know if she knows

187

what really happened to the *Splendor*, but I'm not going to be the one to tell her. "I'm going to fix it. We'll wait a week or so, then Holden and I will announce that we've decided to see other people. A week after that, he and Pen can be seen together. Queen of the uneven bars and the pharmaceutical prince. Everyone will love them."

"Okay, but Luke and Maddie went on my webshow and told the world you and Holden had broken up. Which means that you two are now officially tabloid fodder," she says as Indiana leans forward to say something to the driver. "You *have* to do my show this afternoon. You totally owe me the exclusive."

I groan and roll my eyes at the interior of the car. But maybe she's right. Maybe Neda's show will give me a chance to tell the story *I* want to see in print—without Holden.

"Fine. I'll be there."

She'll call the police.

MADDIE

Like most kids, Ryan and I got invited to a bunch of birthday parties at various "fun zones" when we were kids. Places with bowling lanes, laser tag, rock climbing, and about a hundred flashing, buzzing digital video games. That's the kind of place I expect when I pull into a parking space in front of the building Luke has led me to.

But one step inside shows me how wrong I was.

"What is this?" There are no zombie shoot-outs, or motorcycle racing games, or dance move competitions with bright, shiny graphics. The machines set up around the room are hardly even recognizable as games.

"Classic arcade games." Luke leads me to the nearest one. "This is *Mario Brothers*, from 1983. And there's *Pac-Man*. And over there is *Galaga*. In the back they have a whole section just for pinball. The real machines, with the springs. Not digital."

"So these are, like, antiques?"

"Vintage. Refurbished," Luke says.

The pure joy on his face makes me smile. "I would have thought you'd go for the newest, highest-tech games."

He shrugs. "In movies and video games you can't beat a classic."

My phone buzzes. The screen shows a text from my mother.

Maddie, the hospital is releasing me. Please meet me at home so we can talk. I love you, *mija*.

I shove my phone into my pocket and head for the *Ms. Pac-Man* game I've just noticed along the opposite wall.

"I'll get us something to drink," Luke says, walking backward toward the snack bar in one corner of the huge open space.

There are only two other people at the arcade in the middle of the day, both college-age guys who look like they just rolled out of bed. Neither of them even glances my way as I drop a quarter into the *Ms. Pac-Man* machine.

Nothing happens.

I squat to look closer at the instructions and discover that it actually takes a dollar to play.

"Here you go." Luke sets an open glass bottle of soda on a nearby pub-height table, while I'm still digging in my purse for another coin.

"I thought vintage video games only cost a quarter," I grumble.

He laughs and sets a paper cup full of coins on the table next to my drink. "Refurbishment includes an upgrade in the name of inflation. Help yourself." He digs a few quarters from the cup and drops them into the *Donkey Kong* machine next to mine.

For the next hour, I ignore the occasional buzz from my phone while I try to beat Luke's *Frogger* record. When I turn out to have two left thumbs, we move on to a bank of Skee-Ball machines—I beat him in three games out of five—then to air hockey, where we're locked in a tie, smacking around the floating puck, until I finally manage to get past his maniacal defensive stance in front of the goal.

"You do know this is just a game, right?" I tease as he digs the puck from the slot beneath his goal. "You're not actually going to be picked last for the air hockey draft if a girl scores on you."

"Football is just a game. Chess is just a game." Luke smiles as he sends the puck toward me, bouncing it off the left side of the table. "Air hockey is a way of life."

I shoot the puck back at him and score *again*. "Maybe you should start looking into other ways of life. Something simpler. Like gluten-free baking or Tibetan throat singing."

"Ha ha." He bounces the puck off the right side this time, and I smack it back at him easily. "But for the record, being scored on by a girl is a dramatic improvement upon my social life from two weeks ago."

By the time we tire of the game, we've each won four times and have agreed to a rematch on our next visit. I haven't laughed so much since before my father ~~died~~ faked his death.

As we're heading to the snack bar, Luke checks his

phone. His face goes pale, and I glance at his screen to see that he's missed three calls, all from his mother. There's a text from her at the bottom of the screen, but I can't read it.

"I *might* have forgotten to tell my mom I was leaving the house." He flinches. "If I'm not home in ten minutes, she says she'll call the police."

"Come on. I'll drive you." I don't know whether or not her threat is empty, but I can't keep getting Luke in trouble with his parents. The genetic train wreck that is my family shouldn't be his problem.

We toss our empty soda bottles into the recycling on the way out the door, and I take him to his house, less than a mile away. After he retrieves his bike from my trunk and heads inside, I sit in his driveway, reading through the texts from my mother. She's begging me to come home and let her explain, and my anger grows with every text I read.

My brother was murdered and my mother tried to kill herself, and *now* she wants to explain?

I call Genesis, hoping to find out what she knows—if anything—before I talk to my mother. But my call goes straight to voice mail.

With a sigh, I back out of Luke's driveway and head home.

I do this all the time.

GENESIS

"*This* is your favorite club?" Indiana looks more amused than truly disbelieving as he takes in the empty dance floor, scanning unoccupied tables around the perimeter.

"Okay, but it's ten thirty in the morning. You have to picture it at night, with a few hundred people in here, and the lights flashing, and the music blasting."

And the bar functioning . . .

"Are we going to get arrested for breaking in?" He doesn't seem bothered by that possibility.

"No, I do this all the time. The owners are friends of Neda's parents. They've been letting us sneak in since we were thirteen. That's how I know where the key is." Worst-case scenario, they'll charge me the private party rate for our before-hours . . . private party. "Come on!" I pull him into the DJ booth and press buttons until things start powering up.

High-tech lights—check.

Speakers—check.

The only other thing I know how to work is the phone dock, but that's all we really need. I plug my phone in and set my music app to random. The first song comes on, and the light show changes, synchronizing the flashes and swoops of color with the beat. *Now* it's a party.

"Come on!" I pull Indiana onto the dance floor, and he looks so surprised that for a moment I wonder if this isn't his thing. I've done a sexy Cuban salsa with him on the beach, and I've heard him play acoustic guitar, but maybe he's not a club kind of guy.

Then he starts to move, and I can only smile as I watch him. He's seriously sexy, and suddenly I'm *so* glad this is a private show.

I join him, and two songs later, my heart is pumping and I'm damp with sweat. "Thirsty?" I ask as I head for the bar.

Indiana follows me. "Yes."

I pull a twenty from my phone case and set it on the counter next to the register, then I take two bottles of my favorite microbrew from the cold case under the bar. I open both bottles and leave the caps on top of the twenty. The owners will see the security footage. They'll know I paid for our drinks.

Not that it really matters. We're underage and the source of my cash is the illegal drug trade. I'm avoiding one crime but diving headfirst into two others. Karmically speaking, I'm in the hole pretty deep.

Turns out I have been my entire life.

Indiana lifts one brow at me as he takes a bottle. "Didn't

you just tell Neda it's too early to drink?"

"It's too early for *her* to drink. She wasn't kidnapped, or starved, or threatened with murder. The universe owes us a couple of cold beers."

We take our bottles around the bar and claim two bar stools. I can't help but smile as I watch Indiana take a sip. He notices me staring and smiles. Then he leans toward me for a beer-flavored kiss.

I push everything else away and decide to live in the moment, because that's all I can do. Holden may have a choke hold on my public image, but he can't touch this private moment. And for now, this is enough. Indiana, and beer, and dancing.

We finish our drinks, and I slide off my bar stool. I'm heading toward the sound booth to play something that might inspire another sexy salsa when the front door of the club opens, throwing harsh daylight all over our private party.

The owner of the club steps inside. "Genesis." He doesn't seem surprised to see me, nor does he seem angry. He looks . . . worried. Two men in nondescript suits step past him into the club, and one of them flashes some kind of identification at us.

"Genesis Valencia?"

I nod as I grab my phone from the dock with one shaking hand. I know the drill. I've seen Holden arrested twice, and both times he's been sprung by his family's attorneys within the hour.

Kids in my tax bracket don't get in serious trouble.

But then, kids in my tax bracket don't usually kill twelve hundred people, then try to pay for legal services with drug money.

Indiana stands, studying me in concern.

"Homeland Security," the man with the badge tells me. "We need you and your friend to come with us. Now."

Anxiety sends adrenaline straight to my chest, and for a moment, I wonder if I'm having a heart attack. Theoretically speaking, I no longer want to be dependent upon my dad's illicit income. But if that means spending the rest of my life in prison, I can't swear that my moral stand will win out over self-preservation.

I've already spent enough time locked up.

6 DAYS, 8 HOURS EARLIER

There was never a good time to tell you.

MADDIE

I've hardly been alone with my mother since Pen, Luke, and I got back to Miami. That wasn't intentional. But as I open the front door of our apartment, the dread churning in my gut tells me that maybe, at least subconsciously, it really was.

My mother is sitting at the table, sipping from a cup of coffee. The funeral catalogues are gone. She's just staring at the woven placemat until I close the door at my back. Then she looks up and sees me.

"Maddie, hon, I am so sorry." She stands, but keeps her distance, as if she's not sure how I'll react if she tries to touch me.

Good call.

"For what? Trying to kill yourself? Or sleeping with Uncle Hernán? Or lying to me and Ryan for our whole lives?" What else is she not telling me?

She bites her lip, but that isn't the guilty expression I'm looking for. That's the expression that tells me there's more. Something she's trying not to say.

"What?" I demand, and she starts to shake her head, but I cut her off. "Just tell me, Mom."

Her expression crumples and fresh tears fill her eyes. "Ryan knew."

My hand falls to my side. The car keys jingle as they hit the carpet. *No.* He would have told me. Ryan *always* told me the truth.

He stole ten dollars from Dad's wallet when he was twelve. He ate the last sugar-free brownie, even though I'd called diabetic-dibs, because he was too lazy to go to the store. He wasn't sure he could stop drinking on his own.

Letting me believe a lie was as bad as lying to me himself. Why would he do that?

My father. My mother. My uncle. My brother.

It's too late to get answers from Ryan, but my *mother* . . .

"Why would you tell him, but not me?"

"I didn't tell him. He . . . figured it out. And we didn't tell you because your father had just died, and that seemed like more than enough for you to deal with. Then Ryan went into rehab, and things just . . . There was never a good time to tell you. There was never a good *reason*."

"I've always found the truth to be reason enough."

My mother flinches, and I feel a twinge of guilt. I've never been so mad at her, but hurting her only makes me feel worse.

"Dad didn't die," I point out in as rational a voice as I can manage.

She sinks into the chair at her back, as if the truth has

somehow punctured the bubble of denial she's evidently been living in. As if it's deflating all around her. Sapping her energy.

She isn't healthy enough for this conversation. I know that. But neither of us can move on until we've had it.

I cross the small living room into the dining area, and the fact that I'm coming closer—voluntarily—seems to prop her up a little. "Did you know?"

She exhales slowly. "He . . . He put too many things in order before he left for Colombia that last time. I suspected he might not come back. And when they told me they'd found his body, it was easier to believe he'd died than that he'd just left. Even if deep down, I knew better. But I had *no idea* about the rest of it, Maddie. About what he did . . . I'm not sure I truly believed it until—" She bites off the rest of her sentence, but I can hear what she isn't saying.

"Until Uncle Hernán told you."

She nods. "I just . . . It sounded so surreal."

"If you didn't believe it, why did you take a whole bottle of pills?"

For a moment, she only stares at her placemat. As if she's searching for the right words.

I don't care if they're right. I just want them to be true.

"That wasn't about your father," she says at last, and her voice sounds fragile. Flimsy. As if it could be torn like a sheet of paper. "Not entirely. I just . . . I made a really bad call. In that moment, all I could think about was everything I've lost. I felt like I had nothing left."

I stumble back from the table. My face burns as if she's slapped me.

Too late, she realizes what she's said. "No, Maddie, that's not what I meant. Obviously I still have you. But at the time, all I could see was what I'd lost. I was sick, honey. I've been sick for a while now and the truth is that when Ryan died, that light at the end of the tunnel died with him. I couldn't even imagine a time when I would feel better, and I thought . . ." Her tears spill over. "I thought you'd be better off without me."

"That's not true." My voice sounds strange. I feel oddly numb. As if I'm hearing someone else say the words.

"I know. I know that now. I knew that then. It was just . . . That was really hard to keep in focus at the time. I just . . . I need to know that you'll forgive me."

I can only blink at her. I know I'm supposed to say something, but all I can do is stare.

"It doesn't have to be right now. I know you need some time, after what I've done. But I'm going to get better. I'm going to do whatever it takes. For you and for me. I just need to know that it can happen. Eventually. I just need that hope, Maddie. Can you give me that?"

I nod.

Then I turn and walk back to my room. I close the door. Then I lock it.

This can't be happening.

GENESIS

"How did you find us?" I know there are more important questions I could be asking the agent sitting across the table, but that one is stuck in my head. "Did you use some kind of high-tech spy gear, or have you been following me?"

The man in the suit checks the setting on the recorder sitting in the middle of the table, as if he didn't even hear my question.

A minute later, the door opens and another man in a suit escorts my father into the room. And suddenly I understand how this happened.

I pull my phone out and disable the "track my phone" option, making sure my dad can see what I'm doing. I half expect him to threaten to take my phone away, but he doesn't. If I didn't have a phone, he'd have no way to get in contact with me, and I'd have no way to call for help, should I need it.

So he only frowns and sinks into the chair next to mine while the man who escorted him into the room closes the door and stands next to it like a guard.

"Thank you for coming, Ms. Valencia," the man on the other side of the table begins. As if I'm here of my own volition. "We have a few questions about your time in the jungle."

If the FBI had brought me home, they probably would have questioned me immediately, as they did Pen, Luke, and Maddie. But since we came home on my father's jet, without government assistance . . .

Indiana is in another room somewhere in this same building. With another set of men in suits.

"Okay." My thoughts whirl so fast that the room seems to be spinning around me. My dad doesn't look worried. But then, my dad wouldn't look worried if he were balanced on one foot on the rim of a churning volcano. He doesn't believe in tipping his hand.

"As you may already know, we've had several chats with Sebastián Cardenas since he was transferred into US custody overnight."

Cardenas. I never even knew Sebastián's last name.

Then what the man in the suit is saying finally sinks in. What has Sebastián told them? How much does he know?

"Am I under arrest?" The second the words are out of my mouth, I realize I've revealed too much. My father stiffens next to me, confirming that, and for a second, I hate that I've disappointed him.

Then I remember that *I'm* disappointed in *him.*

"You are not under arrest at this time," the man in the suit says. "Whether or not that changes depends on how this meeting goes."

"Do I need an attorney?" I ask.

My father nods. "I've already called—"

"An attorney would not be appropriate at this time," the man says.

My father stands. "You're not interrogating my daughter without an attorney present."

"Mr. Valencia, we're not characterizing this as an interrogation at the moment, but I want you both to understand that should that change, we are legally permitted to question persons of interest without a lawyer present under the Patriot Act."

"The Patriot Act?" My father sits again, but it feels more like he's collapsing into his chair. "You're questioning her as a terrorism suspect?"

Terrorism? Because of the explosion. The *Splendor* victims.

A jolt of fear burns through me.

"Not as a suspect. As a material witness. Unless something changes." The man in the suit leans toward me over the table. "Ms. Valencia, it is our hope that we can resolve this today. It's in your best interest to cooperate with us at this juncture to avoid more . . . extreme measures later."

Suddenly I can hear my pulse rush in my ears. This can't be happening. Everything I did *had* to be done. "Look, none of this was my fault. I got kidnapped. I had a gun pointed at my head and a machete held to my throat. I found out that there were bombs, and I tried to—"

"Genesis, stop talking." My father's voice is low and sharp.

My mouth snaps shut.

"We already know what happened to the *Splendor*," the man in the suit says. "We understand that you didn't intend for anyone to die. In exchange for your cooperation—for filling in some blanks for us—we are willing to stipulate to that in writing and to agree to forgo any reckless endangerment charges—"

"Reckless . . . ?" The room feels too bright. My voice sounds too high. "I just spent a week starving at the hands of terrorists, and now you're threatening to put me in prison. I'm a US citizen. Am I supposed to be as scared of my own government as I am of a terrorist?"

The man standing guard by the door snorts.

"I'm giving you a choice here, Ms. Valencia. You can answer our questions and leave this room formally cleared of all guilt in the deaths of more than twelve hundred people, or you can elect to explain your actions in a court of law instead."

Cleared of all guilt. No charges. If I do this, Holden will have nothing to hold over me. I'll be rid of him.

I lean forward, my elbows propped on the table, and look the man right in the eye. "I'll tell you whatever you want to know. But not with him here." I nod in my dad's direction.

"Genesis, I'm not going to—"

The man across the table stands. "I'm sorry, sir, but I'm going to have to ask you to step outside."

6 DAYS, 4 HOURS EARLIER

I don't care.

MADDIE

My phone rings, and I struggle up from an accidental nap to answer it.

"Hey," Luke says when I answer. "I've been paroled. Want some company?"

"Yes." I don't even have to think about it. "Your house?"

"No way. Parole means I'm allowed to leave the grounds. Can I come over?"

I roll onto my back and stare up at the ceiling. "I have to get out of here. Wanna hit the arcade again?" I'd found it pleasantly impossible to think about real life while we were chomping pixelated ghosts and shooting floating hockey pucks at each other.

"How 'bout someplace quiet?"

"The coffee shop a block from my apartment," I suggest as I sit up and dig under my bed for my shoes.

"I'll meet you there."

I hang up my phone and slide it into my pocket, then sneak into my mother's room to make sure her nap isn't of the permanent variety. Her chest rises softly as I watch, and the only thing on her nightstand is a glass of water. On my way out, I grab my house key and slap a Post-it note on the inside of the front door telling her that I'll be back for dinner.

The afternoon is clear and beautiful, but I can only glare into the spring sunshine, well aware that I'm channeling Eeyore. *No one* in my position would be in a good mood.

Then I see Luke get off the bus half a block away, and I can feel my mood lift. It doesn't seem fair to him that he's the only ray of light in my life. That feels like too much to pin on a guy who hasn't even turned sixteen yet.

But he keeps coming around, so I have to believe that he welcomes the challenge.

I speed up and we get to the coffeehouse at the same time. "You get a table, I'll get coffee?" he suggests. I nod, then I pick out a spot in the corner by the window, where I can stare out at the world. I'd much rather watch it than be in it these days.

A few minutes later, Luke sets two lattes on the table, then lets his backpack swing carefully to the floor. He sits in the chair opposite mine and pulls a tablet from the front pocket of his backpack, and when I see that he's trying to log into the free Wi-Fi, I read the password to him. It's written in chalk on the blackboard-painted rear wall, along with the daily muffin and cupcake selections.

Luke opens an app that turns his tablet into a virtual air

hockey table and sets it on the table between us with a grin. "Ready?"

I've just decided we're the cutest couple on the face of the planet when a bright light flashes in my face.

Stunned, I look up, blinking, and I find a photographer standing a few feet away, zooming in for a second shot with his huge, expensive camera.

I have no idea what to do, and Luke's so focused on his air hockey defense that he hasn't even noticed. But the barista behind the counter has.

"Hey. Buy something or get out!" she shouts. She's trying to be helpful, obviously, but all she's really done is call attention to our presence.

The photographer heads outside, where he's evidently content to take pictures of us through the window, and before I can tell Luke that we should leave, half of the customers in the coffee shop are staring.

Then the whispers begin. I hear our names. Then I hear Ryan's. I hear my mother's. Someone mentions the *Splendor*.

"Luke."

"Maddie, you just let me score." He looks up from the tablet, where the electronic puck now floats in front of his goal, waiting for him to send it flying with one finger. Then he notices my expression. "What's wrong?"

"Let's go."

"What? Why?"

"Because everyone's staring."

Finally, he looks around, and now there are phones

aimed at us. People are taking pictures. Some of them seem to be recording.

"I don't care," he says, but his jaw is clenched. "They don't own the coffee shop. We have every right to be here."

And I want to be here. But I don't want to be on their social media accounts and YouTube channels.

"Ignore them," Luke says. "They'll get bored when they realize how normal we are."

But I don't feel normal. I feel like a fraud. "Thank you." I tap the pause button on the app and meet his gaze from across the table. "For this, and for everything else. You're the only connection I have to 'normal' these days. And I'm starting to think that you and Genesis are the only people in my entire life who've never lied to me."

Luke gives me an amused look as he lifts his coffee cup. "Didn't she tell you she was taking you to the Bahamas for spring break?"

I'm almost startled by the realization that he's right. "Okay, yes, technically she lies semi-regularly. But she's different since we got out of the jungle. And now that Ryan's gone, she's the only family I have left. The only person I feel like I can trust, other than you. Which means I have to tell her about my brother." I lower my voice to make sure none of the phone cameras can hear me. "*Our* brother . . ."

My phone beeps. A text from Neda pops up on the screen.

Where the hell are you?

I only reply to give myself something to do other than stare back at all the assholes still talking about us.

???

I hunch down in my chair, trying to hide behind Luke's head.

We go live in 5 min. For my show. I texted you the details.

Neda did text me earlier, but I never read the message because I don't want to encourage an open dialogue with her. Genesis is home. We don't need any more publicity. Which means Neda's just another journalist—in her case, a "journalist"—trying to use Luke and me for exposure.

We have more than enough of that already.

"What's wrong?" Luke asks.

"Neda seem to think we're going live on her channel in five minutes."

"We never agreed to another show."

"She tends to miss details like that," I say as I type.

Not gonna happen.

I start to slide my phone into my pocket, but it begins to buzz in my hand. Neda's calling. She must be desperate.

"What?" I snap into my phone, in lieu of a greeting.

"I was supposed to be interviewing Genesis and Indiana, but they're a no-show, so you're up!" Her voice is too high-pitched. She sounds upset.

"We're not doing your show again. Get Penelope," I whisper into the phone as I hold my coffee higher than necessary, to block a particularly intrusive coffee shop patron's less-than-subtle shot.

"Pen won't come out of her room. She's been crying all day. Holden's going live on the radio this afternoon—ungrateful bastard—and Genesis is MIA. You *have* to do this, Maddie. I told everyone I'd have an exclusive."

"What do you mean, MIA?" I stand and head toward the bathroom, for at least the illusion of privacy.

"I mean she's totally off the grid. So is her dad. And Indiana. No one's heard from them in hours."

I hang up the phone and race back to the table. "Luke. Do you have your laptop? I need you to find my cousin."

We won't need to.

GENESIS

My father follows the man in the suit back into the small room where I've been answering questions all afternoon. "Well?" he says as he sinks into the chair next to mine.

The man in the suit sets a folder on the table, then sits across from us. "We're satisfied, for now, though we reserve the right to ask more questions later, should the need arise. Here is the paperwork we mentioned." He removes two identical sheets of paper from the folder, then pulls a pen from the inner pocket of his jacket. "We'll need you each to sign one."

"What is it?" I ask as I glance over the document.

"It's an NDA. A nondisclosure agreement. It says that you agree not to talk about anything we've discussed here today, to keep from hampering our ongoing investigation into the Moreno cartel and its connections to David Valencia. If you violate the nondisclosure agreement, you will be subject to monetary damages in an amount to be determined by the courts, for whatever damage our investigation incurs as the result of your revelation, and our agreement not to prosecute will be null and void."

"Wait, *what?*" As I mentally untangle his cruel knot of words, one thing becomes clear. "And if I don't sign, what are you going to do? Sue us and prosecute me?"

"More accurately, we will leave the decision of whether or not to charge you for the damages or the loss of life on board the *Splendor* up to the federal prosecutor, and we will, of course, be obligated to provide whatever information he or she needs in order to best make that decision."

"Charge me with what?"

"With the reckless handling of a potentially lethal weapon—three conventional warheads and a detonator— that resulted in the deaths of more than twelve hundred souls. One thousand two hundred thirty-four counts of involuntary manslaughter. If you're found guilty, you'll never see the light of day again. Assuming they don't go for the death penalty."

Shock crashes over me in a frigid wave, stealing my breath. Leaving me stunned. "But I didn't know the bombs were on the boat! I was trying to—!"

"Genesis, stop talking," my father orders, and my mouth snaps closed.

"Thus the 'involuntary' in involuntary manslaughter. All they have to prove is that you knew the bombs could kill someone and you detonated them anyway. That's reckless endangerment. If you refuse to sign . . ."

"You'll sell me out? I cooperated! I answered every question you asked!"

"Genesis, just sign the paper." The way my father says it tells me this is not his first NDA. "They're agreeing not to prosecute if you do."

I turn on him, fear and anger coursing through my veins like adrenaline. "But if I sign that, we can't tell anyone that I'm not guilty of murder."

My father exhales slowly. Then he takes the pen the man across the table offers. "We won't need to, because if you sign the document, no one will ever know you pressed the button," he points out, in his most reasonable, no-nonsense voice.

But he's wrong. Holden knows. And if I sign this paper, I will be at his mercy for . . . well, maybe forever.

I want to be free of Holden. I *need* to be rid of him.

"You should know that whether or not you sign, if you reveal classified information about our investigation, not only could you both face criminal charges, but I suspect my superiors will want to revisit their decision not to touch assets that we are legally entitled to seize, for the duration of our investigation."

"What assets?" I ask.

My father is already signing. "*Our* assets. Genesis Shipping. The houses. The money. The cars. Everything." He turns to me and hands me the pen. "If you don't sign, they're going to prosecute you, and we won't have enough money to pay our lawyers."

I'm sure that would be cozy.

MADDIE

I realize my mistake the second Neda's car pulls up to the curb. She drives something sporty. Bright red, low-slung, and topless. Her goal in life is to stand out, and in my neighborhood, she's getting twice the bang for her father's buck.

Holden is in her passenger seat. When he opens the door, it takes everything I have to resist kicking him in the balls in greeting.

People turn to stare when Neda gets out wearing designer sunglasses, a top that is more straps than material—I can't quite figure out how she got into it—and expensive sandals that look like they've never actually come into contact with the pavement. If my neighbors don't know who she is yet, they will soon.

And they already recognize Holden. The national hero.

"Let's go inside," I say. But Neda leans against the hood of her convertible, practically posing for the cameras she imagines follow her everywhere. Lately, she's right about that more often than not.

She glances up at my apartment building in obvious disgust. "I'm sure that would be cozy, but I get claustrophobic in buildings with low ceilings and poor lighting. And Luke looks like he could use some sun." She crosses her arms over her chest. "Let's just do this out here."

"Quickly," Holden adds. "I have a radio interview in an hour."

"What did you find out?" Neda asks.

"Not much," Luke says through clenched teeth. "Genesis hasn't logged into any of her social media accounts in more than a week. I ran an open-source facial recognition software, looking for new pictures of her online. There are *thousands* of posts since yesterday, but most of them are just the same few pictures over and over. The one of Holden carrying her out of the jungle. Genesis getting off the jet. And a bunch of screenshots of *Good Morning America* from this morning. But nothing new in the past four hours."

"Did she say where she was going when she left the studio?" I ask.

Holden shrugs. "She and Indiana just stormed out. She's not answering my texts either. If she doesn't show up for this radio thing . . ." He leaves his threat unspoken, and if I weren't worried about what his revenge on Genesis could do to my mother, I'd call him out for his blackmail right here and now.

Neda's gaze scans my block, and she actually shivers in disgust. I can practically see her urge to flee. "You could *both* blow off the radio and come on my show."

Holden acts like he didn't even hear her.

"Indiana isn't answering his phone either," Luke points out, hiking his backpack higher on one shoulder. "And there are no new pictures of him in the past day. They're probably together. Probably alone. I'm sure they'll start answering their phones when they've had enough privacy."

He clearly isn't worried about Genesis, and I'm not sure I should be. But . . . "Uncle Hernán isn't answering either. Not even when my mom calls him." I kick at a pebble on the sidewalk. "If he could answer, he would. I think they're all three somewhere with no cell signal."

Luke's eyes widen. "They're being questioned." He sounds certain. Like he can't believe we didn't think of it before.

"For five hours?" I frown. "Agent Moore was done with us in under one."

He shrugs. "We weren't held in the jungle for an extra few days, with—" He bites off the rest, because Neda doesn't know, but I hear it anyway. *With Maddie's dad.*

Holden smirks, well aware of what Luke was about to say. "I'm being interviewed by Homeland Security tomorrow," he says. "She could be there now." His phone buzzes and he frowns at the screen. Then he gives me a weird look as he answers the text.

"That has to be it," Luke says. "I'm sure her dad and Indiana are with her."

Neda shrugs as she rounds the hood of her car, clearly ready to flee my neighborhood. "That, or they threw her in a deep dark hole, with Domenica."

But if the United States government has Sebastián, then they know that Genesis pushed the button. Which means Neda's joke might be more accurate than she knows.

I'll be able to forgive him.

GENESIS

Indiana is waiting in the hall when they finally let my father and me out of that little room. He stands when he sees us coming. "You okay?"

He looks tired, but he's worried about me.

"Yeah. Did they make you sign anything?"

"No. They just threatened to charge me with obstruction of justice if I say anything that might compromise their investigation into our kidnapping and the explosion of the *Splendor.*" He huffs. "You'd think they'd want to help us, rather than threaten us, considering that we're the *victims.*"

Huh. No NDA for Indiana. Because he doesn't have assets that can be seized? Or because he didn't actually see me blow up the ship?

In the parking lot, my dad tries to usher us toward his car. I only give in when I remember that Indiana and I were absconded with in an official government vehicle, but no return service was offered.

"Will you drop us at Maddie's?" I ask as he clicks the key fob to unlock the doors.

My father frowns. "Genesis, I want you to come home. You're going to have to talk to me eventually."

He's right. His money is dirty, but I'm still taking it. Still living on it. I just sold my soul—my First Amendment rights, at least—to the United States government to protect that dirty money, because the sad truth is that I don't know how to live without it.

Especially if I find myself under arrest.

But I'm not ready to talk to my dad about that. Not yet.

"Indiana is welcome to stay as long as he likes," my father adds as he opens the driver's door, but I'm already shaking my head.

"I'm going back to school tomorrow, but I'm staying at Maddie's."

My father exhales, as if he's grasping for patience. "Daniela came home from the hospital today. I think she and your cousin need some time alone, *princesa*." I can tell from the stress he's putting on my nickname that there's more to that than he's saying out loud. Because Indiana isn't family.

Damn it.

"Get in the car. We'll pick up dinner on the way home." He turns to Indiana. "Please join us." Then my father slides behind the wheel, as if there's no question his order will be followed.

I've never openly disobeyed him before. I've always

gone along, then done whatever I truly want to do afterward. In the past, he's been willing to turn a blind eye to that, because obeying shows him that I respect him as a parent—and I truly did—and quietly disobeying shows that I've learned from his example.

But things are different now.

Businessmen lie and call it negotiation. They grease wheels and make deals. I've always known that about my father, but I'd believed he was straight with me. That he let me see beyond the curtain. That he was teaching me.

But really, he was lying. I'll be able to forgive him, eventually, but I won't be able to trust him, because I can't ever be sure that he's not still lying to me.

Beyond that, I'm not sure that I can trust myself and my own instincts, considering that I believed his lies for seventeen years.

"I'll be home by midnight." I pull my phone from my pocket to open the ride-share app and realize I missed six phone calls and twenty text messages—most from Neda and Maddie—while I was being questioned in that black hole of an interview room.

My father frowns and gets out of the car, but he doesn't argue. While I click through the app to request a ride, I hear him talking softly with Indiana. I can't make out what he's saying, but I can guess the subject matter.

"I'll see you both tonight," my father says when I slide my phone back into my pocket. Then he gets in his car and drives out of the parking lot.

"Did he try to recruit you as his spy?" I ask Indiana. "To keep him in the loop?"

Indiana laughs. "No. He asked me to look out for you."

"Because I can't take care of myself?" Does he seriously think he wasted all the money he spent on my self-defense classes?

"He's just worried about you. With good reason, considering where we were two days ago."

Our car pulls up to the curb and I call Maddie as Indiana gets in. She answers before I even hear the phone ring. "Where the hell have you been?" my cousin demands into my ear.

"Being questioned by Homeland Security," I whisper. "It's a long story involving the Patriot Act and the theory that I might actually be a terrorist. Why?" I climb into the car next to Indiana.

"So you're okay? Neda seems to think they threw you in some kind of federally funded hole in the ground with Domenica."

"They very nearly did. But I'm fine." Except for the governmental gag order that just gave Holden virtually limitless power over me. But she doesn't need to know about that.

"Did they know about . . . my dad?"

"Yes. But they didn't seem to be in any hurry to publicize that fact."

As our ride pulls into traffic, my gazes catches on a familiar form looking back at me from a parking lot across the street from the police station where we were questioned.

Silvana. Chill bumps rise all over my arms. This time I can see her face. It's really her.

She's watching me. She's *following* me.

If she's still alive—if she's *real*—my uncle's plan B could be real too. . . .

6 DAYS, 2 HOURS EARLIER

I don't even like her.

MADDIE

The surreality of this moment hits me as I glance around the wrought-iron table stretching the length of the cabana. This jungle hostage reunion is bizarre, and I'm not sure what Genesis was thinking.

We weren't exactly a cohesive unit before the kidnapping—most of us didn't even know Luke or Indiana a week ago—and throwing us together now isn't going to change that.

We haven't been together as a group since the day we hiked into the jungle, and tonight we're all every bit as tense as we were that day.

"What do you think they're talking about?" Luke leans closer to whisper as he stares down the stretch of private beach at Holden and Penelope. Indiana, Neda, and I are all staring with him.

Genesis's jaw is clenched so tightly I have a feeling she'll have to go get her caps repaired in the morning. Yet she's not focused on the beach drama. Her gaze is constantly skipping from Holden and Penelope to the stretch of sand behind them, to other tables in private cabanas, then behind us to the clubhouse itself.

She looks like she's waiting for something. Her unease is setting me on edge.

I try to catch her gaze, but Genesis is focused everywhere but on the people at this table. The people she's brought together.

"I think he's dumping her," Neda says, drawing my attention back to Holden and Penelope. We've all been thinking it, but she's the only one who would ever say it out loud. "'I know I told you this was real, but a tiger can't change his stripes, baby,'" she continues in a cartoonish approximation of Holden's voice. "'I'm a lying dick.'"

Luke and Indiana laugh, and I fight an unexpected urge to give Neda a fist bump.

Genesis's teeth make a terrible grinding noise. Then she drains her wineglass.

Immediately, the waiter steps forward to pour more.

It's harder to get served alcohol in public in Miami than it is in Cartagena, where there's no legal drinking age, but my uncle has spent large sums of money over the past decade contributing to the beachside country club where he and Genesis have a lifetime membership. She can get whatever she wants with a smile and the unspoken promise of a big tip.

Luke picks up his glass and sniffs the contents. I know he doesn't like wine, but he accepted a glass to be polite, and now he looks curious. "Did you see the wine your cousin ordered?" he whispers near my ear, while two more waiters set a plate of salad in front of each of us. "It's five hundred dollars a bottle."

I did not see that. I'm not surprised to see my cousin spending her father's money with abandon, but I *am* surprised that she doesn't seem to be enjoying it.

She looks like she wants to march down the beach and punch Holden in the head. We caught a rebroadcast of his radio interview in the car on the way here. He told all of Miami that it was true that they'd had a fight in the jungle, during the trauma of the kidnapping. But that ultimately, stress had brought them back together, and that they are closer now than ever, despite the rumors to the contrary.

Even from fifty feet away, I can see that Penelope is upset. She's hugging herself with both arms, nodding with every word Holden says, as if she agrees. Or at least understands why he's saying whatever asinine thing he's saying. When the truth is that he's clearly breaking her heart.

I don't even like her, but at this point I would gladly hold Holden down so she could kick him in the balls.

Holden and Penelope start back toward the cabana, and he has his arm around her shoulder. He looks like a smug coach comforting a disappointed player forced to take one for the team.

I wish Sebastián had killed him in the jungle.

We all turn back to our food, as if we haven't been watching them the whole time.

The plate on the table in front of me holds a thick slice of tomato between two slices of mozzarella, drizzled with vinaigrette and sprinkled with cilantro. On what planet is this a salad?

Luke looks just as confounded by his identical serving, but Neda has already cut hers into several tiny bites.

Uncomfortable silence descends as Pen and Holden step into the cabana. She returns to her seat with her spine straight and her head held high, but her eyes are downcast and damp.

Holden sits in the chair across from my cousin and accepts the glass of wine a waiter sets in front of him. He smiles at Genesis, but she stands to address the entire table, as if she didn't even see him.

"I know this is supposed to be super casual," she begins while I stare at the artfully arranged hunks of tomato and cheese sitting in front of a gold-rimmed one hundred twenty-five dollar glass of wine. "But I just wanted to say a quick thank-you to everyone for coming. We've all been through a lot over the past week and a half, and tomorrow most of us are going back to school. Moving on with our lives. Let's try to think of this dinner as closure. As putting the past behind us. Will you all toast with me?" She lifts her wineglass, and everyone else mimics the motion.

I raise my glass, but I feel like a kid playing dress-up.

Penelope still has tears in her eyes. Holden looks smug. Neda has her phone in one hand with her camera app open, obviously debating the wisdom of pressing the record button without permission.

"To the future," Genesis says, and now she *is* looking at Holden. "May the past burn in hell."

"To the future." Luke looks at me as he says it, and in his wide-eyed look of wonder at the display of wealth all around us, I see a glimpse of the boy I invited to tag along on a camping trip that would change both of our lives.

"To the future." Penelope sounds despondent, while she watches Holden stare up at Genesis.

"To the future." Indiana's eyes are closed as he sips from his glass, as if he's truly thinking about what the toast means.

But I'm not ready to let the past burn in hell. Not quite yet.

We each take a sip of our wine, then silverware clinks as everyone begins to eat.

Except Genesis. She's still standing, her brows drawn low as she scans the beach, as if she's looking for something. Or someone. Her posture is stiff. Her glass shakes a little in her unsteady hand.

Something is wrong.

When she excuses herself to head for the bathroom in the main clubhouse, I follow her onto the beach. "Genesis," I call, and she turns slowly. Reluctantly.

"Ryan was your brother too." I don't know where the words came from. I meant to ask her why she's so tense. But she deserves the truth. "I overheard your dad and my mom . . ."

I let the rest fade between us, waiting for her to draw the painful conclusion and spare me from saying it. But she only blinks at me. Then her gaze drops to our feet, where the toes of her designer sandals and my vintage ones are practically meeting in the sand.

She doesn't look hurt. She doesn't even look surprised.

"You knew."

Genesis's gaze snaps back up to me. She frowns. "I'm sorry, Maddie. Ryan made me promise not to tell you."

5 DAYS, 12 HOURS EARLIER

I'm still me.

GENESIS

People turn to stare the moment I step into the marble-floored foyer. That in itself is not unusual. Even in a school populated almost exclusively by children of the extremely rich and/or politically powerful, I am wealthier than most. And I know how to get what I want.

I've spent four years crafting my reputation. Building the Genesis I want to be—at least the Genesis I want them to *see*—out of a careful blend of rumor, fact, and artfully arranged couture ensembles.

That was the whole point behind my campaign, during my freshman year, to do away with school uniforms.

But for the first time in four years, this attention isn't of my own doing.

I toss my hair over my shoulder and paste on a smile. A small one that says I've been through hell, but I'm still strong. I'm still me. I make eye contact with everyone I pass. I nod and murmur hellos, complete with names, and I make it halfway to my locker without betraying the fact that I'd rather be at home on the couch with Indiana. Or under the boardwalk at the beach with Indiana. Or picking up dog poop on the front lawn—as long as it's with Indiana.

The first person to brave an approach is Hedda Rogers. President of the Unity Club and founder in chief of the local teen chapter of Worth the Wait. The abstinence society. To say we have differences of opinion is like saying the surface of the sun is a little warm.

"Genesis!" She tosses her Givenchy backpack over her shoulder and links her arm through mine as if we've been best friends since the hospital nursery. "We're all so glad you're home, safe and sound. Is it true you were kidnapped? Because Kaye Williams is saying you just got lost in the jungle, and the whole thing was blown out of proportion to spare your ego. But I told her you would never make something like that up."

"How sweet of you." I extract my arm and give her a big smile. "I told her the same thing last year when you were gone for two weeks with mono, and she told everyone you'd had a second nose job. I mean, why would you bother, when the first one was such a success?"

I leave her standing in the middle of the hall, staring after me with a smile frozen in place beneath her *totally* fake nose.

My locker is fifteen feet away. I'm almost there. More smiles and nods, and a hug from a girl I've never seen before who stops to tell me that her church youth group prayed for the Miami Six every night that we were missing and handed out remembrance bracelets at the candlelight vigil.

It's strange to hear about what happened while we were in the jungle. I've worked hard to make sure everyone at school associates the name Genesis Valencia with the version of myself I've chosen to show them. And now, suddenly, they all seem to think they know the "real" me.

I dial in my locker combination and open the door, and I'm about to grab my European History text when a set of designer sandals stop next to my feet.

Penelope.

In August, I paid a scholarship student five hundred dollars to trade lockers with her so we could be next to each other. That was before I knew she was in love with my boyfriend.

They both stabbed me in the back. I could kill Holden, but for Pen, I feel only pity.

I close my locker. She's staring into hers without truly seeming to see it. "Hey," I say.

"Hey." She pulls out an anatomy text. But she doesn't have anatomy until fifth period.

"Listen." I lower my voice to keep all the hangers-on from hearing. "I don't know what he told you last night, but what Holden's saying in public isn't true."

She turns to me, and her gaze is cold. I taught her that look, back in middle school. The key is that the ice has to start in your heart, then slowly work its way out until it's visible in your eyes. We've used it on many a former friend. But we've never turned the weapon on each other before.

"Right," Penelope says. "You're holding hands on TV because you're *not* a couple again. I'm done with you both." Then she slams her locker and heads off in the direction opposite her first-period class.

So much for putting the past behind us.

I'm ready.

MADDIE

"You sure about this?" Luke already has his hand on the car door handle.

I nod. "I'm ready. I need just another minute." I picked him up in my mom's car. She probably won't be leaving the apartment today, and if she needs to go somewhere, she has Ryan's . . .

Crap.

"I should have taken Ryan's car." I've been driving my mom's because driving Ryan's is as difficult as going into his bedroom. It smells like him. It feels like him.

My mom isn't ready to drive around with his ghost in the passenger seat next to her.

"So, your uncle bought your brother a car but he didn't buy you one, and no one got suspicious about his motivations?" Luke's talking to fill the silence. To try to distract me from my own thoughts.

"He bought me one too. Brand-new. I sold it and gave the money to Habitat for Humanity."

"You did not." His eyes are wide again.

"I did. In my father's name." Because I was the dumbest, most naive and gullible sixteen-year-old on the face of the planet. "He'd been dead for a couple of months. Or so we thought."

"Did you at least drive it first?"

"Yeah. I took my road test in it. Then I drove it straight to a used car dealership and cashed out." I shrugged. "I was trying to make a statement to my uncle, about how I didn't need his money and he couldn't buy my love. And I was trying to memorialize my dad." Another shrug. "I guess I got it half right."

"Damn." Luke looks half shocked, half impressed. "I've never known anyone better at putting her money where her mouth is than you are."

I laugh. I can't help it. That's the most flattering characterization I've ever heard of one of the dumbest things I've ever done.

"But I guess they helped build a house with the money you donated, so there's that."

I laugh again. "They built *three* houses with the money I donated."

"Holy crap! What kind of car was it?"

"I can't tell you that," I say as I push open my door, indulging an unexpected smile. "It'll make you very, very sad."

I own you.

GENESIS

The lunch bell rings, and I head for the parking lot. We only have an hour, but I placed an order online for sushi at my favorite restaurant. I can't eat in the quad today. Not with Penelope shooting daggers at me and Neda trying to film every word either of us says in hopes that the "exclusive content" will boost her page views.

And Holden . . .

"Hey, beautiful." He appears out of nowhere in the hallway and slides his arm around my waist. I try to shrug him off, but his grip tightens. "Don't be a bitch, Gen," he leans closer to whisper, and I know that to everyone watching, that probably looks like some kind of romantic gesture.

I want to punch him in the groin.

Instead, I stop walking and turn to face him with my most sincere screw-you smile. Then I lean in until my lips brush his earlobe. "The fairy tale you're telling in public doesn't change anything between us, Holden. Only a fool believes his own lies."

When I step back, I expect to find angry-Holden staring back at me. Instead, he's giving me a half grin I can't believe I ever found sexy.

"This isn't about what I believe. It's about you making *everyone else* believe. Lucky for you, I'm willing to contribute to the effort." He wraps one arm around me again, and his hand slides down to squeeze my ass.

I tense, ready to drive my knee into his favorite parts, but for once, he anticipates the blow.

"Twelve hundred bodies," he hisses into my ear, and I freeze. "Billions in illegal profit. An undead uncle heading up a terrorist organization." He squeezes me again, and his lips brush my ear as he whispers, "I *own* you, Genesis. All I'm asking for right now is some public goodwill. A little show for the cameras. But if you piss me off, I might just take this act in a much more *private* direction. . . ."

"Get your hands off me," I growl, infuriated by the fact that I can't afford to shove him off me. Or rupture his scrotum with my Valentino leather wrap sandal.

"You're not calling the shots anymore." He slides one knee between my thighs, and bile burns its way up my throat. "I'll put my hands wherever I want. But all you have to do to stop me is neutralize my threat, Gen. Tell the truth about yourself and your family. Then I'll have nothing to hold over you."

He's daring *me* to tell the truth. The knowing look in his eyes makes my stomach twist with nausea.

He knows.

Holden *knows* about the NDA. He knows I couldn't tell the truth, even if I were willing to sacrifice my family.

He knows his grip on me is ironclad.

Holden gives me one more nauseating squeeze, then lets me go, even as he whispers into my ear, "I'll let you know when I need you. And you damn well better be available." With that, he turns and walks off down the hall, *humming* to himself. While I shake with rage.

When I realize people are staring, I shove my anger down deep and head out the door into the parking lot. The moment I step outside, I carefully scan the school grounds, gripped by a new tension that has nothing to do with Holden. I've seen Silvana in Miami twice in the past couple of days, which either means that I'm hallucinating, or she's actually here.

Stalking me.

I'm so consumed by my search of the grounds—still cursing at Holden in my head—that I don't even notice there's a guy leaning against the hood of my car until I'm practically stepping on him.

"I thought you might want company for lunch." Indiana pushes away from the car and leans in for a kiss. When he tries to pull away, I wrap my arms around his neck and deepen the kiss instead.

"I am *so* glad you're here," I whisper when I finally let him go.

He laughs. "Rough day?"

I can't tell him about Holden's new, salacious threat.

He's taken the public appearances pretty well so far, but *no* boyfriend would be okay with some other guy groping his girlfriend, and if Indiana confronts him, Holden might make good on at least part of his threat.

And that's when I realize just how bad—and prolonged—this could be. Holden could tell the world that I pressed the button, and *still* have both my uncle's and my father's crimes to hold over my head.

But I have to tell Indiana something, before he figures out the truth from what I'm not saying.

"School doesn't feel the same." Though the truth is that school is exactly the same; I'm the one who's changed. "Penelope hates me, even though *she* slept with *my* boyfriend, and Holden is . . . Holden." I shrug as I press a button on my key fob to unlock the car. "Not gonna lie. There are times I wish he'd never made it out of the jungle."

"You don't mean that."

"No." As badly as I hate Holden, I still don't want to see him dead. That much has not changed. "But I *really* needed to say it."

"Want to eat on the beach?"

"Yes," I say as I slide behind the wheel. "How do you feel about sushi?"

Indiana sinks into the passenger's seat. "Not as good as I feel about teriyaki."

"Coming up." Pulling forward out of my parking space, I use the hands-free system to call the sushi place and add Indiana's order to mine and explain—politely—that we're in a hurry. They know me by name. They're used to my rush requests. And they know I'll leave a tip as big as the bill.

As I turn left out of the lot, an uneasy feeling crawls over the back of my neck. As if I'm being watched. I glance into the rearview mirror, my hand clenching around the steering wheel. I fully expect to find Silvana standing beneath the huge oak tree in front of the academic complex—my school's main building.

Instead, I see Holden, watching with a dark scowl as I drive off with Indiana.

People will listen.

MADDIE

I walk into the cafeteria with Kathryn Coppela, just like I have after fourth period all year long. Trying to pretend this is just a normal day.

Back to school: take two.

Today, I've managed to avoid reading about the *Splendor* victims on my phone *and* getting called on in physics.

Carrying my tray of lasagna and iceberg salad, I glance at the table where we usually sit. Then I glance at Luke's table.

Kathryn elbows me and smiles. "You want to sit with him?"

"Is it that obvious?" My face feels warm. I feel like everyone's watching me. Because they are.

She shrugs. "I'm just glad something good came out of the whole thing. Especially after . . ."

She doesn't need to finish the sentence. It doesn't matter whether she was going to mention my dead brother, my secretly-not-dead father, or my wishes-she-were-dead mother. It's the depressing thought that counts.

"Thanks." I head for Luke's table, and Kathryn follows me. When I turn back to glance at her in surprise, she shrugs. "Can I sit with you guys?"

"Yeah. Please."

Luke stands when he sees us coming and introduces Kathryn to Michael, Landon, and Jayesh, who are already seated at the table, along with Jayesh's girlfriend, Ashley. We're short one chair, but before I can even ask, Landon has pulled one over from another table.

"Thanks," I say as I set my tray on the table next to Luke's.

Kathryn and I sit and everyone is friendly. Everyone gets along. And for just a minute, I feel like two halves of my life have peacefully merged.

Then I notice that the buzz of conversation has gotten much softer than usual. I twist in my chair to find that half of the cafeteria is staring at me. A few people don't even bother to look away when I make eye contact.

The stares don't look mean. They just look . . . curious. Interested. I'd hoped that the attention would fade over the weekend, but that clearly hasn't happened.

Luke wasn't the only one around here who no one noticed before spring break.

"How long do you think this'll last?" I ask as I turn back to the table.

"Probably as long as Holden keeps the story alive," Luke says.

"Well then, that could be forever. He loves nothing so much as the sound of his own voice."

Ashley gestures in my direction with a cherry tomato speared on the end of her fork. "You know what they say—if you can't stop people from talking, change the conversation."

I nod as I cut a corner from my slab of lasagna. "What happened to us isn't even what we should be talking about. Our kidnapping was only noteworthy because of how rarely it actually happens. What we should be talking about are Colombia's real issues."

Luke shrugs as he pours a tiny cup of Italian dressing onto his salad. "So talk about it. You have a platform now. People will listen."

"Talking about it isn't enough," I tell them as a new idea begins to form. "We need to *do* something about it." I turn to Luke. "We need to find a way to take action. To give back." To make up, in some way, for the damage my father has done. To get back to the cause he fought for, before his passion became a psychotic obsession.

"What do you suggest?" Luke asks.

"I don't know." I have to think about that for a minute.

We eat in an awkward silence for a while, Kathryn's gaze flitting from one of Luke's friends to the next while she chews. Eventually Jayesh and Ashley break the silence with a good-natured argument about some kind of open-source software I've never heard of, and his other friends each take a side.

Kathryn glances at me almost shyly. "Thanks for letting me join you," she whispers, as if the discussion going on around us is a shield, letting her talk to me privately beneath its cover. "I'm sorry I kind of ran out on you the other day. At your apartment. But I didn't know how to . . . I mean, everything I started to say seemed so . . ."

"I get it." I mean, what do you say to the girl who saw her brother murdered and barely escaped the jungle with her life?

So glad you didn't die?

I bet my stay-cation looks great now?

Can you recommend a good mosquito repellent?

I mean, it's not like Hallmark makes a greeting card for this.

"I'm so sorry about Ryan," she says, holding my gaze though the subject obviously makes her uncomfortable. "I always liked him. He and I . . . I guess you knew that we went out for a while. Last year. After your dad . . ."

My fork drops onto my tray with a startling clang, and the software discussion dies as everyone around us turns to look at me.

"No, I didn't know."

"I . . ." Kathryn's forehead furrows. "We didn't want to tell you at the time. In case it didn't work out, we didn't want there to be any awkwardness between you and me. But I figured afterward he would have told you. . . ."

No one told me. Another lie of omission.

"Excuse me. I have to—" I stand and race-walk out of

the cafeteria, desperate for some space.

My father. My mother. My uncle. My brother. My cousin. My friend.

Was *anything* true about my life before the jungle?

When I finally look up, I realize my feet have carried me on autopilot to the science hall, where my locker—

I stumble to a stop in the middle of the empty hallway. Chills race over my arms, raising goose bumps.

"Liar" is written across the front of my locker in black block letters.

4 DAYS, 4 HOURS EARLIER

Intent matters.

GENESIS

"There has to be a way out of this," I say as I pick up my mug. The ocean breeze blows over a page from my textbook. My second day back at school was no better than my first, and I cannot spend another moment under Holden's thumb.

Indiana arches one brow at me. "A way out of European History? I suspect most of Germany feels the same way."

"Ha." I close the book. I haven't processed a sentence I've read in the past hour anyway. "A way out of the warped mythology Holden is creating to replace our actual breakup." Though he doesn't know the extent of Holden's latest threats. "At this rate, I'll wake up tomorrow and turn on the TV to find that he and I are married, and the country is eagerly anticipating the national symbol of hope that is our love child. How can so many people believe so many lies, just because a rich white guy says them on television?"

Indiana laughs. "The solution seems obvious." He shrugs. "Stop playing along."

"That makes a certain crazy sense." I give him a facetious

nod. "Yet the premise seems flawed. If he throws me under the bus, I can't defend myself thanks to the NDA—"

"Genesis!"

I jump in my seat, startled by the woman in her thirties who's just shouted my name from across the outdoor café. I've never seen her before, yet she seems to know me—not an entirely unusual situation.

She stops next to our table and smiles down at me, as if she can't even see Indiana. Or the fact that we were having a private conversation. "I wasn't sure that was actually you. You looked different on TV. But then I shouted your name, and you looked up, so . . ." Her smile is so bright it's giving me a migraine.

"Is there something I can do for you?" I ask. Then I add a smile.

Indiana hides his grin behind his mug as he raises it for a sip.

"I just wanted to tell you that we were all praying for you while you were out there. What you and those others went through . . . It was a wake-up call for America. It really brought us together. It's terrifying to realize how unsafe some third-world countries still are. For Americans."

The hair on the back of my neck rises as my blood begins to boil. "First of all, Colombia isn't a third-world country. It's an emerging economy." Thank you, World Geography, freshman year. "Second of all, the people kidnapped with us weren't even all from the US—you just didn't hear about the victims the US media doesn't consider relevant to its viewership. And *third* . . ." Indiana is covering a huge grin while the lady stares at me in utter confusion. "What happened to us was an isolated incident, and you can't draw sweeping conclusions about the world's sociological climate from a single event."

I'm well aware that I sound just like Maddie. I'm equally well aware that the truth has just gone right over this woman's head with an almost audible *swoosh* sound.

Imagine how confused she'd be if I reminded her that Colombia is in South *America*.

The frown lines in her forehead smooth out, and I can practically see her donning sociopolitical blinders—an adult's security blanket. "Well, either way, you sure were lucky to have your boyfriend in the jungle with you. Can you imagine what might have happened to you out there without him?"

Easily. I might not have been asked to sleep with our kidnappers so he could grab a gun.

I might not have to talk to idiots like this woman, because I would have limped out of the jungle on my own, instead of in the arms of a self-centered, opportunistic jackass like Holden Wainwright.

Indiana sets his mug on the table and looks at me with faux shocked-wide eyes. "You might have had to carry your own backpack or fight your own battles."

I fan my face with one hand. "How would I *ever* have survived?"

The woman makes an insulted sound at the back of her

throat, then walks back to her table looking confused.

"Seriously," Indiana says when she's out of earshot and we're done laughing, "if you want to suck the wind out of Holden's sails, stop legitimizing his fantasy with your participation. Tell the world that you dumped him."

Sounds easy, but . . . "Even if this were just about what *I* did—"

"Genesis." Indiana lowers his voice to a whisper and leans toward me across the small table. "You took on a huge personal risk in an attempt to save lives, when Holden was willing to let people die to save himself. You had no idea the bombs had already changed hands. People will understand that."

"Will they?" Would the relatives of the victims believe I was justified in what I did?

"I have to believe that most people will." His gaze is optimistic, but intense. "Intent matters."

"I hope you're right, but I don't know that I can take that chance." I don't have the right to choose my happiness—and a very satisfying blow to Holden's ego—over the well-being of my family. "He'll tell the world about Maddie's dad." I can't do that to my cousin or her mom.

"Honestly, G, I don't think it'll come to that," Indiana says. "Homeland Security made you sign an NDA and threatened to charge me with obstruction if I talked about their investigation. Shouldn't we assume they said the same thing to Holden?"

"Maybe." I nod slowly, thinking it through as I blow

into my steaming mug. "But I doubt that'll keep Holden quiet." In fact, based on yesterday's confrontation, I *know* it won't. "He's not afraid of an obstruction charge. His parents' lawyers cast a long shadow." As do my father's—assuming we can afford to pay them. If the government were only threatening me with obstruction, I might not be afraid of the charges either.

But if Holden calls me a murderer and I defend myself in the media, Homeland Security will let the state of Florida charge me with involuntary manslaughter.

I could *actually* wind up in prison. For telling the truth.

4 DAYS, 1 HOUR EARLIER

You'll be a hero.

MADDIE

"You want me to *what*?" Holden demands in a fierce whisper as a woman wearing a headset pins a microphone to his shirt.

"Don't act like this makes no sense," I snap. Normally this is the point at which Genesis would step between me and Holden, but this time she seems willing to let things play out. Probably because Holden so clearly hates my idea. "Your family's annual benefit is already in the works. We all know that. I'm just asking you to ask your parents to donate some of the proceeds to a charity to help Colombian farmers."

And frankly, I'm proud of the idea. For having found a way to shine the spotlight where it should be—on ways to help the Colombian people—and shift the national conversation from the Holden-Genesis faux romance.

Holden rolls his eyes. "The benefit is this weekend, Maddie. It's not just in the works. It's in the bag. My mom works on this thing all year long. I may be her kid, but the

Wainwright Foundation's benefit is her *baby*."

"It's never too late until it's over," I insist.

"It's too late," he insists. "They've already announced that the money's going to the homeless."

"To the children's cancer ward," Genesis corrects him as the production assistant fits her with her own microphone.

"Whatever," Holden growls. It's like he doesn't even see the staff buzzing around getting things ready, easily within earshot of his apathy. "My point is that they can't just take money away from those sick, homeless children. It's already been announced."

"So make it a multi-platform charity," I insist. Genesis isn't the only Valencia who knows how to dig in and get what she wants. "Half of the money could go to the cancer ward—those kids aren't homeless, by the way—and half to disenfranchised Colombian farmers. With your celebrity, an announcement like that could increase attendance by forty or fifty percent. You could even raise the price of tickets. What is it now, thirty thousand a plate?"

"Fifty," he says, and the production assistant's eyes widen.

I know how she feels. That's way more than my mother makes in a year—assuming she doesn't lose her job over the work she's currently missing.

"Think about it," I say as the assistant begins herding Holden and Genesis toward two chairs in front of a big green screen. In five minutes, they'll be live via satellite with Jimmy Fallon. "More media coverage. More money going to charity. And all thanks to you. You'll be a hero."

Genesis rolls her eyes, but I can tell when Holden glances at her, both brows arched into question marks, that he didn't see. I'm surprised he still seems to want her opinion, after everything that's gone down between them. But then, that kind of makes sense. Genesis is the resident expert in the field of public opinion.

She shrugs as she takes a seat in her assigned chair. "You wanted to play the hero. We both know you're not going to go hammer nails into houses in person, so you might as well try philanthropy."

Holden glances from her back to me as the guy behind the camera begins to count down. Then Holden nods. "I'll talk to my mother."

I am always in control.

GENESIS

I can't get out of the chair fast enough. The lights are too bright. The woman trying to unhook my microphone is too slow. Too clumsy.

That's not true.

But it *feels* true, because I have to get out of here.

I pull the microphone from my shirt and slap the battery pack into the production assistant's hand, then I'm out. I want to run, but I know better. People who are in control don't run away.

I am always in control.

"Genesis," Holden snaps, and I walk past him.

"Genesis!" Maddie looks like she wants to say something, but I brush right by her.

Outside, I suck in a deep breath. The night tastes bitter, but the darkness feels calm. The sound of traffic is reassuring, because there was no traffic in the jungle.

My hand is still sweaty from being trapped in Holden's. I wipe my palm on my shorts, but I can't get the feel of him off my flesh. Out of my mind.

"Hey," Indiana says as he steps out of the building. "You okay?" He pulls me into a hug without waiting for some visual cue from me. For an invitation. He hugs me just because he thinks I need a hug.

And that turns out to be exactly what I need.

"I can't do this anymore." I wrap my arms around his neck and hold on hard, speaking right into his collarbone. I clench my jaw to hold back tears. I don't know what's wrong with me.

I'm stronger than this.

"I didn't watch." Indiana's hands slide down my back, and the chaste touch feels strangely comforting. "Did something happen?"

"Nothing new. He just . . ." I step back so I can see his face in the light from the security fixture overhead. "I feel trapped. We're out of the jungle, and I'm sleeping in my own bed, but every time I see Holden—every time I hear his name or see him on TV—I feel like I'm still back there. Still being held hostage."

"Okay, so do what you did then," Indiana suggests softly.

"Blow something up?" My bitter laugh sounds harsher than I intended. "That's how I got into this mess in the first place."

"No. Fight back. There wasn't a single moment in the jungle when you weren't plotting something, or in someone's face, or generally being awesome out loud. Why would you feel any more powerless here than you did out there?"

"I . . ." I frown, thinking that over. Why *would* I feel more powerless here?

Because the threat of prison and love for my family are preventing me from taking away Holden's advantage, by simply telling the world what I did.

What I need is a way to put *his* freedom in jeopardy. Something that incriminates him. A mutually assured destruction kind of truce.

Rog.

Holden killed Rog, and there was no one around to verify his claim of self-defense, other than Indiana and me.

Holden doesn't know that I don't still have the clothes he wore onto my father's jet that day—still stained with Rog's blood. Immortalized in the very picture that made him look like a hero to the rest of the world.

"You're right." I smile up at Indiana and already I feel better. I have a plan. "Tomorrow, I'm going to get Holden alone and put an end to this bullshit. Once and for all." I'm going to reclaim my life, and kick him out of it.

Indiana smiles. "Good. I look forward to the return of the beautiful badass I met on a beach at Cabo San Juan."

"Yeah, me too."

Her son is a friend of yours.

MADDIE

"How many multiple-choice questions are there?" Kathryn asks.

Anna Wilson grabs a handful of peanut butter M&M's from the bowl across my small dinner table and rolls them around in her palm. "Between fifty-two and fifty-five."

I wasn't sure they were actually going to show up for study group, after the locker incident. I was still scrubbing the paint—I think it was liquid shoe polish—when the bell rang. Surely they saw it.

Surely *everyone* saw it.

"I'd do a hundred multiple-choice questions if that would get me out of the essays," Kathryn says.

When they go quiet, except for Anna's crunching, I look up to find them both staring at me. It's been at least five minutes since I said anything. Or maybe one of them asked me a question. "Sorry." I grab an M&M and toss it into my mouth, but it's tasteless. "What were we talking about?"

"We can do this later." Kathryn closes her study guide

and stands. "You just got back. This isn't the time to—"

"There *is* no more time," Anna objects. "The exam is next week, and you already skipped the practice test."

I cringe, hoping my mother can't hear us over the sound of running water in the kitchen, where she's doing dishes. The practice test began and ended while I was in the hospital with my mother. I hadn't even realized I'd missed it until it was already over.

My mom doesn't need to add the AP practice test to the list of things she's worried about.

"Do you want us to go?" Kathryn says. "You shouldn't have to think about this the night before . . ."

Ryan's funeral.

"No." I shake my head and try to focus on the study guide. "This is what I need to be doing." I should be glad for the distraction.

As we're quizzing each other from the study guide, my phone rings. I don't recognize the number, so I don't answer.

A minute later, it rings again. From the same number.

Huffing in frustration, I reach for the phone, but my mother beats me to it. "I'm sorry, but we're not speaking to the press. So please stop—" Her eyes widen and her mouth snaps closed. She listens for a moment.

I don't recognize the female voice I can hear from the other end of the line.

My mother presses the mute button on my phone. "Madalena, do you know a woman named Elizabeth Wainwright? She says her son is a friend of yours?"

"Wainwright?" Anna says. "As in, Holden Wainwright? Your cousin's boyfriend? You're so lucky he was out there in the jungle with you. He is *so* hot."

I didn't know so many fallacies could be uttered in a single breath.

"Maddie?" My mom has good reason to look confused. I've never once mentioned Holden as a friend. But his mother, founder and executive director of the Wainwright Foundation, could be a very good friend, both to me and to the Colombian people.

"Yes. Thanks." I take my cell from her and unmute the phone. "Mrs. Wainwright? This is Maddie Valencia."

"Hello, Maddie. It's late, and I'm sure that you're busy, so let me get right to the point. My son tells me that the dual charity idea for our annual benefit was your idea."

"Um . . . yes. I hope I haven't overstepped. I just thought it might be nice to—"

"I think it's a wonderful idea. I've already sent out a press release announcing the change, and I wondered if you'd like to be an active part of the benefit. Beyond the idea phase, I mean. High-level participation in an event of this scale looks very good on college scholarship applications. In fact, the Wainwright Foundation itself sponsors several of those scholarships. . . ."

I don't really hear the rest of what she's saying because I'm already ready to jump at the opportunity. Even though Holden has clearly pitched me to his mother as a two-for-one good press opportunity: be seen giving money to poor

Colombian farmers *while* helping a less fortunate and publicly sympathetic kid pay for college.

Whatever. I can live with her using me as long as I get to use her back.

"Yes. Thank you. I'm in."

"Oh, I'm so glad!" Her voice has that over-the-top delighted quality that my cousin and her friends always seem to develop when something brand-new and exciting goes their way. As if they didn't see it coming.

"All of our positions at the Wainwright Foundation are volunteer positions, of course. We can give more to charity if we don't also have to pay salaries."

"Of course," I say, as if I didn't know that Holden's mother's annual salon budget could probably feed a small island nation for a year.

"I'll be in touch again soon with a summary of your responsibilities."

"I'll be looking forward to it."

"Wonderful. Oh, and if you can, tune into CNN tonight. The national press has been alerted to the change, and the Foundation's publicist tells me that they'll be mentioning it on air!"

"Great!" That, I truly mean. This is the kind of thing the media *should* be covering, instead of what kind of shoes Genesis and her friends were wearing when they were kidnapped in the jungle.

"What was that all about?" my mother asks as I hang up the phone and grab the remote control. Kathryn and Anna look just as interested in my conversation with one of the wealthiest women in the country.

"I'll explain in a minute," I say as I turn the TV to CNN.

On screen, an attractive man with prematurely silver hair sits behind the anchor's desk, talking about the ever-evolving conflict in the Middle East. I turn the volume down a little but leave it playing as I explain about my idea for the Wainwright Foundation's benefit. While Kathryn and Anna gossip-gush about Holden—whom they've obviously never met—I text Genesis to tell her about the phone call. Then I drag Kathryn and Anna back into study mode, listening to the television in the background.

Half an hour later, as they're packing up their stuff to go home, a new voice from the TV catches my attention. The male anchor is gone, and I don't recognize the woman who's taken his place, but hearing my own last name on the news makes my ears perk up. I raise the volume, expecting to hear about my contribution to the Wainwright Foundation's annual benefit, but instead, I see Neda's face on the screen, frozen in midword in an inset above the anchor's right shoulder.

That takes me a minute to process. And finally I understand.

Anger crawls across my skin, stinging like a sunburn. Rather than run a story about a philanthropic foundation's contribution to charity, they've chosen to run gossip.

The national news has picked up Neda's webcast.

I accidentally stood her up.

GENESIS

"Why do you keep looking at your phone?" Indiana asks as I set my cell down on the couch for the fifth time in as many minutes. He runs one hand up my arm, and warmth echoes across my skin in the wake of his touch. "I mean, if you don't want to do homework, I know of a much more pleasant way to waste time than waiting for a text."

"I'm not exactly waiting for a text. More like . . . hoping for one. I extended an olive branch to Penelope and I'm hoping she'll take it." And frankly, I think that was pretty big of me. Her anger should be at the guy who dumped her, not at her best friend since the fourth grade. "But I like the way you think."

I turn away from my phone and scoot closer to Indiana. His mouth turns up in a slow, smoldering smile when I slide one leg between him and the leather cushions. I lean forward and press my lips against the back of his jaw, near his left ear. His stubble scratches me, and I like it. It feels real. It grounds me in this moment and helps me push out everything else.

Indiana pulls back, and the caution in his expression frustrates me. "I feel obligated to mention that your dad could come home at any minute."

"Not likely." I lean in again and let my lips skim his neck as I speak. "He's meeting with his lawyers, and he's not a low-maintenance client. Especially now."

"Well, in that case . . ." Indiana slides one hand beneath my lower back and lifts me, then pulls me toward him. Beneath him. He's stretched out, half pressed between the length of my body and the back of the couch, half over me, and I—

"Wait." I put one hand on his chest. "You promised to tell me your real name when we got out of the jungle, yet somehow I still have no idea who you are." Though the truth is that I know exactly who Indiana is—just not what his parents named him.

His laugh sends a delicious spark up my spine. "My plan was to tell you as soon as the plane landed, but then there were paparazzi, and your dad and Holden were there."

"No one else is here now," I point out as I run my hands up his chest.

"But now the suspense has been built up so much that the reality can only be a disappointment." He grins. "You're just going to have to call me Indiana forever."

"I'm going to call you single if you don't tell me your name."

His brows rise. "You're bluffing."

I am totally bluffing. But I'm also desperate to know who I'm making out with. "Tell me your name, or I'm going to let my dad hire a private detective. Or ask Luke to run your picture through his facial recognition software."

"Fine." Indiana heaves a dramatic sigh. "My real name is Cole Benton. But if you send your dad's detective after me, tell him the thirty-two-year-old Cole Benton who was arrested for stealing beer from a convenience store is not me."

"Too bad." I grin at him, mentally trying to attach the new name to a face I already know by heart. But I'm not sure I can think of him as anything but Indiana. "That would have made you sound pretty interesting."

"And hiking back into the jungle to find you—with a head wound—doesn't?"

"You're right. That's much hotter than stealing beer." I slide my hand behind his neck and tug him down again until—

My phone buzzes, and I fumble for it.

Indiana groans, but a smile peeks out from his frustration as he reaches over me, then hands me my cell. He can see that I'm relieved.

Until I realize the text is from Maddie, not Penelope. I frown as I read it.

"What's wrong?"

"Nothing." I drop my phone on the floor without returning the text. "Holden's mom offered Maddie a volunteer position at the Wainwright Foundation. Now where were we?"

"Just about . . . here." Indiana's hand slides beneath my shirt and up my side. His touch demands nothing yet promises everything.

How could I ever have settled for a guy like Holden? How could I have demanded so much from life, and from school, and from *myself*, yet so little from him?

"Before this goes any further, are you sure you don't need to be doing homework right now?" he whispers. His breath on my neck gives me chills.

"I'm pretty sure I can get most of my teachers to exempt me from makeup work, considering the trauma I've been through."

I block out thoughts of the jungle with a kiss, then I slide my hands beneath his shirt and pull it over his head. It lands on the floor over my phone. Just as my phone begins to ring.

Indiana lowers himself to move his shirt, and his chest is pressed against me. It's a delicious weight.

"It's Maddie." His voice rumbles through me, and it takes me a second to focus on what he's said. "You want to answer?"

"No. I can hear about the benefit tomorrow."

"I agree." He presses a button to reject the call, then settles over me with one knee between my thighs.

My phone begins to ring again almost immediately.

Growling in frustration, I fumble blindly on the floor for my phone. It's my cousin again. I answer the call. "Maddie. I'm busy. I'm happy for you, but—"

"Turn on the TV."

"What?" Something in her tone leaves me cold with dread. "What's going on?" I sit up, and Indiana is already searching for the remote control.

"Did you know Neda did a webshow today?"

"Damn it. I told her I'd go on it, since I accidentally stood her up last time."

"Well, she went on without you," Maddie says. "And CNN picked up the story."

"Why would CNN care about Neda's webshow?" I turn to Indiana, who's managed to get the TV on, but is struggling with the satellite cable. "I think it's channel 200."

"She has nearly half a million followers, Genesis. More than a million hits per video."

"I know, but—"

Indiana changes the channel, and my voice fades into shocked silence. Over the anchor's shoulder, there's an inset screen, frozen on a single image.

There I am on TV again. Making out with Indiana in the school parking lot.

Holden is going to *lose his shit*.

3 DAYS, 21 HOURS EARLIER

He wouldn't be that *cruel.*

MADDIE

"They are *crucifying* Genesis in the comments." Neda's video is like a train wreck. And as with any train wreck, I can't look away. "The internet is full of horrible people," I mumble as I scan the thread.

"Why are you reading that crap?" Luke asks as he types. "They're all assholes. Especially the idiot who said she ought to be thrown in jail for cheating on a national hero."

Stretched across my comforter on my stomach, I look over my own screen at him. He's hardly glanced up in the past hour. "How would you know that if you aren't reading the posts?"

"I read a few. But then I moved on." He still isn't looking up at me. Neither of us is even pretending to do homework anymore.

"What are you doing?" Curious, I shut my laptop and set it on my desk, then sit at the head of the bed with him, leaning against my pillows.

He's running a search, and it's brought up a full page of

results. "I'm looking for collateral damage. The real problem here isn't what strangers online are saying about your cousin."

Fresh fear burns along my nerve endings as what he's saying sinks in. "The real problem is what Holden will say. And do."

Luke knows about Holden's threats to ruin not just Genesis and her dad, but my mom and me as well. "If Neda's video pissed him off, he might have already started. The sooner we know what he's saying, and to whom, the better prepared we'll be."

We.

Holden didn't threaten to ruin Luke or his family, yet Luke is accepting my burden—my potential shame and humiliation—as his own.

A new warmth blossoms deep in my chest as I watch him. "I'm not finding anything yet," he says. "If Holden is going to start something, I'm guessing he'll wait until he can do it in front of a national audience."

"Tomorrow." He wouldn't be *that* cruel. Would he? Could he turn the world against my family on the day we bury my brother?

Luke closes his laptop and takes my hand.

"This is the last thing any of us needs. Especially Genesis. She's been different since she got back from the jungle." And though I know whatever my dad did to her isn't my fault, I still feel oddly guilty. Because he's *my* dad.

"Different how?" Luke asks. He only knew Genesis for a

matter of hours before we were kidnapped.

"She doesn't shop anymore. She was a social media *queen* before, but she hasn't posted anything at all since she got back. She's stopped hanging out with most of her friends. And she's stopped taking shots at my wardrobe entirely."

Luke shrugs, still glued to his screen. "Those sound like reasonable reactions to trauma, Maddie. And improvements upon her personality in general. And I don't think *any* of us are the same as we were before the kidnapping."

"I know. But it's more than that." I hesitate. I haven't told him this part yet. "She thinks she's seen Silvana. That crazy bitch who helped Sebastián march us into the jungle."

Luke looks at me over the screen, his fingers still on the keyboard. "Really?"

"Yeah. But no one else has seen her."

"And you don't believe her?"

"Flashbacks and reliving the traumatic event are hallmark symptoms of PTSD. It's entirely possible that's what's happening. But—" I hesitate. "The problem is that I think I *do* believe her. My dad and Sebastián both told her they would try to use us here, in the States, to trigger some kind of 'plan B.' I *really* want to believe they were just messing with her. But if Silvana *is* in Miami . . ."

The fear that thought brings—the idea that something as terrifying as what happened to us in the jungle could have followed us here, to our *home*—is more than I can truly process.

Even worse is the idea that one of us could unknowingly

be the trigger. As I think about that, an overwhelming sense of fear washes over me, like nothing I've felt since we made it out of the jungle.

How the hell are we supposed to stop something we don't even know we *may* be causing?

3 DAYS, 13 HOURS EARLIER

You gave me no choice!

GENESIS

I've never been at school this early in my life. First period doesn't start for another hour, but I was driving myself nuts sitting at home, refreshing Neda's YouTube page. Reading the comments. Searching for a reason not to *burn her site to the ground.* Metaphorically speaking.

Yet that's all I'm doing here in my car. Clicking refresh. Reading the comments.

Waiting for Neda to get to school.

How could she do this the night before Ryan's funeral?

What a tramp!

One guy isn't enough for Genesis Valencia?

How stupid can she be, making out with this guy right there in public. Did she think no one would see that?

Poor Holden. National hero, humiliated by his slut of a girlfriend on national television. Hey, Holden! I'm still available! And loyal!

I feel sick, which may be in part because I've had three cups of coffee, but no food.

A text appears on my screen. It's from Indiana.

Stop reading the comments.

I smile in spite of everything.

But I can't stop reading, and my smile is short-lived.

Slowly, the parking lot begins to fill up. People get out of their cars. Those who notice me stare and whisper, and I don't need to hear them to know what they're saying. This is the live version of Neda's comment thread.

Finally, Neda pulls into the lot with ten minutes to spare before first period. Holden hasn't shown up. Neither has Penelope.

I get out of the car and close my door softly. When I get close enough, I grab Neda's arm with one hand and rip the earbuds from her ears with the other. Shocked off balance, she turns to me, mouth open, ready to start screaming. A flicker of fear flashes over her expression, but it's much too little to mollify me.

"What. The. Hell?" I demand softly. She can—and has—ignored my texts, but she can't ignore me, live and in her face. "How could you do that? Today, of all days?" My father is at the airport right now, picking up my grandmother.

Neda frowns for a second, then her eyes widen. "The funeral. I didn't think about that last night—"

"That much is *crystal* clear," I snap. "Why, Neda? Why would you do that to me? Why would you do that to *Indiana*? We've never done anything to you!"

"You gave me no choice!" She scowls up at me with perfectly glossed lips, and I can't even remember if I put on mascara. "Twice you left me hanging, Genesis. Live on the air, with nothing to say and no one to interview. After I'd told my entire following that you'd be there. They wanted to see you. They wanted to talk to you. And you just turned your back on us all."

She can*not* be serious.

"In case you haven't noticed, I've been a little busy. Or did you forget that I nearly got put on the *terrorist watch list*?" I hiss the last three words, because people are still getting out of their cars, and though I can't stop them from staring, I can't let them hear any of this.

"Oh, please. You got the same interview with Homeland Security that we all got with the FBI, and that didn't stop anyone else from going on my show. But it's not just about that. You and Pen are supposed to be my best friends. We used to tell each other everything. And since you got back, I've been waiting for that to happen. I spent the whole time you were gone making sure the world didn't forget about you. I told stories on the air, and organized vigils, and took up donations to contribute to a ransom. And now you're back, and you've hardly said two words to me. Not even, 'I'm fine, Neda, but I need a little time to myself.' You just disappeared from my life. Then I get this footage . . ." She shrugs.

"Wait, what? Someone *sent* you the video?"

"Yeah. You thought I shot that?" Neda has the nerve to look offended. As if shooting the video herself is so much worse than airing it in front of the whole world.

"Who sent it?"

She rolls her eyes and tugs her designer bag higher on her shoulder. "I don't know. That's how anonymity works, Genesis."

Panic makes my pulse race. Someone's been watching me. *Spying* on me. Manipulating me through Neda.

Silvana? Uncle David?

I shake off paranoid thoughts and refocus on Neda, clutching my car keys so tightly they cut into my hand. "So you don't even know who sent the video, but you put it on your show and felt justified speculating on who my new 'boy toy' is?"

"Okay, you can get mad about the video, but you can't get mad about that. My coverage was totally flattering. I said you two make a hot couple, and I wasn't lying when I said I don't know who the guy is. We don't even know his real name. Don't you think that's a little weird? Because Maddie, Luke, and I do."

"I know his real name, Neda. I haven't told anyone else because I don't want him dragged into the spotlight—especially now. And since when are you friends with Maddie and Luke?" Have they been talking behind my back?

"I don't know if I'd call them *friends*, but they answer my calls! And they went on my show!"

I cross my arms over my chest and press my lips together as a trio of girls walks by us on their way into the building, obviously trying to listen.

They probably didn't expect me to come to school, because of the funeral this afternoon. But I won't hide behind Ryan.

Valencias face their problems head-on.

"Okay." I close my eyes and take a deep breath when I hear the door close at my back. "All of that is beside the point."

"It is not beside the point. Friendship *matters*, Genesis! At least, it used to. And by the way, I didn't just do this for me. I did it for Penelope too. Holden *humiliated* her on national television. He deserves to be humiliated in return."

"Yeah. Only you haven't humiliated Holden. You've turned him into some kind of romantic martyr. Girls are offering him their virginity in the comments!"

Neda shrugs, but I can see regret beginning to develop behind her eyes. She's finally starting to get it. "Hey, it's my job to report the news. I can't be held responsible for what people do with it."

"That is not your job—"

"Yes it is," she snaps. "I'm getting paid by my sponsors."

As if she needs money.

"Neda, do you have *any idea* what you've done?" I demand at last. But of course she doesn't. Because she doesn't understand the agreement Holden and I had, or what the consequences for me and my family will be, now that she's stomped all over our tense truce.

She doesn't understand that I was *this close* to putting him in his place, but that won't be possible now, because when Holden gets mad, he wants to burn down the whole building. Even if he's still standing in it.

3 DAYS, 7 HOURS EARLIER

It's all we have.

MADDIE

My uncle, my mother, my *abuela*, Genesis, and I sit in the limo in silence punctuated by sniffles. We are a Franken-family—the patched-together pieces of two normal families somehow lumbering along in defiance of several natural laws.

This is not normal. But it's all we have.

My mom is sedated. She stares blankly through tear-filled eyes, her head on my uncle's shoulder. His arm around her back.

Genesis and I sit across from them, watching this parental grief play out with a mismatched set of parents. Abuela sits next to my uncle, and I want to ask her how much she truly understands about the twisted branches of our family tree, but this is not the right time.

There may never be a right time.

No one speaks. No one's really crying. This drive to the cemetery is like putting the ceremony on pause, so we can relocate from the church to the graveside and start saying good-bye all over again.

I want this to be over. Yet I don't want it to happen at all.

Ryan's death has come at me in stages, from the sharp horror of the moment I saw him gunned down in defense of me to the miles and miles of denial while we were marched into the jungle by our captors. Since then, his absence has become a painful and constant ache, which is more pronounced with quiet and solitude.

But today . . .

Sitting through his funeral was like reopening that wound. Like twisting the knife in my gut.

Like losing him all over again.

"Oh, shit," Genesis whispers as the limo turns into the cemetery. I follow her gaze to see that reporters have descended upon the grave site.

"Vultures," Abuela murmurs.

"We anticipated this," her father says, his voice soothing as he rubs my mother's back. "Let security handle it."

But security can only keep the photographers back, and distance won't stop photography or filming.

I can feel cameras aimed at me as we get out of the car, my heels clicking a little on the pavement. Luke and Indiana join us for the short walk to the grave, where the rest of the mourners have already gathered, but there are only five graveside chairs.

Abuela, Genesis, her dad, my mother, and I sit. I try to focus on the prayer. On the beautiful things the pastor is saying about my brother. But I am hyperaware of the cameras. Of the blogs and gossip sites that will criticize my dress and declare that I'm either coldly unaffected by my brother's death or completely crippled by grief.

Forget about them.

As if he can hear my thoughts, Luke puts his hand on my shoulder, a silent reminder that he's there. That he's with me.

On his left, Penelope and Neda wear black designer dresses and identical tearful expressions. They may be spoiled, but they did love Ryan.

On the edge of the crowd, Holden is alternately texting and glaring at Genesis. I wish he hadn't come.

I wish I'd had the nerve to tell him not to.

My mother cries softly as the casket disappears into the ground. I should lean over and comfort her. At least take her hand. But Uncle Hernán already has his arm around her shoulders, and despite the part he unwittingly played in my brother's death, I can't bring myself to hate him today.

People are leaving. Uncle Hernán helps my mother up, and I rise with them, my gaze scanning the crowd. Kathryn Coppela stands on the other side of the grave, with some friends from school. The principal has come, and I recognize several of Ryan's teachers.

Penelope and Neda are already heading for their car, balanced awkwardly on the toes of their stilettos so their heels won't sink into the earth. Indiana stands next to Genesis with his hands in the pockets of his black suit pants.

My mother looks like she'd blow over in a strong breeze. I don't think she's eaten anything all day. I should help her to the car, but Uncle Hernán has one arm around her waist, already escorting her to the limo. He's practically holding her up. Abuela follows them, dabbing her damp eyes with a tissue.

"You ready?" Luke whispers, and his hand slides into my grip.

I shake my head. It can't be over already. I don't want to leave Ryan.

Not again.

But when the workers remove the device that lowered the coffin, I realize I don't want to see him buried again either. Luke and I head for the limo.

Abuela, my mother, my uncle, and my cousin are already inside, and as Indiana ducks in to take the seat next to Genesis, I notice a car idling across the way, on the narrow paved road that winds through the cemetery. The tinted window rolls up as I watch, but not before I catch a glimpse of the driver's face.

Silvana.

Genesis isn't imagining things. She's real. She's here, in Miami.

But *why* is she here?

Luke clears his throat, waiting for me to get into the car, and I turn back to the limo, rubbing the chill bumps that have risen on my arms. I need to talk to Genesis, both about Silvana and about the anonymous texts.

But this isn't the time.

I've forgiven you.

GENESIS

My father insisted on holding the reception at our house. The caterers have set up a beautiful buffet and several waiters circulate unobtrusively, making sure everyone who wants a drink has one.

I take a single glass of white wine, and my dad only lets me have that because my hands are visibly shaking. Though the truth is that I could probably get away with much more.

My grandmother refuses to leave the kitchen, where she's harassing the caterers in an attempt to be helpful, and every time I try to get her to come out she pats my arm and tells me what a handful Ryan was as a toddler, then tries to get me to eat something.

My dad's responding to questions with monosyllabic answers and his eyes are unfocused. He hasn't wandered more than two feet away from my aunt Daniela since the funeral. I've never seen him like this.

I was young when my mother died, but I remember her funeral, and I remember my father. He was shattered but strong. He never even cried in front of me.

On an intellectual level, I know that he buried his child today. But he never publicly acknowledged Ryan as his, so it never occurred to me that he would mourn him not as a nephew, but as a son. That he would be just as devastated as Maddie and Aunt Daniela are.

As I am.

Ryan is gone.

Somehow that feels more true now that I've seen the coffin.

"Want me to get you a plate?" Indiana sinks onto the couch next to me.

I shake my head and sip my wine, staring out at the beach through the wall of glass that defines the far side of my living room. The beach used to feel peaceful. Now it's a reminder of everything that went down in the jungle. "Thanks, but I'm not hungry." If anything, I need a pain-killer.

My head is killing me, and my thoughts feel mushy— the mental equivalent of slurred speech.

Indiana nods and winds his fingers between mine, and I take a break from self-pity to be glad he's not the kind of guy who tries to tell me how to take care of myself. I know I shouldn't have wine on an empty stomach and I've decided to do it anyway.

Today we buried my brother and the internet declared me a whore.

I feel like drinking.

People mill all around us, eating and whispering to one another. Staring out at the waves and in at the mourners. Penelope and Neda are here, but they keep their distance. Indiana and I have turned this couch into a private island, and my expression is a clear warning for people to stay away.

Which is how I know, when someone sinks onto the couch on my other side, exactly who it is.

"Gen." Holden doesn't sound mad. I'm immediately suspicious. "Let's talk."

Indiana's hand tightens around mine, and though I can feel true anger emanating from him for only the second time since we met, he says nothing. This is my decision.

I'm too tired to mentally spar with Holden. My head hurts. My heart hurts. But a Valencia never backs down from a fight.

I finish my wine and set the stemmed glass on the coffee table, an irregular slab of white granite on steel legs, then I stand. "I'll be back in five," I whisper to Indiana.

Holden follows me out the oversized sliding glass door, and I close it behind us, then lead him to a corner of the deck not visible from inside the house. The crash of waves over the sand is a clock counting down the seconds. The scent of the water takes me right back to Cabo San Juan.

"Are you really going to do this today?" I demand in as soft a voice as I can manage. "This is a new low."

"You can't blame me for the timing. This was all you. And Neda." He pulls his phone from his pocket and opens the browser, then shows me the screen.

It's the home page of an online tabloid, and there at the top is a still shot of Indiana and me making out in the school parking lot.

The headline reads:

Trouble in Paradise? America's Sweetheart Betrays National Hero.

"The print version is even more . . . impactful," he tells me.

The world no longer makes sense.

If he's expecting an apology, he's about to be sorely disappointed.

I shrug. "You and I are not a couple. *You're* the one who's been lying on national television."

"You went along with it," he points out. "We both look like idiots today. So here's what's going to happen. Raina's booked us on a talk show at eight tomorrow morning. We're going to go on and say that trauma and the stress of the spotlight has gotten to us both. To you especially. That you're still suffering from PTSD and that you're seeing things. We'll tell them that you're in therapy, and that I've forgiven you. That I'm dedicated to helping you through this difficult time." He shrugs with a smile, as if I should be proud of the bullshit "solution" he—or maybe Raina—has come up with. "Lemons into lemonade."

I can't believe this is happening. He's giving me detailed instructions on how to participate in my own humiliation, twenty feet from where two hundred people are gathered to mourn my brother. Holden *truly* has no shame.

"No." I should probably start with something less directly oppositional, considering the ammunition he has against me, but I can't. "This is a *funeral*, Holden. Get out, before I have you thrown out."

"Gen . . ." His eyes narrow and his jaw clenches. He runs one finger down my cheek, and I slap his hand away, fuming. "They *just* put Ryan in the ground. Your aunt *just* tried to kill herself. How is she going to react to the world knowing that her 'dead' husband is actually a living terrorist?" He shrugs. "I'm sure the stress won't make her want to try again with a bigger bottle."

I'm supposed to be afraid of him, but I'm actually a little relieved by how predictable his threat is. This is the Holden of old. The one who only needs to *think* he's won.

"Why do you even want people to think we're a couple?" So that he can be the one to dump me? Or just to keep Indiana and me from being happy?

I put one hand on his arm and swallow my revulsion. "The whole country loves you, Holden. This is your chance to enjoy being an eligible hero instead of being stuck with your ex. So you go on TV and tell the world that you're newly single. Laugh it off. The video will be an inside joke between you and the rest of the world, and they'll love it. They'll feel like they know you personally." My father taught me that. It's one of the best ways to manipulate a wannabe. "You're the world's most eligible bachelor, but you're not ready to settle down. You want to take your time. Find the right girl. And girls will *line up* for the chance to prove they're the one."

Holden's brows dip. "You just don't want to answer questions about the video."

"Yes, and you shouldn't want me to either. It'll look like you lost me to Indiana. Don't be the victim, Holden. Be the victor. Show them this is my loss." I pause and give him a thoughtful frown. "This is a solid PR move, Holden. I'm surprised it's not what Raina's suggesting."

He blinks, trying a little too hard to hide his thoughts, and I realize that's *exactly* what his publicist has suggested. But he was too stubborn to let me go on my own terms rather than keeping me at his mercy. Or dumping me in some publicly humiliating way.

Or both.

He studies me, obviously suspicious. "You're okay with the world calling you a slut and me a hero?"

For a moment, I can only stare at him. "People see what they want to see. I couldn't change that even if you went on TV with the letter A drawn on your chest in your own blood." And the world has been in love with the slut-hero dichotomy since long before women had the legal right to make their own decisions. "So I'll be the girl who cheated on you until I fade out of the spotlight. This way we both win. You get fame, and I get anonymity."

Holden thinks about that, and I can practically see the gears turning behind his eyes. Then he nods slowly. "Okay,

I'll give you anonymity," he agrees, and I want to smack the magnanimous look off his face. "But you're still coming on the show. We'll just announce that we're parting ways and we'll show that it's amicable. That way I look even better. For not holding a grudge."

"Holden—"

His gaze hardens. "This will be the last time. If you show up, you'll be done with me. If you don't, I *will* destroy your whole family on national television."

I nod, because I clearly have no choice. Still, I'm a little surprised that we've actually come to an agreement, because Holden typically considers compromise to be a subcategory of loss. But he's talked me into doing television with him again, so in his mind, he's probably won. And the truth is that if I don't perform to his satisfaction on the air, there's nothing to stop him from painting me as a devious slut in front of the entire world.

As he leaves, flaunting a victorious strut wholly inappropriate for a funeral, I realize that this time, he may be right.

In compromising with Holden, I might very well have accepted a loss.

I need to be alone.

MADDIE

The crowd is too much. The continuous line of friends and strangers all telling me how much my brother meant to them—as if the fact that *they've* suffered a loss too could possibly make me feel better about my own. . . .

I know they mean well. But I don't care.

I push my way through the crowd toward one of the sliding glass doors and exhale as I step off the porch onto the private stretch of beach. I've always found it obscene that a strip of beach can be declared off-limits to the public, but suddenly I'm grateful that this one is.

I need to be alone.

Inhaling the sea air, I step out of my shoes and sit in a grassy patch of sand in front of the deck, where no one inside can see me. I don't care if the sand ruins my dress. I can't remember Ryan with people constantly offering me food and asking me how I am.

I can't say good-bye to him in the middle of a crowd.

Behind me, the door slides open, and I start to stand,

assuming Luke has followed me out. But then Holden's voice freezes me where I am.

The sliding door clicks shut. "She seems to think she can talk her way out of it," he says, and when there's no reply, I realize he's on his phone. "As if everything's up for negotiation."

I can't hear the voice on the other end of the line.

Holden's footsteps come closer, and I scoot back until I'm practically under the deck. "Yeah. The scotch was a good idea. Thanks." He pauses. "I'll let you know how it goes. But you can't call me—"

The door slides open again, and Holden's shoes squeak as he spins around. "I gotta go."

"Hey," Luke says.

"Hey." Then Holden's steps clomp toward the door and disappear into Genesis's house.

The door slides shut again and Luke jogs down the steps. "Maddie? Are you out here?"

"Yeah," I say, and he jumps, startled to find me just a couple of feet away. And on the ground.

"Are you hiding?"

"No." I tug him down next to me. "I'm declining company. Except for yours." His arm slides around my waist and I lay my head on his shoulder.

"And Holden's?"

I snort. "He didn't see me." I sit up and meet Luke's gaze, frowning. "Would you believe that bastard's *bragging* to someone about blackmailing Genesis?"

"To whom?"

"No idea. I can't think of anyone other than Pen who's truly loyal to Holden."

"*Is* she loyal to him? I mean, after he dumped her like that . . ."

"I don't know. I think she'd take him back, if he wanted her." I shake my head, mystified. "That girl can do, like, fifty backflips in a row and walk on her hands for a solid mile. You'd think she'd have a pretty strong spine, but she falls all over him every time Holden so much as smiles at her."

"I don't understand what she sees in him. What your cousin saw in him for so long."

"Well, you're asking the wrong person. I'd take you over Holden any day of the week. And twice on Wednesday."

Luke chuckles. "Today is Wednesday."

I lean forward until my mouth meets his. "What an incredible coincidence."

2 DAYS, 13 HOURS EARLIER

I can move on with my life.

GENESIS

"Are you ready?" the production assistant asks.

"Yes." *No.* But admitting that you're not ready for something never helps. "I'm sorry, what is your name?" I've seen her so often now that I can identify her perfume and her chewing gum, but I don't know what to call her.

She looks surprised by the question. "Marlena."

"Yes, Marlena, I think I'm ready. Thanks." I pat the microphone clipped to my shirt and decide to live with the fact that the battery pack is scraping my back raw again. I'm ready . . . to get this over with.

This time, there's no green screen. This time we're in a studio with an actual set: a chair and a love seat, angled to semi-face each other. There's a lamp and a rug, and a coffee table, where three steaming mugs have already been set out.

This time there's a reporter on set to interview us. In person. And she's not local. I recognize her face from the entertainment segment of a national news show, though I can't remember her name. The station sent her to us, last minute.

That realization resonates, and suddenly my nerves are back. Is this *that* big a story? How can they possibly justify this kind of expense for a segment that will end on a note of forgiveness with both of us deciding to move on?

"There they are." Marlena nods at the set, where both Holden and the reporter are taking their seats. Holden laughs at something the host says as she settles into her chair, and I take a deep breath.

Just get through it. Then I can move on with my life. Free from Holden.

I climb three steps onto the set and Holden moves down so I can have the half of the love seat closest to our interviewer.

"Hi, Genesis." She extends her hand for me to shake as I sit. "I just want to make sure you both understand that this is live television. So no profanity. Nothing crazy, or we'll be fined by the FCC."

"Yes, we've been briefed." This isn't my first rodeo, but with any luck, it'll be my last.

"Okay!" She settles back into her chair and tugs her skirt over her knees as she crosses her legs at the ankles. The cameraman begins counting down.

Holden looks too calm.

Unease crawls up my spine. Something isn't right. Suddenly I can feel his impending betrayal like the tip of a knife poking into my back.

Holden's going to go back on his word. He's going to talk about the video and "confirm" that it's me. That I cheated on him. Or he'll announce that he's forgiven me and we're moving on, totally abandoning his promise to let me go.

I stand, ready to walk off the set. But he grabs my hand and pulls me down next to him just as the cameraman mouths "one" and points his finger at us. We're live.

I freeze, staring at the camera. Unable to smile. Unable to *breathe*.

"Thanks, Don," the host says to her cohost, several hundred miles away. "I'm thrilled to be here today with Holden Wainwright and Genesis Valencia. By now most of you are familiar with the story of how they survived not just being kidnapped by terrorists in the Colombian jungle, but being *re*captured by those same terrorists after their friends had escaped. I can't even imagine." She turns a sympathetic gaze on us, and I don't realize that we're supposed to respond until Holden is already talking.

"It was tough," he says. "Demoralizing. It was like that moment in a scary movie where the girl gets her hand on the doorknob, but before she can escape into the yard, the killer grabs her and pulls her back."

"Except we didn't die," I point out. Then I feel like a fool. Of course we didn't die. How else would we be on live television?

"Yes. Well, this morning Holden and Genesis are here to make a little confession . . . !" Her voice rises into an excited pitch and she leans forward in anticipation.

292

Chills roll across my skin. This kind of excitement is usually reserved for cheesy talk show hosts announcing the results of paternity tests. What the hell has Holden's publicist told her we're going to say?

"Holden?" the host prompts with a supportive nod.

"Okay." He swallows thickly, visibly, and I can practically feel sympathy pouring in for him over the airwaves. "This isn't an easy thing for us to admit, and I want to thank Genesis for the courage she's shown by coming on with me today."

The knot in my stomach grows until it's all I can feel, pinning me to my chair like an anchor to the ocean floor.

"I'm sure many of you saw the video that surfaced recently."

My face is on fire. I should have known he'd do this. That he'd say whatever it took to get me on TV, then stab me in the back.

"And I know most of you are thinking some pretty uncharitable things about Genesis right now. But I want to ask you to stop. You don't know her. You don't know what she's going through. You don't know what she's been through."

I am frozen—a painful irony considering how flushed every inch of my skin feels. I've become a human coal burning from the inside out with fear and humiliation.

"Genesis is seeing a therapist to help her deal with what happened last week in the jungle. But it's been rough going. She's struggling to adjust to being back and to put everything behind her. And I think you'll all understand why she did what she did on that video if you knew what she's privately trying to overcome."

Nonononono.

"Holden," I croak, but his name hardly carries any sound.

"What you don't know is that while we were out there, Genesis fought hard to get us all free. To stop what our captors were trying to do. And when an opportunity came, she felt she had to seize it. She got ahold of one of our captors' detonators and blew up the bombs, hoping to disarm them."

My nails dig into his hand, but he continues as if he can't feel a thing. "Instead, she blew up the cruise ship *Splendor.*"

She didn't—

MADDIE

Ignoring the stares, I set my books on my desk and sink into my chair. The ten minutes before school starts are the worst ten minutes of my day, because I have no real friends in first period. I have no one to talk to and nothing to do but pretend I can't hear the whispers or feel the gazes trained on me.

I feel like a fish in a bowl, swimming in circles for the entertainment of the voyeuristic masses. Which of us is more pathetic: the fish with nothing better to do or the people with nothing better to watch?

My phone buzzes, and I'm relieved to see a text from Luke. It's come with a video, so I dig my earbuds from my purse and step into the hall as I read the text, ignoring the new stares and the way people slow down on their way to class to stare at me.

It's still going live, so I rewound and recorded this.
Watch NOW.

I press the play button, and shaky video begins. Luke has recorded something playing on television with his phone.

It's Holden and Genesis on the national news.

"Wait." The host blinks. She looks confused. "Did you just say . . . ?"

"Don't get me wrong." Holden leans forward and stares earnestly into the camera, as if he's horrified by the idea that he might be misunderstood. "It was totally an accident. She didn't know the bombs were on the ship. Did you, Gen?"

Oh my God. He practically pushed her in front of a bus on national television.

"Is it true?" a voice asks, and I pull my earbuds free as I look up. A girl stands in front of an open locker a foot away, and she can see what I'm watching. "Did your cousin kill all those people? Is she one of the terrorists?"

"No!" I didn't mean to shout, but now everyone's looking. "She didn't—"

But she did.

And suddenly I understand what Holden has obviously already figured out—sometimes it's easier to believe a simple lie than a complicated truth.

I was destined to lose.

GENESIS

Holden waits for my answer with wide eyes, and I can only stare at him in shock while control of my life slides out of my grasp like the tide receding from the shore.

When I don't reply, Holden turns back to the camera. "She had no idea. I mean, she obviously knew someone could get killed from an explosion of that size, but she certainly never meant to hurt anyone innocent."

I can't breathe.

He's just made the case for reckless endangerment against me. On national television.

"Genesis?" The host's voice sounds hollow. She's not smiling. Holden may be playing the idiot-who-was-trying-to-help role, but she clearly understands just how bad this is for me. "Is that true? Did you . . . ?" She can't bring herself to say the words.

I can't either.

I stare at the camera. Silence builds all around me. I can't see the crew members behind the bright studio lights,

297

but I can feel how still they've gone. How attentive.

I can almost feel Marlena, the friendly production assistant, looking at me. Waiting for me to deny it. To somehow exonerate myself. But I can't, because after four years and at least a thousand lies, Holden has just eviscerated me with the truth.

The moment stretches around me, and every second that passes drives his knife deeper into my back. Finally, I stand and run from the set. I hit my knee on the coffee table and overturn one of the mugs, but I keep going. I hardly feel the bruise.

I run out of the studio and down the hall, heading for a red exit sign blurred by my tears.

I press the release bar on the door, and when it swings open, I practically fall into the parking lot. I gulp air and squint against the sun, shocked to realize that though this is the darkest moment of my entire life, somehow it's still broad daylight outside.

The worst day of my life has really just begun.

My phone rings. It's Maddie. I don't answer.

The sore spot on my lower back reminds me that I'm still wearing the microphone, earpiece, and battery pack. I pull them all free and drop them in a heap in front of the door. Then I run for my car.

Maddie calls again as I pull out of the parking lot. I nearly swerve into the next lane as I reject her call, and the moment I make the ringing stop, another call begins. It's my dad.

The next call comes from Neda.

Then from my father again.

Then the texts start rolling in.

I roll down my window, ready to throw the phone out to smash against the curb, but then I freeze with my cell in my hand. What if someone finds the ruins of my phone and manages to reconstruct enough of it to get to the data?

What have I said that could add to the damage Holden has just done?

I turn my phone off and drop it in the center console.

Two news vans are already parked near the gate in front of my house. Their sliding doors open as I approach, and reporters climb out, shouting questions at me through my car window as I pull through the gate.

"Genesis, is it true? Did you blow up the *Splendor*?"

"Are you currently under investigation by US or Colombian authorities?"

"Do you have anything to say to the survivors and family members of the victims?"

As the gate closes behind me, they're still shouting. Hoping for a response.

I pull into the garage, then race across the three empty spaces and into the house. The second I step into my living room, an anguished sob wrenches free from my throat so violently that I feel like I've swallowed a mouthful of thorns.

I've spent most of my life learning how to fight, and deep down, I think I always knew that someday I'd have to. When we were kidnapped, I thought that moment had come. I fought, and I thought I was doing the right thing.

But I had no idea that the real battle would be a war of words, or that whether I armed myself with the truth or with lies, I was destined to lose before I even began.

I couldn't face the stares.

MADDIE

I stare at my phone in the shadow of the school gymnasium, as far from the huge trash bins as I can get without being seen. The only people who ever come back here are the janitorial staff, and they don't care that I'm supposed to be in class.

"How's she doing?" Luke asks as he rounds the corner. I don't think he's ever skipped class before—neither have I— and I probably shouldn't have asked him to. But I couldn't face the stares in the hall or the silence behind the gym alone.

"I don't know. Her phone's going straight to voice mail."

"I assume you tried texting?"

I roll my eyes. "Yes, Luke, I tried texting. That's no longer a last-ditch effort at communication. But thanks for trying to help."

He laughs as he wraps his arms around my waist, pulling me close. "So I guess I shouldn't bother with my second- and third-place suggestions?"

"Psychic communication and Morse code?" I guess.

"Close. Carrier pigeons and sky writing."

I try to laugh, but what comes out sounds more like choking back tears.

He tugs me toward the relatively clean curb at the edge of the sidewalk behind the gym. "So . . . it's true? I knew her plan was to detonate the bombs on the mini-subs, but when the cruise ship blew, I assumed that was Sebastián or Silvana."

"It was Genesis. But it could just as easily have been me." I've never said that out loud before, and the admission feels terrifying. Yet there's no judgment in Luke's eyes. "We had no idea the explosives had been transferred to the *Splendor*. We thought we were blowing up bombs and cocaine. And Holden knows that."

"Holden's an asshole."

"He's psychotic." I sink onto the curb and Luke sits next to me. "You should see the chatter online. There are already death threats. I wish there was something we could *do*."

"You can't refute the truth, so I'm not sure how you could help her."

"Right now I'd settle for hurting him."

Luke crosses his arms over his chest and stares at the side of the trash bin. Then he sits straighter and gives me an odd smile. "That might be doable."

"You want to take on Holden Wainwright? A billionaire with more lawyers than actual friends?"

"Well, when you say it like that . . . hell yes." His smile

grows into a grin. "I don't think we're going to learn anything else today. Let's get out of here." He stands and picks up his backpack, then pulls me up by one hand. "So what would hurt him the most?"

"A baseball bat." I'm only kind of kidding.

"Ha ha," Luke says as we round the far side of the gym, headed off campus the long way to avoid seeing anyone.

"Money," I say as we cross the street, and I realize we're headed for a park about a block down. "But we can't sue him for telling the truth, and even if we could, he wouldn't feel the loss unless we could take *billions*." I grunt in disgust.

My uncle. Holden. Why do all the worst people seem to have the most money?

"Genesis might actually be brought up on charges thanks to him, and *he's* going to be a billionaire someday. I wish we could even that score and send him to . . ."

"Prison." Luke's eyes practically sparkle with anticipation. "You have an idea. I can see it."

I *do* have an idea. . . . "Holden sells."

"Drugs?" Luke frowns as we step into the park. "Like, pot? Because that's not really much of a—"

"Not just pot." I lead us toward the swings, which are empty at eight thirty in the morning. "Prescription meds, mostly."

"Why? He doesn't need the money."

"Genesis says he does it because it puts him in demand." I sink into the left-hand swing and grip the chains, rocking back and forth softly with my feet still on the ground. "He likes to be the guy everyone's looking for at any party." As if Holden Wainwright isn't already popular enough.

"Wow." Luke drops his bag and takes the swing next to mine, but his gaze is unfocused, and I know what that means. He's thinking. "Okay, so all we need is proof."

"What kind of proof?"

"Well, a witness would be ideal, but no one's going to come forward. So, a record of a deal? A text, maybe?" He twists in his swing to face me, brows arched high. Smile wide. "My parents will be at work until six. How do you feel about a skip-day pizza-and-text-reading extravaganza at my house?"

"I feel *great* about that."

"I'll buy if you drive," he says as he grabs his bag.

"Deal." We're already headed back toward school, to get my car. "But how are we going to get Holden's texts? Do we need to steal his phone?"

"Nope." Luke's almost left me behind, as if his brain is moving so fast the rest of him has to too. "His phone is new since the jungle, right?" he asks, and I nod. "So it won't get us much, unless he's sold something in the past few days. Which isn't likely, considering the microscope he's been under. But his *old* phone . . ."

"His old phone got left—and probably blown up—in the jungle."

"Yes, but his cloud account didn't," Luke points out. "If he's like most of us, every text, email, and photo he ever had on that old phone is still up on the cloud, waiting to be discovered. Or used in a plot to send him to prison."

"And you know how to hack into the cloud?"

Luke turns to give me the hottest nerd smile in the world. "I know how to do a *lot* of things."

I don't want to see anyone.

GENESIS

"G?" Indiana's voice echoes from down the hall, but I don't answer. I don't want to see anyone right now. Not even him. "Genesis?"

He pushes my bedroom door open, and I realize too late that I should have locked it. Or at least closed it. "Hey." He rounds the end of the bed and sinks onto the floor next to me. "I've been calling you."

"I left my phone in my car." On purpose. "Did the reporters see you come in?"

"Yeah, but they might not have been able to tell it was me through the tinted windows. And the plates are registered to your dad, so . . ."

My dad had lent Indiana his SUV so he wouldn't be stuck at the house while I was at school.

"It doesn't matter anymore," I tell him. "I still can't believe he did it." I sniffle and press my palms to my eyes. They come away smeared with eyeliner. "I mean, I knew he was mad about the video, but I didn't think he'd go nuclear."

Indiana shrugs, and somehow the gesture actually looks comforting. "The thing about playing your big card is that once you've played it, your hand is empty."

"Only Holden's hand isn't empty. He's still got the drug-trafficking card. And the terrorist card. And the illegitimate half-brother card, if he *really* wants to humiliate my dad and Aunt Daniela."

"But how much worse could those cards be, G?" Indiana puts a hand on each of my knees and turns me on the floor to face him. "You've been trying to protect your family this whole time, but did it ever occur to you that they might want to protect you, if they knew they had that option? That if they knew he was holding you hostage, they might *rather* the truth come out than see you suffer?"

I shake my head. "I can't put Maddie and her mom through anything more."

"But, G, I don't think Holden can either. Not really. What Maddie's dad did isn't her fault and it isn't her mother's fault. And those of us who were in the jungle with you, we all know Maddie wasn't in on it. She and her mother are David's victims just as much as anyone. Most people will understand that, if you give them the chance. And at least then it'll be out in the open."

I want to believe he's right. But my faith in humanity isn't exactly soaring at the moment. And even if he is right . . . "Indiana, my dad—"

He takes my hands and squeezes them. "Your dad's already cut his deal with the feds. So as long as you don't violate the NDA you signed, can things *really* get worse than they are right now? Hasn't Holden already done all the damage he can?"

"I . . ." I frown, trying to think through the chaos in my head. "I mean, *maybe.*" Outting my dad and my uncle might earn him another news cycle's worth of attention, but legally, that wouldn't hurt my family or me any more than what he's already done. And emotionally . . . we're *already* traumatized.

"Stop living like a hostage and you won't be one, G."

I nod slowly. Then I climb into his lap and lay my head on his shoulder. Indiana's arms wrap around my back and I press my face into his neck, breathing him in.

Something about him—about being this close to him—is calming. It's as if chaos can't quite touch him. As if it can't touch me, when I'm with him.

I relax against his chest, sinking into this moment of calm, and for the first time since I can remember, in spite of the mayhem my life has become, I feel focused.

The way forward seems clear.

I'm not sure everything will be quite as easy as he's made it sound, but Indiana's right about at least one thing: I can't let Holden Wainwright have any more power over me.

2 DAYS, 9 HOURS EARLIER

The rules don't apply to him.

MADDIE

"How's it coming?" I ask as I pick up another slice of pizza. There's a grease stain on Luke's comforter because we put the box on the bed, but he hasn't noticed. I don't think he cares.

"Asking that every five minutes doesn't help."

"But if I don't ask, I don't know." I set the slice on the greasy napkin next to his mouse pad.

"Fair enough. I haven't found his account yet."

"So, what are we hoping to get from this? Do you honestly think he'd keep records of drug deals?"

"No. But then again, I'm surprised every time I hear about some idiot getting arrested because of something he posted on YouTube. Even smart people are stupid, and Holden's the kind of guy who thinks the rules don't apply to him."

"Truer words were never said."

Luke gives me a smile as he picks up his pizza.

A few minutes later, he leans back in his chair and rolls

it toward me on the worn carpet. "Okay. I'm in." He looks both relieved and astonished, and for the first time, I realize he wasn't at all sure he could do this. Until he did.

"Holy crap. Will he be able to tell someone was in his account?"

"Maybe. But that won't matter. If we find something, we're turning him in, right? He'll definitely know then." Luke scoots his chair up to the desk again. "Do you know who he sold to most often?"

"No idea. Ryan went to a bunch of their parties, but that wasn't my thing."

"You went to at least one," Luke points out, and I follow his gaze to the jagged scar on my left upper arm. The scar I got when I tried to match Ryan drink for drink—my misguided attempt to make a point about his drinking problem—and passed out on a glass bottle. "Did you see anything? Have any names that might help?"

"Um . . ." I close my eyes and think back. That night is mostly a blur. "I didn't know most of the people there."

"Okay then." He clears his throat and turns back to the keyboard. "I guess we're reading texts."

After two hours of reading Holden's messages, I am both exhausted and disgusted. It turns out there is no truer window into the human soul than a peek at someone's texts and as I'd already suspected, Holden's soul is as dark as espresso, and twice as bitter. Unfortunately, other than a few vague and suspicious agreements he made with his friends to "meet at the place" and "bring the stuff," we find nothing concrete.

Veronica Mars, I am not.

"Okay, I need a break," I declare, pushing my folding chair back from Luke's desk. "Can you pull up his pictures? If we can't find anything incriminating in his texts"—and we've already discovered he rarely uses email—"maybe we can just post a humiliating picture of him."

"Nothing nude," Luke insists as he pulls up Holden's pictures. "I don't think my eyes could take it."

For a few minutes, we laugh at Holden's selfies. Then Luke decides to run some numbers. As it turns out, Holden takes an average of twenty-eight selfie variations of any one pose/location before he comes up with an image he likes well enough to post. But he doesn't delete them. It's as if he can't bear to part with a single picture of himself.

"Oooh, what's that one?" I point at a thumbnail image with a triangular play button in the middle. I hate to admit it, but this has become fun. "He has a bunch of videos. *Please* let him have one where he's singing with a brush for a microphone."

Luke clicks play. The video is somehow both repulsive and boring. It's Holden complaining about the barista who made his coffee wrong a week before we left for Colombia. His condescending and insulting tone makes my blood boil. "Even if he never posted this anywhere, we could use it to show the world what an arrogant, entitled, bigoted asshole he is."

"I think the part of the world that would care already knows." Luke plays the next video, which is frozen on a familiar face—Penelope's.

"Hey, Holden!" she says into the camera, and the angle of her arm makes it clear that she's the one holding it. "So, we've stolen your phone so we can record a few secret birthday messages for you."

The camera spins around unsteadily and I catch a blurry glimpse of a dimly lit room full of people. Music pounds from speakers in the background, and most of the bodies are moving in time with the beat.

"I think that's his eighteenth birthday party. That would have been . . . a month ago?"

"March eighth, according to the date in the metadata," Luke confirms.

"Aaron!" Penelope calls off screen as the shot zooms in on a guy I've never seen before, holding a damp bottle of beer. "What do you want to say to Holden on his birthday?"

We watch for several minutes as Holden's mostly drunk friends record shout-outs for him. Most of them are depressingly uninspired and delivered with slurred speech.

I'm about to tell Luke to click on the next video when the camera catches Holden himself, from several feet away. He's talking to another guy I've never seen before, both of them illuminated in a fall of light from an open doorway.

Neda's voice giggles over the speaker. "He still doesn't know we have his phone!"

Penelope appears in front of the lens again, still talking to the future-Holden who will later find this video. But over her shoulder, the other guy gives Holden a folded bill. In return, Holden gives him something in a small clear plastic bag. The other guy opens the bag immediately and throws two pills into his mouth. Then he swallows them dry.

"Holy crap . . . ," I breathe.

Luke turns to me with a smile. "Maddie, I think we've got him."

I don't want to talk.

GENESIS

"Genesis!" A door slams downstairs. My father is home. And he's clearly seen the news.

"Princesa!" he shouts again, and I hear his footsteps clomping up the stairs, then down the hall toward us.

"I don't want to talk to him," I whisper, hunkering down behind my bed. I know Indiana's been texting him, and I suspect he asked my dad to give me some space. That's the only reason I can think of that he would wait until lunchtime to come home.

"He's going to find you, even if you don't answer," Indiana points out in a matching whisper. "Your own room isn't a very stealthy place to hide."

I laugh because I've cried all I can cry. And because he's right.

"Genesis!" My bedroom door flies open and crashes into the wall.

"She's fine." Indiana lets go of me to stand, and reluctantly, I let him pull me up. Then I meet my father's gaze. I

314

don't know what to say. So I say nothing.

"Why didn't you answer your phone?" he asks from the doorway.

"Because I don't want to talk."

My father steps into the room and his gaze takes me in, lingering on my face. I'm sure it's swollen from crying. He doesn't ask if I'm okay. I'm clearly not.

He doesn't ask if what Holden said is true.

It clearly is.

"We're meeting with my lawyers at nine in the morning," he says at last. "The whole team will be there. Jeff"—his primary attorney—"thinks we have grounds for a lawsuit, but I'm not sold on that because it may ultimately shoot us in the foot."

"Dad, I don't want—"

"Genesis, if the government brings charges, we need to be prepared. And we *will* be." He won't let this go. And maybe he's right. But . . .

"School starts at eight. I can't go see your lawyers."

My father blinks at me in incomprehension, as if that's the most ridiculous thing I've ever said. Indiana only smiles and squeezes my hand.

"No one will expect you to be at school." My father exhales slowly and catches my gaze as if whatever he's going to say next will be significant.

"I'm not going to hide." I stand up straighter. This pity party is over. "That's what Holden expects. That's what he *wants*."

"Meeting with our attorneys isn't hiding, Genesis." My father turns toward the door. "Lunch will be here in half an hour. We'll talk about this then."

"No, we won't," I snap, and he turns around sharply, anger and pity at war behind his eyes. "You don't need me there when you meet with your lawyers."

"I most certainly—"

"You don't even know if you can *pay* for your damn lawyers!" I don't realize how angry I am at him until the words burst from my throat. "If I comment on this, even through an attorney, they'll come after me for violating the non-disclosure agreement and we'll lose everything we've ever had!" I didn't intend to shout, but now that I am, I can't go back. These words have been burning a hole in my heart since the moment I found out that my father was a drug trafficker. That my entire life was built upon a foundation of lies and corruption.

"This is all your fault!" I shout, and my father flinches as if I slapped him. "You're the reason those men held a gun to my head and a knife to my throat. The reason Ryan died. You're the reason I made a phone call and killed twelve hundred people. If you'd never started working for Moreno, I wouldn't be a murderer!"

Pain flickers across my father's face. Then it hardens into anger. "If I hadn't—"

"I know. We wouldn't have all this." I sweep one arm out, gesturing at all of our ill-gotten gains. "Maybe we *shouldn't* have all this. Maybe I would have been happy growing up like Maddie if I'd never known anything different. Maybe it would have been okay to wear cheap shoes and go to public school if that meant not getting kidnapped and not accidentally killing twelve hundred people. Maybe my mother wouldn't have been murdered right in front of me if you'd never started working for Gael Moreno in the first place!"

My father stares at me, stunned. Then his expression collapses into a twisted mask of pain.

Those are the words I've never said. That's the thing he didn't know I knew. Until now.

"I *know* he had her killed, and I *know* it was because you tried to quit. I know you kept working for them to keep me safe, and I know I should probably be grateful for that. But here's the thing about working for the devil. You can't take it back. Going legit didn't bring Mom back and it didn't protect me, and there's nothing you can do now to make either of those things happen. You didn't just choose this life for yourself. You chose it for Mom and me too." I take a deep breath. Then I spread my arms, taking in the disaster my existence has become. "Welcome to your decision, Dad. Now get the hell out of my room."

You have ten minutes.

MADDIE

"I can't believe he's that stupid." Luke shakes his head at the screen, yet he's clearly pleased with his own work.

"It's not just stupidity. It's arrogance," I insist, watching over his shoulder as I sink onto the end of his bed.

Luke shrugs. "Anyone that arrogant should be smart enough to enable the two-factor authentication on his cloud account."

"Let's just be glad he isn't." This is the first break I've caught since I got on that stupid plane to Colombia. Well, other than running into Luke on the beach . . .

"So, what do you want to do with the video?" He turns to me, his eyes bright with anticipation. "Send it to the news?"

I pull my phone from my pocket. "I have a better idea. We know someone who owes Genesis a favor."

Luke glances at my cell screen as I make the call. His smile makes me feel warm all over.

My first call goes to voice mail. Instead of leaving a

message, I hang up and dial again. Then again. Until finally, she answers.

"Maddie," Neda snaps into my ear, and distantly I hear the click of her heels on the floor. "If I don't answer, it's because I *don't* want to talk to you."

"Genesis needs a favor."

"Then Genesis can ask me."

"She doesn't know about it. But you *owe* her, after you posted that video."

Neda makes a gurgling growl of irritation right in my ear. "What do you *want*, Maddie?"

"I want you to post another video. Luke's getting it ready right now." He trimmed the video so that it shows only the incriminating transaction and zoomed in so that Penelope isn't shown.

He also deleted the audio, to keep from incriminating her accidentally.

"Done." He brushes his hands together, then holds them in the air in a gesture of triumph. "I'm sending it now. Tell her to check her email."

"Email?" Neda groans, clearly having heard him. "Text it to me."

"It's too big for a text," Luke says, and he doesn't seem to care whether or not she can still hear him.

"Open your email," I snap at Neda. She groans, then the sound changes when she puts us on speaker so she can navigate through her phone menu.

"Okay, I've got it." There's a pause. "If I play this and get some kind of virus, I'm coming after you both."

"If I promise we're quaking in fear, will you open the damn video?"

She huffs. "What's on it?"

"It's . . . scandalous." It's actually evidence, but I suspect she'll be more motivated by a bump in viewership than by helping us bring a spoiled rich kid—one of her friends—to justice.

"A secret video?" Her voice sounds suddenly perky with interest.

"Yes. And this is a limited-time offer. If you're not willing to post this quickly, we'll send it out wide, and you can watch every major news network in the country scoop you."

"Wow." She still sounds insulted, but now she's also a little impressed. "Let me watch, and I'll call you right back."

"You have ten minutes. Then we're moving on." I hang up on her.

Luke gives me a curious look. "Why *aren't* we going to every major network in the country? They have a far greater reach than one webshow."

"Because they also have journalistic integrity." A code of honor I normally support wholeheartedly. "They'll have to verify the source, and that will take a while. Neda can't even *spell* integrity." I shrug. "That, and I like the symmetry of it. Her video is what ultimately brought Genesis down. Now she can do the same for Holden."

Neda calls back with thirty-nine seconds to spare. "Maddie, I can't post this. Penelope and I shot that video! Our friends are in the background!"

"Genesis is your friend, but you posted footage of her and Indiana," I point out.

"They're not going to get arrested for making out in a parking lot."

"But Genesis *can* get arrested for what Holden said on the news this morning. And he did that to get back at her for what you posted."

"I had no idea he was going to do that," Neda insists. "I didn't even know Genesis pushed the button."

"She wanted to destroy the explosives before they could be used against anyone. And now she might go to prison. Because of you."

"Fine." Neda sighs, but this time I can hear guilt in the sound. "I'll post it after school tomorrow."

"No. Do it now."

"Maddie, my parents are going out of town tomorrow, so they're dragging me out for a family dinner. I can film something tonight and schedule it to go live in the morning, right before school starts."

"Fine." That's obviously the best I'm going to get. "But Neda, if you go back on your word, we'll do this without you. And *I swear to God* you'll go down with Holden." I hang up the phone and find Luke staring at me, brows arched high. "What? I'm sick of being lied to."

"Do you think the timing is cruel, considering that the

Wainwright benefit is this weekend? Or would you call that fitting?"

"After what he did the day after my brother's funeral?" I give him a small smile. "I'm going to have to go with karmically sound."

1 DAY, 12 HOURS EARLIER

I'm sure.

GENESIS

"You sure about this?" Indiana asks from the passenger seat.

I stare out the windshield at the back entrance of my school. "I'm sure."

"Want me to come with you?"

"They won't let you in if you're not a student. And that would defeat the purpose. This is my shitstorm. I have to weather it alone."

And maybe that's how it should be.

"Call me if you need me," Indiana says as I grip the door handle. "I'll be back for lunch."

"You can take my car." I try to hand him the keys, but he pushes them back at me with a smile.

"Nah, I'll take the bus. In case you decide to come home early."

I should argue. Knowing there's a way out might tempt me to take it. But no one could fault me for having a safety net, right?

I glance at the dashboard, my hand still on the car door

handle. School starts in eight minutes. My dad is probably already in his lawyer's office. I could easily put the key back in the ignition and drive down there.

Instead I take a deep breath and open the door. Then I step into the parking lot, because unless I get arrested, I will be graduating with my class in six weeks. If I can't walk down the hall right now, how will I be able to walk the line at graduation?

Thank goodness reporters aren't allowed on school grounds.

"Breathe," Indiana whispers as he closes the passenger's side door. I take another deep breath while he rounds the front of the car toward me. "I'll see you later." He leans in for a kiss, and I let myself linger in the moment. Taking courage from affection that doesn't come with strings—a refreshing novelty, considering I've been betrayed by both my best friends and my ex-boyfriend.

Finally I let Indiana go and click my key fob. The car beeps as it locks. I head for the school. Indiana's footsteps echo behind me, headed in the other direction. I want to look back, but I don't.

The hallway goes silent when I step into the building. Everyone stares. No one greets me. As I start down the hall, the whispers begin. The only word I catch clearly is my name. In itself, that isn't unusual. People have always talked about me, and I've always taken pride in my ability to guide the conversation. But I didn't aim this spotlight at myself, and this time I have no control over what's being said.

I ignore everything else and head for my locker. A crowd blocks my way, but it parts as I approach. I stumble to a shocked stop.

"Murderer" is written across the front of my locker in large red letters. The paint is still wet and dripping. A chill washes over me.

I walk past my locker, headed for my first class, and hope that we don't need a textbook today, because I can't get to mine. I can't open that door.

Behind me, the whispers crescendo. There's no laughter. This isn't a prank. The message is very clear. They don't care why I pushed the button. They only care that I did.

"My sister was on that boat." The voice comes out of nowhere. I don't recognize the face suddenly inches from mine. I try to go around him, but he steps back into my path and makes a rough noise in his throat. Then he spits at me.

A glob of saliva and phlegm lands on my shirt.

For a second, I can only stare at him in shock. Then I step around him and into my first-period class while the whispers in the hallway continue at my back.

I want to run. I want to hide. I want to cry. But the soul-crushing truth is that I am not the victim here. I survived the jungle. The machetes. The bombs.

I will damn well survive Holden Wainwright.

My faith in humanity is dead.

MADDIE

I refresh my phone screen again, but the image doesn't change. There's no new video on Neda's site. "She's not going to do it."

"I think she will." Luke sips from his juice carton, then sets it on his breakfast tray. His waffle is half gone. Mine is untouched. "But in case she doesn't, I'm ready to click send on our backup plan." His laptop sits open on the cafeteria table in front of us, connected to the school's Wi-Fi. The video is already attached to an email addressed to every major television network in the country. As well as a few small and local ones, in case the bigger ones don't read their email very quickly.

The backup video is twice as long as the compilation Neda got, and it's captioned with names and dates. We even found one clip where she walks past in the background. That isn't directly incriminating, but it will make it harder for her to deny that she knew Holden was selling.

Evidently *everyone* in his inner circle knew. Why

shouldn't the rest of the world?

"She lied to us. She's not going to do it." I tap the screen again, and Luke's hand settles onto mine, stilling my fingers.

"Maddie." He sounds . . . worried. "Stop. Have a little faith."

But my faith in humanity is dead.

My phone buzzes, and a text appears on the screen. A single word.

Liar.

"What?" Luke says, and I show him the text. "Wow. I thought that was over. It's been a while since you got an anonymous message, right?"

"Since I got an anonymous text anyway. But someone wrote 'Liar' across my locker the other day."

"Why didn't you say anything?"

I shrug. "Stuff kept coming up. Neda's video. Ryan's funeral. Holden's bombshell. And anyway, there's no way to trace a message left on your locker. But this . . . ?" I hand him the phone. "What can you tell me?"

He opens the third-party app. "We have a phone number. I should be able to find out who it belongs to." He opens a new window on his laptop, while I swirl a bite of waffle around in my syrup.

Most people don't eat breakfast in the cafeteria, but everyone who does is looking at us. It's been nearly a week, but the whispers and stares haven't gone away, and they probably won't as long as Holden keeps the kidnapping—and the *Splendor*—in the news.

I glance at my phone again. "Five minutes. If the video's not up by then, I'll click send myself."

"Should we send her a warning?" Luke asks while he types. "Or a reminder? For all we know, Neda's still trying to capitalize on her beauty rest."

"Yeah, I—" *Crap.* Kathryn Coppela is standing in the cafeteria doorway. I turn back to my phone, pretending I haven't seen her. Our little exposé/revenge plot doesn't need a witness.

Maybe she hasn't seen me.

I refresh my phone's browser again, and there it is. "It's up!" On screen, Neda is sitting on one of the pink couches in her studio. She's perfectly made up and wearing one of her typical designer ensembles, but she's not smiling.

Quickly, I pull my earbuds from my pocket and plug them into my phone, then hand Luke the left half, so we can share. And so that no one else can hear.

"Hey, this is Neda Rahbar. You're watching a special edition of *Survival Mode*, and I'm about to throw three truths at you, so get ready. I know that by now most of you have seen the video I posted the other day of my friend Genesis and her new boyfriend. And I know you've probably also heard Holden's theory about what happened to the *Splendor*. I have no personal knowledge of what happened to the *Splendor*, so I can neither confirm nor deny his account. But what I *do* know from multiple first-hand sources is that he wasn't there either. Holden had already escaped into the jungle, abandoning all of our friends, when the ship exploded.

Which means he did not see for himself what happened."

Neda takes a deep breath and continues. "The second thing I know for a fact is that the video I showed you guys doesn't actually show Genesis cheating on Holden. The truth is that they broke up in the jungle. That's totally verified, and if you don't believe me, you can ask anyone else who was there. Gen and her new boyfriend have been together since then. Holden lied to everyone because he thought it made him look more like a hero, and I'm embarrassed to admit that I helped him do that. I shouldn't have posted the video, and Genesis, I am so damn sorry."

She takes another deep breath and picks up her remote control. "The third thing you guys need to hear is this: Holden Wainwright is no golden boy. He's actually a lying, cheating, drug-dealing bastard who's now hurt *two* of my best friends. Don't believe me? Check this out."

Neda presses a button on her remote and the shot of her studio is replaced with the first image of the compilation video Luke and I sent her.

I watch for a few seconds, then I pause the video and turn to Luke, astonished.

"Holy crap," he whispers. "She almost sounded like a journalist."

"She almost sounded like a *human*!" I tap the address bar at the top of my screen to save the URL, then I text it to Penelope.

FYI, she did this as much for you as for Genesis.

329

I could have handled gossip.

GENESIS

The bell rings to end first period, and I leap out of my chair as if it's on fire. Doors open all along the hallway, and my classmates pour out of them. About half of them are staring at their phones. Neda's voices rings out from several of them, tinny from the cell phone speakers and garbled because I'm hearing several of her at once.

I stifle a groan. They're still watching the video of me and Indiana.

People look up from their phones and stare at me. They start to whisper. My pulse begins to pound.

I turn and walk the other way.

Penelope rounds the corner and sees me. I clutch the strap of my bag and turn again to jog back the way I came, dodging elbows, book bags, and open locker doors. "Genesis, wait!" she calls after me.

I run faster, then burst through the door into the parking lot and head for my car.

I tried. I could have handled gossip. I could have stared

rumors in the face and laughed at myself, if I were being ridiculed for doing something stupid or embarrassing. But this is different.

This is hatred.

I head for my car, but I freeze when I see it, anger rolling over me like the pressure wave from an explosion. "What the *hell?*" I run toward my car, my book bag bouncing on my back.

"*Damn* it . . ." All four of my windows have been bashed in, and my windshield is shattered on the driver's side. Even if I could lean over to see out the passenger's side, I wouldn't get very far. All four of my tires have been slashed.

And the word "murderer" has been painted on the driver's side in huge letters spanning both the front and rear doors.

Fighting angry tears, I pull up my ride share app and request a car. While I'm waiting, I take pictures of my trashed car from every angle, for the insurance. Then I text them to my father.

He was right. I should have stayed home.

My ride arrives, and I open the rear passenger door and toss my book bag inside. Before I can get in, something across the street catches my eye, and I look over the roof of the car at the woman staring back at me.

Silvana.

I can't imagine.

MADDIE

My phone buzzes in my pocket. My physics teacher is staring at something on her computer screen, so I subtly pull my cell out and hold it in my lap. The text is from Genesis. It's a picture of her car, all smashed up, with the word "murderer" written across the driver's side.

Oh my God.

I squint, trying to decide if the writing on her car matches the writing on my locker. I can't tell. Could the same person be stalking us both?

There are only five minutes left in class and everyone else is at least pretending to work on the homework. I stand and take the stupid bathroom pass—a big wooden key—from its hook next to the door and make eye contact with my teacher. She nods, and I step into the hall.

On the way to the bathroom, I dial Genesis, but she doesn't answer. So I send a text.

Call me! We need to compare notes.

In the bathroom, I stare at the number the anonymous texts have come from. Luke said it belongs to a prepaid phone, and there's no way to know who bought it.

I copy the number and paste it into my texting app.

Who is this?

For nearly a minute, there's no answer. Then . . .

A friend.

No friend would vandalize my locker or smash my cousin's car.

Bullshit. What do you want?

The answer comes a minute later.

Truth. I know about your dad.

For a second, I can actually hear my heart pound. Then I realize I'm actually hearing footsteps, coming from the hallway.

Chill, Maddie.

I press the call button before I can chicken out. A phone rings on the other side of the bathroom door. From the hallway.

I blink, staring at the door. *Coincidence. Has to be.*

The ringing from the hallway ends. An electronic voice mail greeting plays in my ear.

I throw the door open and race into the hall. A girl with a brown ponytail is staring at her phone, with her back to me.

"*Kathryn?*" I croak. She whirls toward me, eyes wide. Then her gaze slides down to the phone I'm still clutching, and she seems to understand.

But I don't.

"You . . . ? Why . . . ? Why are you sending me threats?"

Her eyes water. "They're not threats. I just . . . I wanted you to tell the truth. About your dad. I know he's not dead, Maddie. I know he's in Colombia. I also know there are no coincidences."

"What—? How—?" I glance around the empty hallway, then pull her into the bathroom with me. "How do you know that?"

"The night I came to your house, right after you got back, I . . . I missed your brother. I went into his room, to kind of say good-bye, but your mother was in there. She was drunk and upset, and she was saying . . . I don't even think she *knew* what she was saying, but she told me she didn't believe he was dead."

"What?" That was before I told her about my dad. Before I even knew about him.

"She believes he's still alive. In Colombia. Where you were kidnapped. Where Ryan was killed. I know he's involved in that somehow, Maddie. I tried to tell you what he was really like, back when we were twelve. I saw him that night. During our sleepover. He smelled like kerosene and he was carrying a gas can."

"You still think . . ." Oh my God. A warehouse burned down that night and the sirens kept us awake. It was full of chemical pesticides my dad said the United States government would have used against cocaine farmers in Colombia. He said God struck the warehouse down, to keep those chemicals from finding their way into rural drinking water. But Kathryn had said . . .

"There was a night guard in that warehouse. He died, Maddie. Your dad killed him and you didn't believe me. If you'd listened—if you'd helped me tell someone—none of the rest of this would have happened. He wouldn't have made it into Colombia. Ryan would still be alive. That ship—*your uncle's* ship—wouldn't have blown up." Her gaze pins me. "You could have stopped this. But you wouldn't listen."

I couldn't. I *couldn't* believe that my father was capable of . . .

"I'm sorry." I shake my head. It's too late now. "You smashed up my cousin's car because of that? Genesis didn't even know about the fire."

Kathryn frowns. "I didn't smash your cousin's car. I've never even met her. But if she really blew up the *Splendor,* there were probably a lot of people ready to take a bat to her stuff."

That takes me a second to process.

335

My phone rings, and Indiana's name pops up on the screen. "Sorry. I have to take this." Surely he and Genesis have seen Neda's show by now. "I'm sorry, Kathryn."

"Have you seen Genesis?" Indiana asks before I can say hello, and my smile dies.

"No, but she just sent me a picture of her car."

"Her dad got one too. Then the school called and said she's missed two classes."

Of *course* she went to school. Pride would never let her hide out at home.

"But she didn't answer her phone, so I told him I'd find her. I'm in the school parking lot. Her car's still here, but she's gone."

"Can Uncle Hernán track her phone?"

"She turned off the tracking." The groan of metal tells me he's leaning against her car. "Do you have any idea where she might go?"

"Other than home? Maybe my apartment?"

"Is your mom home?"

"No, she has a couple of follow-up appointments. But Genesis has a key. I'll meet you there. I'm leaving now."

"Thanks."

I hang up and text Luke.

Genesis is missing. Leaving to check my apartment. Will you get my stuff from physics?

I head out of the bathroom, and the bell rings before I get halfway to the nearest exit. Doors fly open and people pour into the halls. I should have to fight the flow of traf-fic, but it seems to part all around me. People are staring. Whispering.

If it's this bad for me—the cousin of the girl who pushed the button—I can't imagine what Genesis must have gone through at school.

Someone calls my name from the other end of the hall. I spin and find my physics teacher staring at me expectantly. Which is when I realize I left the restroom pass on the edge of a sink in the girls' bathroom.

Instead of going back for it, I give her an apologetic look and run for the exit.

I live less than a mile from my high school, but Indi-ana's already standing on the sidewalk when I pull into the parking space next to him. "Have you been up there yet?" I ask as we take the concrete steps two at a time toward my second-floor apartment.

"No. I just got here."

The television is on inside. I can hear it as I unlock the door.

I step into my living room to find Genesis sitting on the couch staring at the TV, the remote control threatening to fall from her slack grip. Relief washes over me. She looks up, but doesn't seem surprised to find either of us watching her.

"Have you seen this?" she asks.

Indiana and I sink onto the couch on either side of her. I take the remote from her and aim it at the television—and finally the image on screen catches my attention.

Holden Wainwright. In handcuffs.

This is so not the same thing.

GENESIS

"Holy crap!" The remote control falls from Maddie's grip and thumps to the carpet.

"I know." I can't stop staring.

Indiana nods at the screen. "Check out the headline."

"I know!" Despite the day I've had, I can hardly keep the glee from my voice. Although, truthfully, I'm not actually trying.

"'Heir to billion-dollar pharmaceutical fortune arrested for dealing controlled substances,'" Maddie reads from the screen. "Holy crap!" she repeats.

"They picked him up at home ten minutes ago," I say, staring at the front of the huge three-story beachfront mansion where Holden—an only child—grew up. "They've already played this clip three times. Watch. Here comes his mother."

On screen, Elizabeth Wainwright follows her son down a wide set of marble steps. She's speaking frantically into her cell phone, and I can't decide whether she's calling her husband or her attorney.

"Karma!" Maddie declares, her voice heavy with satisfaction. Then her smile begins to fade. "The day before the big benefit. Do you think they'll cancel?"

"I could not care less." I stare at the screen, and a new line of text runs across the bottom. "Billionaire 'hero' outted as drug dealer by beauty blogger Neda Rahbar."

I grab the remote from the floor and rewind. "Did you see that?" I hit pause, and the words freeze on the screen, a little blurry, thanks to my cousin's outdated television. "Neda did this! She posted something on her show." I pull my phone from my pocket and ignore all the missed calls and messages as I open my browser and type Neda's name into the search bar.

"They're playing it." Indiana takes the remote and turns the TV up, and I hear Neda's voice.

"Hey, this is Neda Rahbar. You're watching a special edition of *Survival Mode*, and I'm about to throw three truths at you, so get ready," Neda says on screen. I lean forward to listen, and my jaw drops lower with every word she says.

"I can't believe she did that."

"I know, right?" Maddie's grinning. She doesn't look surprised.

Still stunned, I text Neda.

Call?

My phone rings a second later, and I accept a video chat. Neda's face appears on my screen and her living room passes in a blur of glass and marble in the background. She clearly didn't go to school today.

"You saw my show?" Her dark eyes are bright with excitement.

"They just played it on CNN. I can't believe you did that."

A smile stretches across her face as she drops onto a leather chaise longue. "I still can't believe they're showing it on TV. And the Huffington Post linked to me! Can you imagine the endorsements that will come from this?"

"I'm still trying to imagine Holden in prison." And *really* hoping I don't wind up there myself.

"Prison? Holden's going to prison?" Neda sits up, looking more surprised than she should, which probably means she didn't see the footage of him being arrested.

"I don't know."

"What did you think would happen?" Maddie frowns at Neda from over my shoulder.

Neda shrugs. "I thought he'd be super embarrassed, and probably grounded. His parents have, like, fifty lawyers. I didn't think he'd go to *prison.*"

"First comes jail, and a bond hearing," Maddie says. "Holden's lawyers will probably get him off, if this even goes to trial, but they can't stop him from being arrested."

I shouldn't be surprised that she knows all that. She wants to be an attorney for the ACLU. And she's seen every episode of *The Good Wife.*

"Hey, where did you get that video?" I ask Neda.

She glances over my shoulder at Maddie. "They didn't tell you?"

"They, who?"

Neda rolls her eyes. "Well, it's not like *I* know how to hack into the cloud."

"I gotta go." I hang up and turn to Maddie. "This was you and Luke?"

She shrugs. "Someone wise once told me that you can get over it, or you can get even."

I pull her into a hug so tight my own arms ache. "This is *so* not the same thing," I whisper as I blink away tears. I outted a cheater in Maddie's defense. She got my ex *arrested*.

"Yeah, well, I also once heard you threaten to leave Holden in a Colombian prison." Finally she smiles. "This was the closest I could get."

1 DAY, 4 HOURS EARLIER

I can't say no.

MADDIE

Someone knocks on the front door, and when I open it, Luke holds out my backpack. "Hey."

"Hey. Thanks." I take the bag and tug him inside. "Sorry, it's been crazy. Someone beat the crap out of my cousin's car."

"Because of Holden?"

"Yeah. Security cameras caught it. Turns out they knew one of the *Splendor* victims."

"Oh. Ouch."

"Yeah. Gen's not pressing charges."

"And she can't tell her side of the story because of the NDA. . . ." Luke's brows draw low as he follows me toward the kitchen. "So she just has to let what Holden said stand?"

"Yes. And I hate to point this out, but he was telling the truth. At least Neda gave them a reason to doubt Holden's account." I frown, surprised by my own words. "I never expected to *hope* that people start doubting the truth."

"This is one of those rare cases when the facts and the

truth aren't the same thing. She was trying to detonate the bombs so they couldn't be used in a terrorist attack. She had no idea they were on a cruise ship." Luke shrugs. "If people have to doubt the facts in order to understand the truth, I'm good with that."

"Okay, no one else in the *world* could have made that make sense."

"I told you." He returns my smile with a heated grin as he leans in for a kiss. "I can do a lot of things."

Luke's mouth meets mine and I run my hand up his arm and into his hair. "Mmmm . . . ," I murmur when he finally pulls away. I'm high on our victory and eager to make this feeling last longer. "My mom will be home soon. Let's go to my—"

My phone buzzes, and I have to lean into Luke to pull it from my back pocket and read the text. "Crap. It's Holden's mom's assistant."

"What does she want?

"'Elizabeth Wainwright is busy with a personal matter,'" I read, and Luke snorts in amusement. "'And if we're going to be ready by tomorrow night, I need all hands on deck to help with the preparations.'"

"For the benefit?" Luke looks skeptical. "Don't they hire people to do the actual setup?"

"Yeah. I'm not sure what they want us to do, but I can't say no. I have a scholarship riding on this." I hesitate, then blurt out what I'm thinking. "I know I've asked way too much of you lately, so you totally don't have to help. But if you wanted to come sit on the sidelines and keep me company, I wouldn't object. . . ."

Luke's eyes widen in mock awe. "A chance to set up chairs and tables for no pay so that a bunch of millionaires can pay fifty thousand dollars a plate for a thirty-dollar catered chicken dinner? How could I ever say no?"

He only ran off because he was scared.

GENESIS

"No, you can't drink yet!" Neda snatches the glass of wine from my hand and sets it on the marble surface of her parents' bar. "We have to toast first."

"Toasts are so cheesy," Pen whines as she slides onto a bar stool.

"Sometimes a little cheese is good," I insist as I sink onto the stool next to her. I'm smiling for what feels like the first time in years. "We survived the jungle. We survived the terrorists. We survived Holden Wainwright. That deserves a toast."

Behind the bar, Neda sets out three large shot glasses, then pulls three bottles from the small refrigerator beneath the counter. Coffee liqueur, Irish cream, and amaretto. I stifle a laugh while I watch Neda layer them into the shot glasses, then top all three with a squirt from a can of whipped cream. She pushes one shot glass toward each of us. "Ready?"

Pen and I pick up our drinks. "What are we toasting to?" she asks.

"To the fact that we're all here, and thanks to my web-show, Holden is sitting pretty at the county jail."

"Actually he's still at the police station," I point out.

Neda rolls her eyes. "The point is that he's behind bars. May he drop the soap at the worst possible moment."

Pen frowns. "Is that the toast? Surely you can come up with something a little classier."

"How's this?" Neda holds up her shot glass. "Chicks before dicks!"

Pen and I laugh as we clink our glasses against hers, then we throw them back.

I lick whipped cream from my lips. "Does anyone else find it even a little ironic that we just toasted to 'chicks before dicks' by drinking a shot called a Blow Job?"

Penelope peers into her glass, as if she hopes to suddenly find it full again. "Is that what I just drank? It tasted like chocolate milk."

"Another?" Neda asks, peering at the shelves beneath the countertop. "I think I have everything for a Red-Headed Slut."

"Where did you learn all that?" Penelope asks. "The internet?"

I shake my head. "Her sister." Nadirah Rahbar was a legendary party girl back in her day.

"So? Another one?" Neda is already digging for more bottles.

"I'm good." Penelope twists on her bar stool to face me. "Gen, I'm *so sorry* for everything I said to you."

"Forget it. Holden was the problem. Not you."

Penelope crosses the room and plops down on one of the overstuffed couches. "But I kinda feel sorry for him."

"Who? Holden?" Neda leaves the bar without bothering to put up the bottles—her parents are out of town and her live-in housekeeper is practically always on duty. "No, you do *not* feel sorry for him."

"I mean, yeah, he's a dick, but we're talking about jail. Maybe *prison*. If that's the appropriate punishment for being an asshole, half our school should be locked up."

I frown as I sink onto the couch with her. "Pen, he's not in jail because he's an asshole. He's in jail because he sold drugs."

"And because I posted that video, which I did because I love you bitches," Neda adds.

"We love you too." I pat her leg, and she looks satisfied by the attention. "But my point is that he's in jail because he broke the law."

"We *all* broke the law." Penelope glances at the bar, where we all just took underage shots. "And not for the first time." She looks torn, and I can practically feel her new stance on Holden wavering.

Why can't she see him for what he really is? Even now?

"Pen." I capture her gaze and hold it. "He ran off and left us in the jungle. And he shot Óscar."

"That was self-defense," Penelope insists. "And he only ran off because he was scared."

"We were all scared," I remind her. "No one else ran.

347

But there's more." I'm not sure why I'm whispering. There's no one else around to hear. "You guys, Holden killed Rog."

"*What?*" Neda's whispering now too.

"He says he thought Rog was one of my uncle's men. But . . . he didn't even hesitate. And he wasn't upset about it. He just moved on, as if it never even happened. And I can't tell that he's even thought about it since we got back."

"Poor old Rog! We should do a shot in his honor." Neda heads back to the bar and begins setting up another round of drinks. "Why didn't you tell anyone?"

"Because I don't have any proof it wasn't self-defense. And I was hoping to hold it over him, to get out of any more interviews." I shrug. "Though now it doesn't look like I need to."

Thanks to Maddie.

My phone buzzes with a text from my cousin, as if she knows I'm thinking about her. I read the text and laugh out loud, welcoming the ironic subject change. "Wanna hear something funny?"

"Based on the look on your face?" Neda says. "No."

"Maddie needs our help with the Wainwright benefit, because Holden's parents are busy trying to get him out of jail."

You guys would be so lost without me.

MADDIE

"No, there are supposed to be three rows of eleven tables and two rows of six, split in half with the dance floor area between them!" I shout. Then I immediately feel guilty. The men setting up the banquet room aren't *trying* to make my life difficult, and they probably aren't being paid much to haul tables and chairs around all night.

But at least they *are* getting paid.

"Hey," a familiar voice says, and I turn to see Genesis standing behind me, one hand propped on her hip, an amused smile riding the corner of her mouth. I don't think I've seen her smile since she made it out of the jungle, and I probably shouldn't be irritated that this one's coming at my expense, but . . .

"Hey." I smile back and gesture at the room behind me. "Thanks for coming. I have *no* idea what I'm doing."

"Which is what?" Neda asks from my cousin's left. "Presiding over the most lopsided ballroom transformation in the history of charity benefits?"

"This wasn't exactly in my job description," I admit. "Until yesterday, I was in charge of checking off RSVPs." I turn and gesture to the room. "We're short two tables, the 'portable party floor' for dancing hasn't arrived yet, and the company who rented us the place settings evidently misplaced fish knives and dessert spoons. I don't know how those are different than regular knives and spoons, so how the hell am I supposed to find them?"

"Okay, slow down." Genesis raises one hand. "First of all, why are you in charge of this? Where's the event coordinator?"

"There isn't one. Elizabeth Wainwright prides herself on planning the whole thing personally. She works on it all year."

"Not by herself, surely," Genesis says. "Doesn't she have an assistant, or something?"

"Yeah. Julia. But she got called away two hours ago to help Mrs. Wainwright call important people—congressmen, or something—to try to get Holden out of jail."

Neda snorts. "And they left *you* in charge?"

I shrug miserably. "I figured most of the work was already done, so I *might* have given them the impression that I was up to the challenge, having chaired the prom committee for the past two years."

"You chaired the prom committee?" Penelope looks doubtful.

"No! I lied, okay?" I'm not even sure I'm *going* to prom. "I had no idea what planning this thing would entail, but if

I hadn't stepped up, they were going to cancel the benefit. It didn't seem fair for two different charities to lose out on all that money just because Holden Wainwright is a lying, drug-dealing asshole. So can you help me?"

"Yes." Genesis plucks the clipboard from me and turns to her friends. "Neda, you go sort out the place settings." She flips through the papers. "If they're actually missing the dessert spoons and fish knives, let me know. I've got the service number."

"Luke is back there digging through boxes," I tell Neda. "But I don't think he knows what a fish knife is either."

Neda rolls her eyes on her way toward the kitchen door at the back of the ballroom. "You guys would be so lost without me."

Genesis pulls a page from the clipboard and hands it to Penelope. "Call the dance floor people. Tell them that if they're not here in half an hour, the Wainwright Foundation will take its business elsewhere and blacklist them all over the state."

Penelope nods and takes the paper, then retreats into a quiet corner with her marching orders.

Genesis turns to me with a smug smile, and I decide to let her get away with it because we've both had a rough week and she's digging me out of a hole. "What's next?"

"Julia ordered two different colors of tablecloth, and I don't know which one she actually intended to use."

"Okay." Genesis says. "Let's go sort this out."

It turns out that the different-colored tablecloths are for

layering. There are also coordinating and contrasting cloth napkins already being folded into fancy shapes by a staff of women in a room off the kitchen, as well as table runners, and thick, lacy sashes to be tied around the backs of the chairs.

This benefit is like prom on steroids. Not that I would actually know.

Indiana arrives with pizza and we take a short break to eat. Two hours later, the tablecloths are layered, the dessert spoons and fish knives have been found, and there's an entire army of napkins folded into the "napkin crown" shape, which looks like a tall column with a point on one side.

The tables don't actually get set until a couple of hours before the banquet, which means we don't have to worry about that tonight. "Okay, what's left?" Luke asks, glancing around the banquet hall, where forty-five round tables have been arranged to face the long head table, elevated on a platform. Around the edges of the room, four empty bars wait to be manned and stocked tomorrow night.

"Um . . ." I glance at the list Julia gave me. "The sound guys will set up in the morning, so I guess that just leaves the balloons."

"What balloons?" Genesis asks. "They've never had balloons at the benefit before."

"They're a last-minute addition. To be dropped from a net at the end of the dinner. I found a huge box of them in the back room, along with a note saying we have to blow them up ourselves, because the company that mounts them in the net will only blow them up if we use *their* balloons."

"Why aren't we using their balloons?" Pen asks.

I shrug. "I think it has something to do with the give-away. One of the balloons has a ticket in it, and whoever pops that one wins some kind of prize. But I assume some-one's bringing that one tomorrow, because they didn't leave me the ticket."

"A prize?" Luke snorts. "This thing is fifty thousand dol-lars a plate. What kind of prize could people with that kind of money possibly want?"

"For your information, there are plenty of things money can't buy," Neda informs us.

"Yeah, but how do you fit personality, talent, and a sense of humor into a balloon?" Indiana asks with a grin.

Neda sticks her tongue out at him. "It's nearly eight." She glances at her phone screen. "I am *not* spending all night blowing up balloons."

"You don't blow them up with your mouth," I say as I lead them toward the room in the back. "There are a couple of pressurized tanks. We just have to inflate them and clip them closed. Tomorrow morning the crew comes to load them into the net and set the rest of it up."

"Come on." Genesis links her arm through Neda's and drags her across the ballroom. "It'll be fun. Don't you remember your birthday party in third grade? You asked for a room knee-deep in balloons, and your mom made it hap-pen. We can reenact that."

"Do *not* pop them!" I call as I follow. "We only have thirteen hundred, and in a room this big, we'll need all of them."

"Can we turn on the TV while we work?" Luke asks as he catches up to me. "I could watch Holden get arrested all day long."

"That makes two of us."

I turn on the television while Luke shows us how to work the tanks, because he's the only one who got the tutorial from the guy who delivered them.

"Why didn't you get helium?" Neda says as she claims the second tank. "We could all be singing Mickey Mouse karaoke right now."

"Helium balloons don't fall when you drop them," Indiana points out with a smile.

Neda sticks her tongue out at him again and fills the first glossy silver balloon.

The rest of us take turns using the other tank, while everyone else seals the full balloons with little white clips, but Neda claims she can't handle the clips because of her long manicure, so we leave her on the tank.

"Nooooo . . . ," Genesis cries a few minutes later, and it's the agonized sound of her voice more than the word itself that captures my attention. I follow her gaze to the TV screen, where the news network is showing a live image of Holden and his parents on the steps of the courthouse, surrounded by men and women in suits, who can only be attorneys. "Turn that up!"

I grab the remote and punch the up arrow several times.

". . . live at the courthouse, where Holden Wainwright has just been released from custody, after the Miami-Dade State Attorney declined to prosecute him on charges rumored to have included possession and distribution of a Schedule I substance."

Genesis inhales sharply. "Son of a bitch!"

13 HOURS EARLIER

I'm not ashamed.

GENESIS

"We knew prison was a long shot, but we thought he'd at least have to stand trial," Indiana says, and I freeze in the hall outside the kitchen, so I can listen. "Any idea what went wrong?"

I'm not ashamed of eavesdropping. When spies do it, they're called national heroes.

"They didn't find anything illegal on Holden or in his house," my father says, accompanied by the sound of pouring liquid. "My lead counsel said the State's Attorney was probably afraid that Neda's tape would be declared inadmissible. Without that, they have nothing left but witnesses who won't testify for fear of incriminating themselves."

"I'm guessing all those witnesses also have teams of lawyers waiting to tear into the prosecutor?" Indiana says.

"That would be my guess as well."

"The Wainwrights paid someone." I step into the kitchen to find my father leaning against the long kitchen island holding a glass of orange juice. Indiana sits at one of the bar stools in front of a bowl of cereal, as comfortable around my father as if they've known each other his whole life. "All the rest of that may be true, but the real reason they dropped the charges is money."

My dad arches one eyebrow at me, and I know what he's thinking. People with money—including us—have always gotten away with things and it's never bothered me before. But it bothers me now.

What can I say? It's personal now. I won't deny that that makes me a hypocrite.

"Speaking of people getting away with things . . ." My father takes my favorite mug from the cabinet and pours coffee into it. "I have good news. Holden's interview didn't change anything at Homeland Security. They're not going to charge you either, Genesis, as long as you uphold the NDA."

Relief washes over me like warmth from the sun. No charges. No jail. Then his phrasing sinks in and I frown. "I'd hardly call that getting away with something," I snap at him. "Other than the coincidental timing, my case and Holden's have nothing in common."

"I know, *princesa*." My father pushes my mug toward me, trying to catch my gaze. "I was joking. Trying to make you smile."

"Did they say why?"

"Because in addition to Moreno, they're still hoping to catch David and Silvana, and if they can get them extradited to the US, they want us both to testify against them."

I glance at Indiana, silently asking for his opinion, and he gives me an encouraging shrug. So I exhale. "They won't have to extradite Silvana. She's already here."

"*What?*" My dad turns to Indiana for confirmation.

"I haven't seen her, but I believe Genesis," he says.

My dad frowns. "Why haven't you said anything about this?"

"Because no one else has seen her, and Holden was already threatening to tell the world I was suffering from PTSD-related hallucinations. I figured everyone would agree with him."

His gaze narrows on me in concern. "Genesis, where did you see her?"

"At school—across the street. And outside the television studio."

"Did she say anything?"

"No, and she disappeared as soon as I'd seen her. But I *know* it was her."

"Okay." My father nods as if he's made a big decision. "I'll have our attorneys pass that along to Homeland Security. They'll probably want to talk to you again, and this time I'm staying in the room."

"I'm fine with that."

"Are you okay with testifying? They promised we'd get round-the-clock protection."

I nod slowly. The fact that we'd need protection is scary, but the truth is that we're in danger from Moreno whether or not we testify against him, because of my father. "Yeah.

I'll do it. But I can only testify to what I saw and heard."

"Of course," my father agrees. "That's how it works."

I glance at the clock over the microwave as I accept the mug. "You haven't had breakfast yet, but you've already spoken to your attorney about Homeland Security not charging me?"

"No, he told me last night, but you never answered your phone. Nor did you wake me up to say goodnight when you got home."

"My phone was on 'do not disturb' all night," I tell him. But the truth is that we've hardly spoken since the argument in my bedroom. I'm not sorry for what I said, so I can't bring myself to apologize. And I don't know how to move forward. How to talk to him.

He's still my father. He's still running Genesis Shipping. We're still living in the same house. But none of it feels normal anymore.

"I need a new number. I'm getting sixty calls a day from the press."

"Me too. I'll take care of it." My dad sighs, and when he pats my shoulder, I don't shrug him off. And I call that progress.

Indiana smiles over the milk-filled spoon he's lifting toward his mouth. "Once again, I tout the advantages of anonymity," he says. Then he crunches into a bite of corn-flakes.

"You're right." I turn toward my father. "Which is why I've decided to withdraw from the public eye."

His brow arches again, but this time he looks amused. "That sounds a bit melodramatic."

"I'm hoping for the exact opposite. No drama. I can't stop people from talking about me and I can't control the conversation, thanks to the NDA preventing me from telling my side of the story. But I *can* let myself fade from the spotlight and refuse to step into it again. No more fashion shows. No premieres. No club openings. People will forget about me, right?"

My question sounds needy, but I don't care. I just want them to agree that at some point, I'll be able to live my life without hearing the word "murderer" whispered behind my back.

Indiana shrugs. "Eventually. Probably. Until they do a 'Where Is She Now?' exposé on some cable network."

I elbow him, and he laughs when milk sloshes over his spoon.

"What about the benefit?" my father asks, and I can't help noticing that he hasn't answered my question. "I bought a whole table."

Crap. "Okay, after tonight, no more appearances."

"*Princesa*, I doubt anyone would blame you for backing out."

"I know, but I've already committed, and Valencias never back down or back out."

5 HOURS EARLIER

We have no doubt.

MADDIE

I'm strangely nervous as I ring the doorbell, in part because I didn't think I'd ever wind up back here. And in part because of why I'm here.

Neda opens the heavy, iron front door and pulls me into her foyer, and the excited shine in her eyes dispels my sense of déjà vu. Neda Rahbar has never been thrilled to see me in her life.

"Maddie! Come on in. We're all set up in my closet."

Before I can ask why they'd be crowded into her closet, she tugs me through her marble-floored entryway and living room, then down the hall into an elegantly decorated bedroom approximately the size of my entire apartment.

"Hey, come on in," Genesis says from the left-hand doorway on the back wall. Through the door on the right, I can see a huge bathroom with a modern freestanding tub and marble countertops, which means the door on the left can only be the closet.

Genesis is holding two champagne flutes full of what

looks and smells like orange juice. "Mimosas," she says as she hands me one and sips from the other. I sniff my glass as I follow her through the doorway.

"Your mom lets you drink champagne?"

Neda laughs. "My parents are out of town."

"That's why we're doing this here." Genesis ushers me into a closet that is literally bigger than my bedroom. And has a *window*. And a window seat.

"Are you sure about this? I was just supposed to help plan the benefit. Elizabeth never said anything about me attending."

Genesis shrugs. "My dad bought a whole table. You and Luke are both coming. I insist."

I do the math, then stumble backward. There are eight seats per table.

Penelope is already sorting through dress after dress on a high closet rod, her own mimosa held lightly in her left hand.

"Pen and I brought these." Genesis gestures to a rolling clothing rack, where at least a dozen formal gowns are hanging. "I know it's a slim selection. We both donated a bunch to charity last year. But with what Neda has, we're bound to find something that looks good on you."

My cousin clearly doesn't understand the backhanded compliment she just gave me, so I decide to let it slide. Considering that I can't afford even one dress like the dozens currently hanging in Neda's closet.

Genesis and Penelope sit on a padded bench standing

on a spotless, shaggy white rug in the center of the room, and I realize that they're the judges in what I stupidly assumed would be a simple, half-hour dress hunt. Evidently it's actually a fashion show, starring everyone's least fashionable charity case: me.

"Start with the Valentino!" Penelope says.

"No, the Dior," Genesis insists.

Neda puts a halt to the argument with one raised hand. "We're going to *start* with the *Schiaparelli*." She pulls a black dress with a mostly sheer bodice from a rack of her own clothes, then throws open a door I'd mistaken for a cabinet.

It's actually a dressing room.

Neda's closet has a dressing room. Evidently just for events like this.

I lose track of the names and styles over the next hour as I try on dresses in every conceivable style and color, made of every possible fabric. My favorite is a sleek white pantsuit with a plunging V-shaped neckline, but Genesis doesn't think I have the "stature" to pull it off, so we dive back into the dresses.

By the time I've tried on twenty of them, I can no longer remember which ones I liked, and the debate continues without me, while my cousin and her friends sip their third mimosas and argue over whether I should look powerful or delicate, and whether my complexion will look better with the green lace or the rose silk Marchesa.

"She looks like the Little Mermaid in the green!" Neda growls, and Genesis agrees.

"But she's not packing enough in the back for the rose!" Penelope insists. And that's when I realize that I might never have left Colombia at all. Maybe I died out there in the jungle, and this is hell.

Out of the corner of my eye, I notice that my phone has lit up on the window seat. I penguin-walk around the arguing divas and sit as best I can in skintight silver satin, then pick up my phone. There's a message from Holden.

Watch your back.

Chills pop up all over my bare arms. "Hey, guys?"
But the divas can't hear me over their own bickering.

"Guys!" I shout, and they turn to me, startled. Penelope's eyes look glazed over, and I realize she can't hold her liquor. Neither can I, which is why I didn't even finish my first mimosa. "Holden's threatening me."

"What?" Genesis marches over and grabs my phone. "What the hell is his problem? He got off." She grabs Neda's tablet from the window seat and types Holden's name into the search bar.

It doesn't take us long to find the story. She taps the top link and a video opens on one of the major news network sites. The banner running across the bottom sums it up.

Wainwright Pharmaceuticals' Stock Plunges; Heir to Pharmaceutical Fortune Disinherited.

"Holy shit," Genesis breathes as she sinks onto the bench seat.

"Turn it up," Penelope mumbles.

Genesis turns up the volume, and we gather around the tablet, listening, shocked, as Holden's father speaks at a formal press conference from behind a podium crowded with microphones.

"While we are obviously relieved that the State's Attorney hasn't found reason to press charges against Holden, as parents, we can't deny that our son's behavior is not in keeping with the values espoused by Wainwright Pharmaceuticals, and we understand the executive board's discomfort with the thought of him someday taking the helm. So it is with a heavy heart but a very hopeful outlook for the future of both our company and our family that we announce that our son, Holden, will not inherit any stock in Wainwright Pharmaceuticals. Nor will he be employed in any way by the company. We have no doubt that he will find great success in the future. But it will not be at Wainwright Pharmaceuticals."

"Damn," Neda breathes. "If my parents disinherited me, I'd sue."

I start to ask how she'd pay her lawyer if she were disinherited. Instead, I laugh. "Let's hope he has the sense to come to you for legal advice."

1.5 HOURS EARLIER

You belong here.

GENESIS

Luke's eyes are wide as he climbs into the limo behind my cousin. "I've always wanted to ride in one of these!" Evidently the one at Ryan's funeral didn't count. He plops down between Neda and Maddie without realizing that he's sitting on both of their skirts. "Have you ever been in a Hummer limo?"

Neda rolls her eyes and pushes him over so she can free her dress. "Hummers are so pedestrian."

Luke laughs—until he realizes no one else is amused. "Wait, was that not a joke? You know, she just called a *car* pedestrian?"

Indiana laughs.

Maddie smiles and takes Luke's hand as the limo begins to roll forward.

"Have you heard from Elizabeth Wainwright today?" I ask Maddie.

"Only through her assistant. She said we did a great job, but they don't need any more help from me. I've basically

366

been politely dismissed." She shrugs. "There goes my scholarship. Thanks to Holden."

"Screw him," Penelope says, and I'm relieved to see that this time she seems to mean it. After everything he's done, it took his threat to Maddie to finally get through to her.

"Yeah. Screw him." But Maddie's voice lacks conviction. She leans forward to see Neda around Luke. "What I can't figure out is how he knew it was me. You didn't tell anyone, did you?"

Neda stares at her feet, clad in a brand-new pair of designer pumps.

"Neda?" I ask as a sick feeling begins to churn in my stomach.

"What. Happened?" Maddie demands, her voice lower and scarier than I've ever heard it.

Neda sighs. "A couple of lawyers came to my door yesterday afternoon. They said they were working on the case against Holden and asked where I got the footage of him dealing at those parties."

"What lawyers? What were their names?" Maddie asks.

Neda rolls her eyes. "How the hell am I supposed to remember that?"

"You didn't have to answer their questions," I tell her, resisting the urge to rub my face in frustration, which would ruin my professionally applied makeup. "Especially without a parent present."

"That's what I said—that a journalist never reveals her sources. Which I totally thought was a thing."

"It *is* a thing." Indiana reaches across the aisle to give her a comforting pat on the knee.

"Well, *they* said that there's no legal protection for a journalist's source, and that the only way I could protect that information is if I were willing to go to jail for refusing to reveal it." She shrugs. "And *obviously* I'm not willing to go to jail."

"Neda!" Maddie snaps. "You'd only go to jail if you refused a *judge's order* for you to reveal your sources. Did they bring a court order?"

She frowns. "I don't know."

Maddie scrubs her face with both hands, heedless of her makeup. "If they had one, they would have shown you."

"What does it matter?" Neda leans back and crosses her arms over her chest as the limo makes a tight right-hand turn. "They were working to put Holden in jail, and that's what we want. Right?"

"Except that if they were on our side, they wouldn't have threatened you," I explain, grasping for patience. "They were probably Holden's attorneys. They used the information you gave them to help get the charges dropped."

Maddie groans. "And Holden used that information to threaten me."

Neda rolls her eyes again. "He's not going to hurt you, Maddie."

"He already has! His mother practically promised me one of the scholarships her charity sponsors, and now that's gone."

"You can have my tuition money. I don't need college anyway. I'll be too busy with my webshow."

Maddie's face turns four different shades of furious, and I realize there's no way to defuse this bomb. "Do you have *any idea* how insulting that is?" she demands. "The one truly good thing your privilege can do for you, you're willing to throw away for some stupid web—"

"Okay." I spread my arm in the space between the seats, calling for a truce. "Neda didn't mean to rat you out, and she's actually trying to be generous, rather than insulting."

Maddie scowls at me as the limo pulls to a stop, and we all rock a little in our seats. She's the first one out when the driver opens the door, but then she just stands there, blocking everyone else's path.

"Maddie?" Luke sounds worried.

I give her a little push and climb out next to her. My cousin looks terrified as she stares at the handful of other attendees getting out of limos. Each of the women wears a dress that costs more than her mother makes in six months.

"Tonight you're a guest," I whisper as I link my arm through hers and subtly pull her away from the car door. "Not an employee. Not a scholarship hopeful. You belong here just as much as the rest of us." I hesitate as the truth burns a hole in my tongue. "And you *deserve* to be here more than any of us."

Maddie is the only reason that half of tonight's proceeds will go to benefit Colombia. She's more of a hero than her father will *ever* be.

Luke climbs out of the car, and he looks as stunned as Maddie. Behind him, Neda and Pen are wearing their A-list smiles, perfectly at ease.

Indiana looks . . . amused as he gets out of the car. I let go of my cousin and link my arm with his, pleased to note that his formal black cowboy hat looks strangely hot with the tux he let me rent, but refused to let me buy.

The man at the door doesn't ask for our tickets. He knows who we are. *Everyone* knows who we are. It feels a little strange to be back in this spotlight, even if only temporarily. I decide to enjoy it. For the last time. Even if the stares aimed at me are more confused and critical than admiring.

Indiana declines to check his hat in the foyer, and I lead us across the lobby.

Just outside the ballroom doors stands an elegant free-standing banner, announcing that at the end of the night, one lucky attendee will walk away with a seventy-thousand-dollar bottle of sixty-four-year-old scotch—one out of a batch of only sixty-one bottles produced.

"The balloon prize?" Indiana guesses.

I nod. It has to be. "Bottles that old rarely go on sale." I know, because my father bought one from that very batch a few years ago, and he had to outbid six other buyers.

In a couple of hours, women in sequins and silk will be trying to drive designer stiletto heels into thirteen hundred balloons to win that bottle. The Wainwright Foundation's annual benefit will close out the night like a damn barn stomp.

Shaking my head in disgust, I head into the ballroom

with my arm tucked into Indiana's.

"Wow . . . ," Maddie breathes, and her awe is warranted. We did a lot of work last night, but the finishing touches put into place this morning have made all the difference. A huge bouquet of red roses sits at the center of every table, on top of the silver and black table runners and tablecloths layered in the same colors. Elegant, eighteen-piece place settings with silver-edged dishes have been perfectly arranged in front of each chair, the salad plates topped with tall black napkin sculptures.

And over all of our heads, where no one else seems to be looking, a huge net has been fastened to the ceiling, bursting at the seams with the black, silver, and red balloons we blew up last night. They'll fall at the end of the evening, when the silent auction has concluded and Elizabeth Wainwright reads the fund-raising grand total.

I lead our group toward my father's table at the front of the room. He buys one every year, but has yet to actually attend. While everyone else takes a seat, I scan the ballroom for familiar faces. For the first time in my life, I'm actually hesitant to mingle.

My gaze lands on Holden. He's standing across the room next to his father, and though Mr. Wainwright is holding a glass of what can only be very expensive whiskey, Holden's hands are stuffed into his pockets.

Last year, they let him wander the ballroom with me. This year he's clearly tethered to his father's side, for obvious reasons.

I give Holden a big, smug smile. Then, as I reach for Indiana's hand, a familiar face behind Holden catches my attention.

"No . . . ," I murmur.

It's probably just an allergy.

MADDIE

Genesis mumbles something about going to the bar, then grabs her clutch and heads into the crowd. I stare after her, surprised. Then I realize she's heading right for Holden. Probably to confront him about threatening me.

I should stop her. A scene is the last thing we need, after the week we've all had. But then she walks right past him and out a side door, and I realize that if she's going to make a scene, it won't be here.

It'll be somewhere private. Where she can rupture his scrotum and concuss his brain without an audience.

Indiana watches Genesis leave with a look of concern, but Luke is oblivious. His eyes are huge as he stares around the room, stunned to find himself among two NFL quarterbacks, four Grammy winners, and more actors and directors than he could count on both hands.

"Maddie, you want a drink?" Neda asks. "It's an open bar, and an extra big tip will usually stand in the place of ID."

I must look extra awkward if she's being this nice to me.

Or maybe she feels bad about giving Holden's lawyers my name.

Neda picks up her clutch and steps around her chair, both brows arched as she waits for my answer. But then my focus lands on the hand clutching her purse. "Neda, what happened to your hand?"

She looks down and frowns. Her clutch clunks onto the table and she holds her hand closer to her face to examine the cluster of small blisters in the web between her right thumb and forefinger.

Penelope leans over to look. "Did you burn yourself?"

"No. And it doesn't hurt."

"Does it itch?" Luke asks, leaning in from his seat on my other side.

"Well, it does *now*," Neda snaps. As if suggesting the possibility brought the itch to life. "You guys, chill." She glances around the room and smiles, as if nothing were wrong. "It's probably just an allergy to my new hand soap. Or something." Then she holds her purse in both hands, strategically hiding the blisters, and heads for the door.

"I'll be right back," I tell Luke. Then I follow her out, walking slower than I'd like, thanks to the stupid heels she insisted I borrow.

I hit the lobby just as Neda disappears into the women's room, and when I follow her inside, I'm relieved to find it empty, other than us. Neda sets her clutch on the counter and runs water over her hand, scowling at the blisters.

"What kind of hand soap did you switch to?" I ask.

"I didn't. But I couldn't let people think I'm *contagious*." She turns off the water and frowns at her hand.

"Could they be bug bites?"

She gives me an angry look in the mirror. "I don't have *bugs*, Maddie."

"That's not what I—"

The bathroom door flies open and Luke bursts into the powder room, holding his phone.

"You can't be in here!" Neda whispers fiercely. In reply, he shoves his phone in our faces. The screen shows a picture of a cluster of blisters that look eerily similar to the ones on Neda's hand. "What is that?" she asks, squinting at the screen.

"*Those*"—he swipes through several more pictures, all identical to Neda's hand—"are .early-stage blisters from a cutaneous anthrax infection."

NOW

I have to give my uncle credit.

GENESIS

I march across the ballroom, past men in tuxedos and women in expensive dresses.

Silvana is here. Dressed like a waitress. She's heading into the kitchen. I can still see the faint traces of a bruise on her face—probably from my uncle's fist.

I hesitate for a second at the swinging door. The last time I saw her, she nearly killed me. But that was in Colombia. In the jungle.

We're in my house now.

I can call the police with the press of a button.

I push my way into the kitchen, expecting to be stopped. I'm wearing a twenty-thousand-dollar custom gown and four-inch heels. I obviously do not belong in here, but no one even looks up from the plates they're preparing or the trays they're loading. They don't have time to notice me.

Thank goodness.

Determined, I lift my skirt to keep from dragging it or tripping over it and follow Silvana down an aisle on the right side of the kitchen, careful not to bump into anything or anyone in the bustling, steam-filled room. She takes a left at the end of the aisle, and I see her in profile.

She's . . . not Silvana. I open another door and rush into a dimly lit hallway, and—

"Good evening, *princesa*."

Startled, I gasp and whirl around . . . and find myself staring up into Silvana's darkly amused eyes.

"Your uncle sends his regards." She cocks the pistol aimed at me, and my throat clenches around nothing. "Toss your phone at my feet."

I consider trying to dial 911 instead, but she can pull the trigger faster than I can scroll to the emergency call screen. Reluctantly, I lob my phone at her.

She stomps it into useless electronic debris.

"Why were you following me? What are you doing here?"

"Cleaning up the mess you made. You might have heard that someone blew up your uncle's arsenal, but David is endlessly resourceful. Plan B is a go, Genesis."

Plan B. Here. Now. At a charity event with two hundred of the wealthiest people in the country in attendance.

I have to give my uncle credit—he does not think small.

"Where are the bombs?" Not that I'll be able to tell anyone if she kills me.

"There are no bombs. We're going for a different kind of drama this time. Something more . . . fitting with the atrocities the US government has visited upon the Colombian people. Your uncle calls it 'poetic justice.'"

More fitting?

Money given in support of one cartel over the others. Pesticides sprayed onto farmland. Deals made with crooked politicians. Raids ending in a hail of bullets and the slaughter of entire families.

Which of those is my uncle planning to unleash on a room full of philanthropists? Bullets seem the most likely, but . . .

"You're going to have to give me more of a hint," I tell her. "Or are you just going to shoot me?"

"Oh no. David wants you to have a front-row seat." She backs toward the door to the kitchen, keeping her gun aimed at me. "So just sit back and enjoy the show. . . ." Then Silvana disappears into the kitchen.

I lurch for what's left of my phone, and it falls apart in my hand. "Damn it!" I have to find a phone. And evacuate the building.

Starting with my father's table . . .

This is crazy.

MADDIE

"No." Neda holds her hand away from her body, as if it's betrayed her. "That doesn't make any sense. Where the hell would I have gotten anthrax? And what's . . . cutaneous?"

"It means 'relating to the skin,'" Luke tells her. "That means you got this infection from touching anthrax, rather than eating or inhaling it."

"Whoa, wait a minute. We don't know that," I insist. "Just because her blisters look like those blisters doesn't mean she has anthrax." I suck in a deep breath, praying that I'm right. Because if Neda's somehow been exposed to anthrax . . . I shake my head firmly. "Googling medical images is *not* a valid way to make a diagnosis."

"Acknowledged. But she's got *some* kind of infection." He turns back to Neda. "If your doctor takes after-hours calls, I'd make one right now. Just to be safe."

"This is crazy." Neda grabs her clutch and heads back into the lobby, still holding her hand out as if she doesn't even recognize it.

Luke and I follow her, and though the ballroom doors have closed, we can hear Holden's mother giving a speech from beyond them. Neda pulls her phone from her clutch with her good hand, and before I can decide whether I should call her a cab or text everyone else from our group with an update, we see Genesis explode from a door leading into a service hallway.

Neda doesn't even glance up from her screen, where she's scrolling through her contacts, probably looking for her doctor's number. She's lost in Neda-land, and this time I can't blame her.

"I need your phone!" Genesis whispers fiercely.

"What's going on?" I dig in my clutch, an uneasy feeling crawling across my skin.

"Silvana's here," Genesis says. "And she's not here to eat catered chicken Kiev. Plan B is a go."

Fear shoots up my spine, leaving chills in its wake. My words carry almost no sound. "Here? With all those people in there?" My father's plan B is targeting two hundred of the wealthiest people in the country. And *again*, he's dragged my friends and me into it.

"Are there bombs?" Luke pulls his phone from his pocket. "We should get out of here."

"She says there aren't, but she could be lying. We need to clear the ballroom without panicking anyone." Genesis is already heading for the double doors.

"You guys, my doctor's not answering," Neda says, oblivious to the turn the conversation has taken. She holds her hand out again. "If this is anthrax, should I just go to the hospital?"

"*What?*" Genesis spins toward us again, and I can see what she's thinking. When she twisted her ankle in the jungle, Neda practically thought she was dying. Her "anthrax" could be a mosquito bite.

Or it could be my father's backup plan.

"Show her," I say, but Luke's already pulling up the pictures on his phone.

"*Noo,*" Genesis says. "That *can't* be anthrax. Did you touch anything weird? Get into anything you don't normally? New soap or lotion?"

"No." Neda frowns. "Well, I washed my hands here last night. With that cheap pump soap in the bathroom at the back of the building. There was some residue after we blew up the . . ."

My gaze slides toward the sign on the wooden tripod, advertising the sixty-four-year-old scotch. To be won through a ridiculously juvenile balloon stomp. At a fifty-thousand-dollar-a-plate benefit.

"The balloons . . ."

"Oh my God," Luke whispers. "They're full of anthrax."

"I thought it was just dust." Neda's voice sounds hollow with shock.

"The balloons were a last-minute addition." Words spill out of my mouth as things begin to fall into place, my thoughts spinning so fast I can hardly focus on them. "Julia said someone approached Holden and donated the scotch, but wanted the giveaway to be part of the celebration of the fund-raising total. They're going to announce the final tally and drop the balloons. Then—"

"Then people will pop them," Luke finishes for me. "Anthrax everywhere."

My head spins while I try to process what I'm hearing. This *can't* be real.

"One of us is supposed to trigger plan B," Genesis whispers. "But we *all* did it. We blew up those balloons. And we helped plan the event." Neda had one tank all to herself. She blew up more balloons than any of us.

"Holden gets to push the button," I tell them, numb with shock. "To drop the balloons. It's his only part in the whole fund-raiser." He's *literally* going to trigger a terrorist act. Just like Genesis did. Except . . . "Oh my God, you guys, he knows."

"What?" Genesis frowns at me.

"He knows about the balloons. He *has* to. I heard him on the phone with whoever donated the scotch. It's someone he knows. And if this is plan B, it has to be my dad. Or . . ."

"Silvana," Genesis says. "She's been in the States for days. Maybe as long as we have."

"But Holden *hates* her. She nearly had him killed," I point out. "Why would he have been in touch with her?"

"And where would she get a seventy-thousand-dollar bottle of scotch?" Luke asks.

Genesis's eyes close. "From my dad. He bought one at auction a few years ago—I think it was the same year as the prize bottle." Her eyes open and her gaze lands on me with the weight of the whole world. "Maddie, he gave it to your dad for his fortieth birthday."

Holy shit. I remember that. My dad thought it was a *huge* waste of money that could have gone to charity.

The irony burns straight into my soul.

Blood drains from my face. I feel cold all over. Plan B was orchestrated by my father. Put into place by Silvana. And will be triggered by Holden. Infecting two hundred of the country's wealthiest philanthropists—people my father believes to be hypocrites who're "part of the problem"—with anthrax.

Does he even care that he'll also be infecting the caterers, waitstaff, and other employees? Not to mention his own niece and daughter?

"So, I should go to the hospital, right?" Neda eyes are wide and scared.

I can only blink at her.

Luke nods. "Take a cab. Go now."

"By myself?" Her hands are shaking. "Am I going to die?"

"No." Luke takes her hand—the one with the blisters—and I realize he's trying to calm her down. To show her he's not afraid, and she shouldn't be either. "Anthrax is a kind of bacteria that forms spores. It isn't contagious. Cutaneous infection is the most common kind, and the least dangerous. All you need is some heavy-duty antibiotics. You're going to be fine."

"Okay." She nods and starts backing toward the front doors. "Okay. I got this."

"I know you do." Genesis smiles at her. "Call 911 from the cab. Tell the police what's going on. We have to get everyone out of here. But then we'll be right behind you."

"We'll all have to get checked out," Luke adds, still smiling confidently at Neda. "We were all handling those balloons. You just got the biggest dose."

She gives us another shaky nod, then disappears out the front doors.

"You're amazing," I tell Luke, fully aware that he just did a very nice thing for someone who's never been anything but rude to him. But he shrugs the compliment off with an embarrassed smile. "Was any of that true?"

"Yes." He nods. "A strong dose of antibiotics will fix all of us right up. A cutaneous infection is really no big deal. But if those balloons pop, the spores will be distributed through the air . . . If people breathe them in . . ." He looks suddenly grim. "If the spores germinate, they can cause internal bleeding and necrosis. Your lungs can fill up with bloody fluid. Anthrax can even cause hemorrhagic meningitis. All of which means that inhaling even a little bit of anthrax can be fatal. And it's a *horrible* way to die."

I know just how to cheer us all up.

GENESIS

"This can't be happening," Maddie whispers. "We have to warn people. We have to get everyone out of here without starting a panic."

"The fire alarm." I spin around, searching the lobby until I find one by the far left set of doors. We race across the slick floor toward it and I pull down the handle, my heart pounding. Braced for a brain-splitting siren. Flashing lights. Chaos.

Nothing happens.

"*Damn* it."

"It's broken?" Maddie frowns. "Tonight? That can't be a coincidence."

"It's been disabled," I guess. "If Silvana snuck in here to leave anthrax-laced balloons, she would damn well have disabled our only quick-and-easy way to evacuate the building. But there are probably dozens of alarms in a place this big. Surely she didn't disable *all* of them."

"She could have snipped the central wire at the control box," Luke says. "Cutting them all off at once."

"We have to be sure. Any idea where are the rest of them are?"

"Building code requires one at each exit," Luke says. "And one in each of the bathrooms. The kitchen . . ."

"I'll take the ladies' room. You take the men's room," Maddie tells him.

"And I'll see if there's one in the ballroom," I say. "If the ones in the bathrooms don't work, meet me in there. We'll have to evacuate this place the hard way."

They take off in different directions, and I slip back into the banquet to find that the first course is being served, a few tables at a time, by several teams of waiters. Elizabeth Wainwright is still at the microphone, but I can tell from her tone and cadence that she's nearing the end of her opening remarks.

Standing against the rear wall, trying to be unobtrusive, I scan the large room and finally find a fire alarm on the far side of another set of doors to my left. I head that way, my heart pounding a staccato rhythm, flinching with every soft click of my heels on the floor.

Indiana catches my eye and lifts one brow in my direction. Silently asking the obvious question. I nod subtly toward the exit as I walk. His brows rise even higher as I reach for the alarm.

I suck in a deep breath. Then I pull the handle.

Nothing happens.

I pull it again. And again. And again. But it only clicks ineffectually.

On the dais, Elizabeth sits at the head table, and Holden stands. His gaze narrows on me, and he smiles.

He actually *smiles!*

Then he calmly steps up to the podium.

"Holden!" Elizabeth snaps softly from her seat, but I can hear her clearly from across the room.

He gives his mother a placating smile. Then he starts speaking into the microphone.

"Good evening, ladies and gentlemen. I'm Holden Wainwright, son of our lovely hostess. For those of you who might not watch the news, I've had a really rough couple of weeks, which began when I was kidnapped at gunpoint by Colombian drug lords—from whom my father *declined to ransom me*—then culminated last night, when I was publicly disinherited by my parents."

Awkward mumbles rise from the audience. Some people seem to think this is a joke. Others realize he's committing the social version of a nosedive off a tall building.

Holden's mother looks humiliated. His father looks ready to breathe fire.

On my right, the lobby door opens, and Maddie and Luke step into the ballroom. She gives me a soft shake of her head.

All of the fire alarms have been disabled. And Holden clearly already knew that. I can't quite wrap my mind around this. This isn't shooting a kidnapper in self-defense. This isn't stabbing a rescuer mistaken for a terrorist.

This is an attack against innocent American citizens.

What the *hell* happened to Holden?

"Anyway," he continues as his mother stares at her plate, her face scarlet. "I thought some of you might also be having a rough week, and I know just how to cheer us all up." He pulls something from his pocket, and for a second, I think it's his phone. But it's a remote control with a single black button.

Shit. Now that he knows we've figured it out, he's expediting the balloon drop.

"I assume you've all heard about the bottle of sixty-four-year-old Glenfiddich donated by a very generous anonymous benefactor. And I assume you know that the only way to go home with that very rare bottle is to find the golden ticket."

"Holden!" his father hisses.

Holden laughs and holds up one hand, palm out, as if his father's anger is something to be shrugged off. "This was supposed to happen at the end of the evening, but I think we could all use a little fun right now." He lifts the remote control.

My pulse spikes so painfully that my vision flashes gray for a second.

Then he presses the button.

Adults gasp and several children squeal in delight as black, red, and silver balloons rain down over the room. The effect is stunning.

"Wait!" I shout, and my shrill cry carries over the excited mumbles of the men and women as they stare around at the display. "Don't move! *Don't touch the balloons!* They're full of poison!"

I don't know anything.

MADDIE

I watch in horror as balloons settle onto the floor all over the ballroom, my cousin's shout echoing in my head. Heads swivel all across the room. Shocked eyes focus on Genesis.

Holden sets the remote control on the podium, then turns and flees in a fast walk across the dais—away from his parents. He jogs down the steps and heads for the nearest door. Quickly.

Genesis turns to Luke and me. "I'll go after Holden. You get up there and tell people not to pop those balloons!" Then she races around the perimeter of the room—where the balloons have not fallen—and out the door without waiting for my reply.

Damn it!

I grab Luke by the arm. "Get Indiana and Penelope out of here!" I whisper urgently into his ear. Then I kick off my heels and rush toward the host table, wading shin deep into a carpet of large, shiny, deadly balloons. "Don't touch them!" I shout as I go. "They're filled with poison!"

A low murmur washes over the crowd as people stare,

trying to decide whether or not to believe me. I dodge balloons as I weave between the tables, and on my way toward the dais, I see a small boy in an adorable and obviously expensive three-piece suit pick up one of the red balloons and squeeze it. I slap it from his hands.

He starts screaming.

"Seriously!" I snap at his parents. "Poison!"

Mr. and Mrs. Wainwright stare at me in shock as I race up the steps and rush past them to the podium. I grab the microphone, and it squeals through the speakers mounted in the corners of the room. But before I can say a single word, the sharp pop of a balloon breaking echoes across the room.

"Shit!" The microphone picks up my curse and amplifies it. Some people laugh. Others stare. I can feel the weight of their focus like an invisible pressure.

"Maddie!" Elizabeth Wainwright stomps toward me in her heels, and I backpedal, determined not to let her have the microphone. Feedback squeals again, and several people drop balloons to clutch their ears.

"Ladies and gentlemen," I begin. "I don't want anyone to panic, but we have reason to believe those balloons are filled with anthrax."

Elizabeth's flush deepens until she looks like a tomato with arms. "Give me the mic!" she demands softly.

"This is not a joke!" I insist into the microphone. "My friends and I blew up those balloons last night, and Neda just left here with anthrax blisters on her hand. She's on her way to the ER. You should all be doing the same thing."

"What the hell is going on?" someone demands from the audience, but I can't see who spoke. "Is this a joke?"

"It's not funny!" someone else shouts.

"I'm sorry. But I'm totally serious. Even if you don't believe me, are you really willing to risk it?"

A grumble rises from the audience, and one parent snatches a balloon from her daughter's hands, her eyes wide and terrified.

"The balloon that popped . . ." I glance across the room, trying to figure out where the sound came from. "Did any white powder come out of it? Any residue?"

"Oh my God!" A woman in a red ball gown stands, still holding the fork she evidently used to pop the balloon. "It's all over me!"

Shouts rise in a panicked cacophony. I can't hear them all clearly, and I don't have any of the answers they're asking for.

"Ma'am, you need to go to the hospital," I say into the microphone. "Everyone near you needs to go to the hospital. Right now. And everyone else, slowly, calmly leave the building. The police are already on their way. No need to rush. There are plenty of exits. So walk calmly and slowly. And do *not* pop any more balloons."

To punctuate my point, I set the microphone down and head for the steps at the end of the raised platform. Slowly. Calmly. But the Wainwrights step into my path.

"Maddie, what the hell is going on?" Elizabeth demands.

"I don't know anything else except that we need to get out of here. Now." I step down from the side of the platform and head for the nearest door, skirting balloons as best I can. "Oh." I turn back to them. "And your son's going to need your lawyers again. Like, the whole team of them."

"The doors are locked!" someone shouts from the left side of the room. "They've been chained from the outside!"

"Okay, everyone calm down!" Indiana calls out over the crowd. "The doors at the back of the room are open. So are the doors into the kitchen. We're all going to get out of here."

Yet all around me, people are running. Panicking.

And as my gaze connects with Luke, where he and Indiana are trying to direct people toward the main exits, I hear another balloon pop.

A shriek rises from the crowd.

The stampede toward the doors becomes a crush of well-dressed bodies, fleeing a sea of party balloons.

You all deserve whatever you get.

GENESIS

"Holden, you son of a bitch, get back here!"

He glances over his shoulder at me, then takes off down the back hallway. As if he could ever outrun me.

I kick my shoes off, and even holding my own skirt, I catch up to him in under a dozen steps. I grab the back of his tux jacket, spin him around, and shove him into the wall. When he tries to free himself, I ram my knee into his groin.

"*Anthrax?* How the hell could you do this?" I demand.

Holden coughs and dry retches. If I weren't holding him up, he'd curl around his wounded privates. "*I didn't do anything but play my part in a charity event. I* had no idea there was anything bad in those balloons. You and your cousin and your friends blew them up. It's *your* fingerprints they'll find on the tanks. On the balloons. On the clips. The balloons were shipped to *you.* From Colombia, where *your* family has notorious and dangerous connections. Who exactly do you think is going to go down for this?"

"You're willing to kill all those people just to get back at me?" This isn't just anger. This is *insanity*. How could I not have seen it?

"It's a return blow for the poison the US government has been spraying over Colombia's farm fields for decades," he chokes out. "But it's just to scare them. To teach them a lesson. Anthrax is survivable."

"Is that what my uncle told you?"

He rolls his eyes, still coughing. "I looked it up. It's not a bomb, Gen. It's a bacterial infection. It'll scare the crap out of them, but they'll be fine. And maybe a little more humble."

I grab a handful of his hair and shove his head against the wall, holding him upright. "It won't just scare them if they inhale it!" I shout at him. "It could kill them. There are *kids* in there! Your *parents* are in there!"

Holden blinks at me. He looks confused. Conflicted. Then his gaze hardens. "The kids will be fine. And my parents deserve whatever they get. My dad was going to leave me in the jungle, Genesis. He had a chance to get me out of there, but he chose the company over me. Over his own kid." He shrugs. "You chose *Indiana* over me. You all deserve whatever you get."

"That is psychotic—"

"Genesis!" Indiana pounds around the corner, and relief floods his face when he sees me. "The police are on the way. We need to get out of here."

"Maddie and Luke?" I ask him. "Penelope?"

"They're outside with everyone else. Waiting for the ambulances."

And that's when I hear the sirens. I exhale slowly. The police have arrived.

This is almost over.

"Come on." I give Holden a shove in Indiana's direction. Toward the front of the building.

He pulls free, backing away from us slowly. Hands up, as if to fend me off. "Everyone will be fine. Just . . . let me go. Your uncle promised to get me out of the country—"

"Yeah. About that."

I whirl toward the familiar voice to find Silvana standing at the other end of the hall. Pointing a pistol at us.

Shit. My pulse whooshes in my ears. The hallway looks a little unsteady.

"There's been a change of plans," Silvana says.

I back away, hands up, palms out, and Indiana steps closer to me. As if he might step between me and the gun. But she isn't even looking at us.

"David thanks you for your service." Silvana aims at Holden. "Consider yourself relieved of duty." Then she pulls the trigger.

Light flashes from the end of her gun in the dim hallway, and I gasp, half deaf. Holden grunts, but I can't hear him. Then he slides to the floor.

Blood blooms on the front of his formal white shirt, low on one side, and spreads rapidly beneath the side of his tux jacket. His face goes pale. Pain flickers behind his eyes and he clutches the wound.

The clogged sound in my ears begins to clear, but they're still ringing. I feel like I'm inside a gong.

Silvana turns to me, and fear becomes fire pumping through my veins. Sharpening my senses. "Silvana . . ."

"Don't worry, *princesa*. David wants you alive, so you can live with the consequences of blowing up his arsenal. Have a great life. And say hi to your cousin for me." Then she turns and disappears down the hall in the other direction.

A second later, I hear the squeal of sturdy hinges. Then a heavy door slams shut.

Silvana is gone.

"Gen . . . ," Holden gasps. "Help me."

"Is there anyone still in here!" a new voice calls from the front of the building.

"Yes! We're back here!" I shout as I kneel next to Holden. Indiana takes off his jacket and presses it against Holden's wound.

Two officers round the corner in the direction Indiana came from. They're wearing gloves and respirators. "Ma'am, we need to get everyone out of the building."

"He's been shot." I stand to make room for the cops, and one of them kneels next to Holden, already pulling a radio from his belt to call for an EMT crew.

"The shooter is a woman," Indiana tells the other cop. "In her early twenties. Dark curly hair. Brown eyes. About five foot eight. Her first name is Silvana. She went around that corner and out the door."

The cop pulls his gun and takes off after her, but I already know he won't find her. This may finally be over, but Silvana and my uncle are gone. They left Sebastián and Holden to pay for their crimes.

And me to be tried in the court of public opinion.

1 WEEK LATER

She's a liar.

MADDIE

I ring Neda's doorbell for the second time in a week, and suddenly I worry that this may become a habit. She's still annoying. But I have to admit, she's grown on me.

Her housekeeper opens the door. "Ms. Rahbar doesn't want any visitors," she says. "But thank you all so much for coming."

"It's okay, Charlotte." Genesis steps past me, and the housekeeper moves back to let her in. Most people don't know how to say no to my cousin. "She'll see us."

Charlotte holds the door open, and Indiana, Penelope, Luke, and I follow Genesis inside, armed with an iced latte, a balloon bouquet, and an envelope containing a gift certificate for a "get well" full-day treatment at my cousin's favorite spa.

"Who was it?" Neda calls out from the chaise longue, where she's wearing earbuds and holding her tablet.

"Only your best friends in the world," Genesis says as we troop into the living room.

"No, you guys, I don't want anyone to see me like this!" Neda sets her tablet down, and before she tucks her hands beneath her thighs, I see that in the past week, the blisters have spread and darkened. But they're nowhere near as bad as some of the ones we've all been looking at online. Probably thanks to prompt treatment in the ER.

"We don't care what you look like." Genesis sets the balloon weight on the coffee table, and the inflated bouquet hovers over it. "We're here to see you, not your hand."

Neda flinches eyeing the balloons. "Get those things away from me!"

"Oh, come on. They're Mylar!" Genesis laughs. "Helium only. So you can do your Mickey Mouse karaoke."

Indiana grins. "I told you she wouldn't think that was funny." He hands her the envelope. "I think you'll like this better."

Neda eyes the envelope suspiciously. Then she rips it open. Her smile looks reluctant, but real when she sees the certificate. "Thank you."

"Gen and I will be joining you." Penelope sinks onto the couch and holds her hand out for Neda to see. "After we've healed." There's a neat ring of blisters on her left hand, and one on her right palm. "No masseuse in the world would touch us right now."

Genesis has a single cluster on her left wrist. Luke's is on the back of his right hand.

Only Indiana and I are unmarked so far. But we're all on strong antibiotics, just in case.

"How are you feeling?" Luke settles onto one of the couches next to me.

"Lousy." Neda eyes her hand.

"Well, I suspect that's psychosomatic," he says. "The survivability of cutaneous anthrax infections is right at eighty percent, even *without* antibiotics, and with the meds we're all on, we're going to be fine. Holden, on the other hand . . ." Luke shrugs, and an uncomfortable silence descends over the room.

Holden is still in the hospital. Handcuffed to his own bed. The doctors think he will survive the gunshot wound, but I'm not sure he'll survive himself. He's been on suicide watch all week, because he's threatened to kill himself rather than go to prison.

Genesis went to see him. Once. To thank him for telling the truth to the FBI, though I'm pretty sure he did that to flip the bird at my dad rather than to help us.

Gen says she went more for her benefit than for Holden's. For closure. But I can't tell that she actually got much out of it.

I feel the same way about my father. I'll never get to ask him why he did what he did. Why he kept in touch with Holden, but not his own daughter. Why he abandoned his own family to pursue a violent, twisted agenda.

I'm never going to get any answers from him. And I will always hate him for that, and for the three people who inhaled anthrax at the benefit and are fighting for their lives in the hospital.

But I'm learning to deal.

"The doctor said it could take sixty days for these things to heal," Neda moans, staring at her hand. "That's most of the summer. I'm going to have to hide out in the house for two months. No parties. No vacation. No umbrellas on the beach. I don't even get to walk the line at graduation."

"Neither do we," Penelope tells her. But I don't think they would, even if they could. Even if the rest of their school weren't terrified of catching anthrax. As if that's even possible.

Genesis is pretty much done with her fancy private school. With the facade of her perfect life. She's a pariah now. A constant topic of speculation on the news and gossip on the internet. Some people still think she's a murderer for blowing up the *Splendor*. Some people think she's a hero for helping save people at the benefit.

The press is pretty sure she's a liar, and that no one should ever believe another word she says.

They're all wrong. She's just a girl who tried to do the right thing and made a lot of mistakes.

She's also my cousin. My brother's other sister. And my best friend.

"Well, you might have heard that my dad and I own a private strip of beach." Genesis sinks onto the end of Neda's chaise longue. "And that I like to throw parties. Though the list of people who might actually show up is pretty much limited to those of us in this room." Genesis gives the rest of us a rueful smile. "I expect to see you all at my house tomorrow night at seven. We're going to put this whole thing behind us the same way it began.

"Together. On the beach."

ACKNOWLEDGMENTS

Every book has its own unique challenges, but because of the structure of the timeline, this one has had more than its fair share. Which is why I must first and foremost thank the outstanding copy editors at Harper Collins who, in addition to fact- and grammar-checking me, double-checked every reference to day and time in the entire manuscript. After all the timeline shifts necessitated by revisions, you made me look good at a point when I could no longer see the manuscript for the trees, and I am grateful. That said, any mistakes that still exist are mine.

Thanks also to Maria Barbo, my long-suffering editor, for more emergency phone calls and plot sessions than I can count. I leave every conversation we have feeling energized and enthusiastic, and I can't tell you what that means to me.

Many thanks to Sophie Jordan, Terra Lynn Childs, and Angela Corbett for retreat plotting, commiseration, cookies, and company. I miss you all.

Thanks as always to Jennifer Lynn Barnes for endless suggestions and support, and to Rinda Elliott for listening to my doubts, fears, and complaints as if she'd never heard any of them before.

More now than ever, a huge thank-you must go to my children for letting me know when my characters said something a twenty-first-century teenager would not, and to my husband for reminding me daily that though I am no longer a teenager, it's perfectly fine for me to consume caffeine like one.

And, of course, thank you to my agent, Merrilee Heifetz, and to everyone at Writers House for getting stuff done. Your job allows me to do my job in peace, and I could not be more thankful.